Catherine Temma Davidson has received numerous accolades for her poetry, including an award from the Academy of American Poets and the Dorothy Daniels Award from PEN. Her novel, *The Priest Fainted*, was a *New York Times* Notable Book of the Year and was listed in the *Los Angeles Times* Best Fiction selection. She teaches at Richmond, the American International University in London.

THE PRIEST FAINTED

Catherine Temma Davidson

Published in Great Britain by The Women's Press Ltd, 1998
A member of the Namara Group
34 Great Sutton Street, London EC1V 0LQ

First published in the United States of America by Henry Holt and
Company, Inc, 1998

This edition published 2000

British Library Cataloguing-in-Publication Data
A catalogue record for this book is available from the British
Library.

ISBN 0 7043 4660 5

Printed and bound in Great Britain by Cox & Wyman Ltd,
Reading, Berkshire

For Christina and Katina, who wove the bread
and made it rise

THE PRIEST FAINTED

İmam Baildi

Imagine a country built on dead rocks. The rocks are dead because they have already been lifted from the ground, shaped, and reworked into temples, houses, and streets. They have been columns where men breathed together in small groups, deciding the fate of civilizations. They have been paving stones that kept the heat of the day in them long past midnight, when courtesans full of intelligence and power would walk barefoot across them, holding jugs of wine.

The people born out of these rocks are broken by the past. They remember, but they do not know. They come of their mothers' wombs looking in the wrong direction: down, not up. They have been sat on for hundreds of years of foreign occupation, and once they lifted the chains they could find nothing to build on but dead rocks. So they keep their women huddled together in houses, and the men go out into the streets day after day, gathering together as if to find a solution.

If you are a man born into this tribe, you might be able to find yourself in the stories of the past, in heroes and glories and the idea

3

that through you and you alone your family's name will pass. What if you are a woman? You have no interest in sifting through dust.

Your grandmothers and your great-grandmothers gave up their names to their husbands, went inside their houses, and were never heard from again. If you wanted to trace the story of their lives and find yourself in them, you could not look in books or history. You would have to start with secret clues. You would have to start with *imam*.

Throughout the Levant, on any given day, the aroma of *imam* rises, a scent of onion and oil, garlic and tomato. There are as many versions of the recipe as there are bays and mountains. In the geologic twists and passages of northern Greece, villages that never make it onto postcards hide in valleys far from the sea. Not much goes in and not much gets out, and little has changed in four hundred years. Recipes are passed hand to hand, mother to daughter. Girls helping their mothers to prepare simple meals acquire an unspoken knowledge in their palms and fingers. If you come from these villages, you must find your history in your body.

This is our version. We take plump, feminine purple eggplants and slice them into round discs, pale as moons. Next, we gather zucchinis, hairy, wiry, and long, and slice them lengthwise so they resemble the bottoms of boats. The piles of vegetables are fried in olive oil and dripped on thick paper. Then we mix a rich paste to marry them together. We chop garlic—more garlic than you think you want—carrots, parsley, tomatoes, and throw them in with lemon and salt and pepper. The mix should have a bite, should make you want to pucker your lips and almost cry, and then should fill your mouth with salty pleasure. Layer the moons and the boats together, bind them with the tangy red paste, and bake.

The full name of the recipe is *Imam Baildi*, and, in my family, it means *The Priest Fainted*. Why did the priest faint? No one knows. Priests in Greece live on high rocks built up to the sky, where they ask for food in baskets to be lifted up to them and where not even the animals they eat are allowed to be feminine. Perhaps the priest was given a bite of bitter and sweet pleasure, and the power of everything behind the dish pushed him off his rock, just for a moment. Perhaps, when he was tumbling through the air, sighing with fear and ecstasy, he saw a glimpse of a new life to come.

A GREEK MYTH:

THERE IS ONLY ONE WAY TO TELL THIS STORY

Every woman needs a story, and perhaps this is how the story should go.

Sometimes, in the middle of a great battle, the taste of blood in your mouth, you close your eyes. Against the dark of your lids a scene rises, a bay encircled by olive trees, morning sun piercing the water clear through to the heart of sand rippled by tiny currents. Maybe you once owned a memory of the island but lost it during years of war. Maybe its name was spoken by a woman in passing who did not know you knew her language. Maybe it is something that does not exist, that you have dreamed up yourself in a moment of pure despair to comfort you in your need. Maybe it sounds like home. One day, you put down your weapons and decide to try to return to the island. You set off.

You come to the land of the Cyclops first. Each has a handsome body, and their one-eyed glances are enough to make you forget where you thought you were going. You stay with them for many years, or one, or a lifetime. Sometimes you bear them children. Sometimes you devour the children or they devour you. One way or another, it turns out to be costly stopover. If you are lucky, the spell breaks early and you continue on your voyage.

When you set out, the storms include various ill winds. A narrow passage with towering cliffs blocks your route. The sea swirls dangerously. Traditionally, monsters who were once beautiful creatures guard the way and demand that you recognize them—or at least pay a bribe—before you go past. When my mother went by here, two women leaned over the edge, one with teeth like knives, wearing an apron and holding the hands of three little children, and another who wore too much makeup and blew dangerous, tobacco-stained, alcoholic fumes down from above.

After you pass the monsters, you come to a lovely bay, an island in a poster ad. Perhaps this is it. A woman there sells pigs, and she tells you to rest and stay with her for a while. The faces of the pigs look strangely familiar; one of them reminds you of an ex-boyfriend. You find you have developed a sudden desire for pork. She feeds you wonderful dinners and long, luxurious lunches, and you have a good time laughing over the antics of the pigs. Eventually, you see that all this feasting will keep you from your true destination, but when you say you want to leave she is so angry you sneak off at dawn.

In this story, when you ask the crew to tie you to the mast, the sirens on shore have the faces of your aunts and the bodies of beautiful birds. They hop around one another, smoking cigarettes and flicking their wings back and forth. Their gossip lifts up over the waves and catches you as you float past. They speak in a language you only half understand, and they know perfectly well where you are going and the best way to get there, but they do not look up. You want to jump ship, ask them a few questions, certain things you always wanted to know. The current pushes you along; their words are almost clear, almost yours.

It seems as if the gods do not want you to land. But if you persist, you will reach the island at last. You will find that the calm face waiting for you is your own calm face. The woman there has fought off every suitor and learned how to spin. She weaves a story every day, a story that has the noisy mist of the ocean in it, and the quiet shift of a pile of sand. At the end of the day, she unravels the story, happy to let it go and begin again, knowing the journey itself is the best thing, knowing she carries the voyage and the island and the day together in the same palm of the same hand.

My mother went to Greece in 1955, or that is what I have been told.

Women in those days wore tight, waist-defining clothing, and I can imagine her stepping out of the green convertible in which she has just driven across Europe. She hands herself over to the impoverished Italian count, who admires the way the wool of her dress winds itself around her body as he helps her step into the street. In the stories, the count has come with her and her best friend, Daphne, and Daphne's new husband as they traveled from London to Athens. The rest of what we know about him has faded around the edges, like a photograph left too long in the garage. After this he goes back to the small apartment where he lives with his mother forever, in a tiny corner of the old palazzo they still own, filled with furniture they can no longer afford. Now, he dusts himself off in our imagination. He is wearing a white dinner jacket, long at the waist, and sports a thin mustache. His skin is sallow, the way men's skin always used to be, with pale purple circles under his eyes. He looks out at the world sadly, since he knows he is destined to play a minor role. But the more I imagine my mother, the clearer she becomes. Across her shoulders she has wrapped a chiffon print scarf, the kind women wear in old movies. She wears dark, sharp, pointed glasses, and she does not take them off as she looks up at Daphne's new honeymoon apartment.

The white of the new building is dazzling as marble, and the sky looks clean and wide and blue. We know they are in Glyphada, which we must imagine not as it is now, with the unfinished air of a suburb that has been surpassed by other suburbs, wearing its

8

age with embarrassment. Their Glyphada is new, freshly minted, pristine. Identical rows of white boxes mark the new end of Athens, and in the distance there are only the honey-colored fields of Attica. Beyond, they can imagine the villages, which still sleep their village sleep, the rhythm of boats gone out and nets pulled in. Behind them, the pulse of traffic reveals a city that moves just quickly enough to spare a few of its citizens to live by the sea on a hill, from which they can feel young and modern and rich.

The apartments have double-basined sinks in their bathrooms, and room for appliances in the kitchen. When he bought it, Daphne's future husband told her she would feel she had never left New York; he was taking her back to modern Greece, the new old world. Their apartment seems to be the biggest, the best, built at the very top of the hill. Like a moat, the street wraps itself around the building and its sleek nautical lines. The asphalt has barely dried. The street will be important later in the story, as will the veranda that opens from the guest bedroom below. A bit of mud has stained the bottom of the wall running the outer length of the building, a rich red that will remind anyone who looks at it of the soil, pungent and wet.

Why is my mother there? A year before, she was in the back room of her parents' apartment. She had dark circles under her eyes because she never went out, and even her parents, who had told her to come home after college to help the family, were worried. She was only twenty, and she thought her life had finished.

How do I know this? Of course, she never told me. She let things slip. Stories spilled accidentally or turned up on the back of old photographs, caught in a box hidden deep in the garage. Neither of us knew there were other ways into the past, other routes. Every story can be told, and in so many different ways.

This is how I know about a scene she has kept—a scene she must have kept—from her childhood.

She is almost eight. Her mother and her mother's sisters are gathered around the kitchen table, heaps of multicolored silk and

9

wire piled on the table and pooled in soft bunches of color around their feet. My mother has been enlisted to wind the wire around the folds of silk the women have molded with their fingers, the large bunches making the shapes of roses and tulips and marigolds. Since the women get paid per flower, they trade fabric across the table quickly. Their hands have been blunted by years of work, cut by knives when they were young and careless, healed over in rough patches, peeling a bit around the fingers where they have touched lime and bleach, broken along the edges of their palms by salt and dryness. (I can confirm this by looking at my own hands, where the skin along the fingers is starting to pucker and go rough; or my mother's, whose thumb after rolling grape leaves is crisscrossed with calluses that withstand the brine.)

My mother's hands are small enough to perform the delicate winding of the wire, but she is impatient. Outside, her brothers play in the street. Her family moved to this apartment, one of a series, small and dark between other buildings. They have moved for so many years, escaping landlords, trying to find a safe harbor, and now they say it will get better with the war. My mother sleeps with her brothers in one room. They have had a hard time making friends; the rough neighborhood boys are still testing them.

My mother listens to her aunts gossiping. They are speaking her first language, the words she was told to put away when she went to school. Their voices are melodious and fluent in a way they never are when they speak to their children, their tongues bumping against the edges of an alien language. They move through the thick vowels of their native language quickly, water running downstream. They know a girl who has just come from Greece who is marrying someone outside the community, and they enjoy their own outrage, passing it between them, kneading it over and over again. My mother imagines Queens outside the window, the tiny box houses and cracked streets that flow all the way to the East River and the bridges that span the waters with the speed of light, the towers of Manhattan and the beautiful women.

On the stove, the women have left a chicken to boil in a large pot of salted water. They are waiting for the meat to be so soft it falls off the bones, and then they will clear the table and begin to separate the sweetness of the meat from the gristle. The windows fog over with steam, leaving a small line of gray to mark the outside. My mother watches the last bit of bright sky outside, waiting for steam to cover the top of the glass. She does not notice when the fire begins, when the flame from the stove, pushing out from the bottom of the wide pan, catches the end of an oil-soaked rag. The women have jumped up, thrown the rag into the sink, and doused it with water. They all laugh, talking to the stove as if it were a child or a god, as if they could convince it not to perform such an evil act in the future. My mother says, without looking up from the wire, *It wasn't the fault of the stove, you left the rag too near the heat.*

Her aunts are amused. Her mother does not look at her but says to her sisters, *So the egg stands up on its legs and gives advice to the chicken.* They come back to the table and do not speak to her, to let her know they disapprove, but they hand her another flower because they still love her and disapproval should be punishment enough. The words she forms in her mind are English, and she builds them block by block, a defensive wall they will never penetrate. She has put her allegiance down on the side of the oven, on the side of steel and pipes, on technology that is not to blame for its own errors.

Now she pulls her sunglasses onto her head and smiles as she looks at the count, who is helping Daphne and her husband pull their luggage out of the trunk. She is scheduled to return to New York in a month, and what she does not know yet is that she will cash in her ticket and stay until the money runs out. Her best friend in the world has just run up the steps and is opening the gate of her new

11

apartment. She hugs her husband with squeals of delight because he found them this home and she is married and wealthy and only nineteen. She is about to run over to my mother and give her what in those times was considered an acceptable girlish squeeze. My mother looks away for a moment, out over the tops of the hills to the horizon. Then it wells up inside of her once more, the feeling that is still new, of an opening into a field that has always been hidden, of looking out a window and expecting darkness and finding, to her surprise, a wide sea bright with sunlight. The sky stuns her, more blue than it will ever be in New York. She has crossed the Atlantic on a luxury liner, the Atlantic her mother crossed years ago in steerage during the First World War. She has driven through Europe with her wealthy young friends and a handsome companion, seen the Bayeux tapestries, and drunk the wines of regions whose roots go deeper than nations and borders.

For the first time in her life she is on her own, away from her family, her country, the ambiguity of first and second languages, and she likes the way the breeze feels on her face. She knows what the world looks like around her. That is all she needs to know.

What she does not see, so far away it might almost be the future, is a tiny dark cloud rising over the horizon. Black at the center, it glows at the edges with a weird green light. It is a cloud that did not want to rise from the earth, a cloud that never meant to be formed, a cloud that is reluctant to rain. It will hold on to its burden for as long as it can, but when the time comes it will fall, pushing the waters back into a new channel. It is a cloud attached to my story, the story of her daughter, who will go to Greece thirty years later.

Psyche and Aphrodite

Aphrodite stepped out of a shell. Like an oyster, a pearl, something soft and shiny, edible and small, safe and contained. In the myths, she floats in and out, flaxen-haired and large-breasted, the Marilyn Monroe of Olympus, a familiar type—tossed by emotions, anger, or lust. The pout of her lips could send a fleet of ships to the bottom of the sea; the flash of her eyes sets fire to a field.

The famous story of Aphrodite and her son, Eros, reveals her worst qualities. In the story, a beautiful girl has been born to a king. Psyche is so lovely she arouses the wrath of the goddess of love, who condemns her never to love or be loved and to die, slain by a serpent. As is often the case, the ancients provide an escape clause: Aphrodite's son, Eros, falls in love with her and whisks her off to his palace. For a time, all is well. He has only one rule, that she never see him. He visits her at night and the sex is marvelous, so Psyche does not complain. One day, her sisters visit her and fill her with suspicions. *Who is he? Does anyone know his family?* Under their influence, she lights a candle and has only a moment to see he is really a god before he disappears, seemingly forever. Trying to find him, she encounters Aphrodite, a typical Greek mom, jealous and overprotective. Aphrodite tries to ruin Psyche's beauty by forcing her to embark on a series of nail-destroying, dirty, and disfiguring tasks. Behind the scenes, her lover magically helps her complete each one. In the end, Aphrodite reluctantly concedes. With a sweep of her red-nailed hand, she gives Psyche her son. Psyche becomes immortal and they live happily ever after.

With a little imagination, it is possible to see the story very differently. In my version, Aphrodite, the goddess of love, drops her disguise to reveal her ancient origins: wise and powerful. She is a goddess old enough to have begun the world, to cause light to desire darkness, earth to lust for water. In this story, Aphrodite and Psyche are allies.

In fact, Psyche dreams up Eros out of her own boredom. Being the daughter of minor royalty, living in the countryside, she waits to be bartered for pigs like her sisters, married off to the fat sons of her father's neighbors. Every evening, she stares at the horizon, imagining fate walking out of the haze. She spends her time filing her nails and trying on new outfits with her sisters, thinking there must be more to life than this. One day, she hears a voice in her ears, lips like velvet brushing her lobes. Predicting her mother's disapproval only makes her desire more fierce, and she follows the voice as it leads her to a marble palace, as it tells her to lie down on the satin pillows, to open and relax. At night, although she cannot see his face, she feels her lover's jaw in her hands, the cleft against her thumb, and knows he is beautiful. Between kisses, he holds her against his chest and talks to her about her life, but whenever she asks him about his, he puts his hand against her lips and whispers, *Shush*.

In my version, Aphrodite herself inspires Psyche to drop hot wax on her lover's chest in the middle of the night, waking him up. Aphrodite is the beat of her blood pounding her inner ear, the part of her that says, *This is not enough*. When Eros disappears in a petulant huff, blaming her for her desire, for not following his rules, at first she is filled with despair. Was it so bad, living with a god? The alternative is returning home, where her sisters and her mother will say they warned her while they wrap themselves around their husbands. She decides to look for him.

By the time Aphrodite finds her, Psyche has lost her looks. Searching for Eros, she is depressed, has stopped washing her hair, and has drunk and seen too much. Aphrodite sets her tasks, true, but not to destroy her. Aphrodite would have known that, in order to live with her son, Psyche would have to face her fears, to be strong. More than anyone, Aphrodite knows how spoiled Eros has become, controlling the hearts of men and gods. Loose with his arrow, sure of his own beauty, he is in danger of becoming another of Psyche's confining horizons. Aphrodite teaches Psyche patience when she forces her to gather a hundred thousand grains of rice. She teaches her bravery when she sends her into hell to gather water. When Aphrodite finishes with her, Psyche knows how to encounter danger and most disasters. She can spend eternity with a god, face-to-face.

— Men have always had war and war games, quests and adventures, to test themselves. In their stories, we women live by love, waiting passively on the sidelines, the reward or the temptation. Underneath that version lies another, where the goddesses do more than chase around the gods; they too shape the world. After all, love can also be a testing ground. Sometimes the goddesses are there to help us tumble into danger. Behind us, Aphrodite moves the air and water, giving us ourselves.

In my mother's story, Aphrodite inhabits the bodies of aunts and mother, girlfriends and cousins. She takes on many disguises to nudge my mother toward adventure. For me, Aphrodite has the voice of a ghost. She has been the desire for something only half remembered,

15

a search that took me from the new world to the old, to find what had always been there, hidden. Aphrodite entered my life through the spirit of my dead grandmother.

It is the third year of my life, and my dead grandmother is trying to speak to me. She is telling me to go outside and visit my grandfather in the backyard. She wants me to learn something.

My parents have asked my grandfather to live with them. They have only been married for a few years, and they have a little house on Serrano Avenue in Los Feliz, California. The sun from the desert city outside the house makes sticky patterns on the walls and I run my fingers along them, feeling their *bump bump* along the ridges of my skin. The stairs are as large as I am, each one a sea of soft brown wood to swim across. Outside, the patio stones are warm on my feet, and then the grass tumbles down in a green wave, scrunching under my toes.

My grandfather tends his new lemon tree. He bought it and planted it next to a row of tomatoes and pots of basil. The tomato plants have curling green tendrils on them, with furry leaves. At eye level, buds of unripe tomatoes sleep against the stalks of the little trees. The fur tickles my nose, and my grandfather lifts me up on his knee. He speaks to me in Greek, pointing out *ta lemonia*. The fruits have waxy skin, a yellow more bright than the sun behind its dusty haze. They pucker and sweat and bend the spiny branches of the tree. I breathe in the scents of the tomatoes, sweet and dusty like clean sand, and the lemons, which smell like the sea, a sharp distant longing. My grandfather looks me in the eyes and nods. He pulls one off for me to hold in my hands, and my dead grandmother smiles.

Eight years later, my grandfather has gone and I have forgotten I ever knew the rhythm and pattern of Greek. We live in a big house on a hill in Los Angeles, and I have a sister and a brother. There are still empty lots in the city, patches in the hills or canyons where no one has yet built over the plowed earth, and the chaparral has begun to climb back at the edges of the fields. Because of the way sharp desire grabs me, watering my eyes, I know the voice that calls my name and leads me outside belongs to my dead grandmother. The lot next to our house looks over a tiny arroyo filled with cactus; below, wide boulevards stretch south and west, the tiny buildings deferring to the wide sky that leads to the ocean. A few winter clouds drift over downtown. Inside, I can hear the sound of the television, my brother and sister fighting, the dog barking. I lie down in the grass and look up into the sky until I am dizzy. I can feel the blue reaching all the way across the continent, across oceans, reducing distance to a moment. It is the blue painted under the dome of the church where my mother takes us once a year, the blue that rises over the face of the Mother of God. I stay in the field looking up and lose track of time.

By the time my mother comes out to find me, I have had a long conversation with my grandmother. How else can I explain the longing that took hold of me, that made me say to my mother that we had to go to church right now, that I wanted to light a candle at Saint Sophia's? Religion has never played a big role in our lives. We go to church for Easter at the bidding of my mother and to Passover dinners with the cousins of my father. I am eleven years old, and only a few years before, I had cried with relief when my parents told me I would not have to go to Saturday school anymore to learn Greek; they gave us the choice and we all said *never again*. My mother explained how during the four hundred years of occupation, the Greek language and religion were actually forbidden, illegal. Greek children had to go to school at night to be taught by monks. *They felt grateful for the chance.* We had even learned a song about it, *Phengaraki mou lambro*, about a little moon that lit up their path. Four hundred years of occupation did not stand a chance against a free Saturday. Now I tell my mother I will not leave the field until she promises to take me to Saint Sophia's. Right after lunch, she swears. We go back to the house, and I play in the kitchen and forget the field and the candle.

I am fifteen and we are in the kitchen with my dead grandmother. For two days, we have been cooking her recipes for my mother's annual Christmas/birthday party. Under pressure, we have had a big fight and are trying not to speak to each other. The turkey that has been roasting in the oven all night has just come out, warming the room. Silently, sullenly, we make the bread. My mother kneads it because she does not trust me to do it right, and her fingers are covered in dough when the phone rings. I hand it to her and she cradles it on her shoulder, the flour getting all over the mouthpiece and the dial. She pushes her hair back under her scarf and gets powder on her forehead. My mother smiles for the first time that day. Her mouth takes the names of her aunts and turns them into endearments, flowing into their language, listening to them pass the phone back and forth between them. She is speaking to another world in a strange voice. The words sound like water rushing over sand. She has deep bells in her vowels; consonants form round roofs in her mouth. The sentences wash together with the thick fluidity of olive oil or honey. She speaks behind an invisible wall that makes what she says disappear into the air. If I close my eyes, I can fall into the rhythm of this speech and believe I understand the meaning of the words. Almost, almost, I am about to break into the blue world of the old language. I can feel my grandmother rising up in me, a perfect wave. My mother puts the phone down and asks me in English why I am not working, why I have stopped. *We have guests coming in five hours*. I stomp out of the room as noisily as I can and get on the phone to my best friend, who can listen to me for hours about how much I hate my mother. The sea rolls back; the sand settles and falls silent. My grandmother will have to find another way.

18

It is my first year at college and I am far from California, in a chilly eastern corner of America. I am in an English lecture. The professor has skin like parchment and a seaman's beard over his dry face. His dull eyes look as if they would like to shut once and for all. Behind the sandpapered fingers sweeping over his beard, he holds secrets he will never share with us. The boys in the class creep toward him. He strokes his beard harder and harder, and the boys move in more closely. I am in the back of the circle, and in my throat words are caught like pieces of wood in a channel. *But, but*, the words say. *But, but*. The room is cold. Outside, the air is getting colder than I have ever felt it before, and it is only November. I imagine my skin drying out and flaking away as I listen to the scratch of his beard. After class, I separate from the boys praising the lecturer and walk out into an afternoon in which the sun has already gone down behind the brick alleyway. A pigeon rises off the wall into the sky, wings beating like tiny drums, and I see a vine leaf tremble in the wind. My tongue has curled into the back of my throat and will not come out again. Pinned and shivering on the wall, a notice announces a new class in modern Greek.

My dead grandmother has almost forgotten me. When I enter the classroom in January and hear the dark-haired woman say *Kalimera; good morning*, my grandmother remembers some work she has to do. When the woman bends her tongue against the back of her mouth and my own tongue uncurls, my grandmother stretches her arms inside me and nudges her memory. She stands. The snow outside disappears. Behind the wood-paneled walls, the blue sea laps.

Sometimes goddesses appear in your dreams. Sometimes they hide among the furniture, moving objects suddenly in your path or freeing your way to something you wanted but once was blocked. In the story of how my mother got to Greece, my grandmother is a silent presence, much more than a ghost. She appears in a cloud of smoke and disappears, a grain of wood my mother rubs herself against. It is an old pattern.

The year before she went to Greece was the worst in my mother's life. Imagine: She had gotten herself into college and was supposed to graduate, the first in her family. She had majored in Victorian literature, because when she was growing up she had loved to read thick, rainy books with lowering clouds and wool-clad heroines. She had minored in Spanish because it was practical (someone's cousin's uncle said he could get her a job as a secretary in an import-export company), but really because she wanted to read the original *Don Quixote*. And it had all been a success, until the very end. On the day of her graduation from Queens College, instead of marching with the class, she stood at the back with her Spanish professor, sobbing. Between the two of them, they went through the entire box of Kleenex before the procession of elegant black gowns wound up. The dean of the college paused for only a moment in the place where her name should have been before moving on with the ceremony. What made it worse for everyone was that she was the president of the student body, the first woman ever elected to that post.

Which was what had caused all the trouble in the first place. My mother still has the editorial from *The New York Times*, written to defend her. I saw it once, brittle and yellow but still clearly showing her name, her original Greek name, in that alluring typeface.

How had she gotten to that point? It probably started years before, the day she had forged her father's signature on the college application and had to break it to him when she was accepted. *My parents didn't want me to go*, she told me once. *But what was I going to do, stay home and iron my brothers' underwear?* (That came later.)

Since her first day in school, when the kids around her spoke an alien language and laughed at her heavy accent, she had learned to negotiate two lives. At home, she lived like the daughter of a proud village family, never raising her voice, always saying yes. Outside, she had learned to speak, with an edge as hard as leather boots, the New York street slang that did not always stop her from getting beaten up on her way home from school. In the streets, she wore lipstick and smoked cigarettes. She always wiped it off before getting within a block of the house and had to sneak her cigarettes in the dark of her room, where her mother complained she was always reading; she was going to pile the books so high one day they would fall over and kill her. When her parents walked into the room unannounced, she would slam her cigarette into her book and hide both behind her. *Luckily, they both smoked so much they never knew.*

She was only sixteen when she started college, but she had already spotted the escape route. After she applied to Queens College with a forged signature and was accepted, she stepped out of the village and was headed for the big city. It is no wonder she had the strength to rebel four years later, not against her father but against the whole establishment. No wonder, when this failed and it seemed she was heading back to the village, she almost lost the strength to crawl out again.

In her final year of college, my mother was elected student body president. She must have run and won the votes; she must have been that popular. The college had been transformed by vets back from the war who were sick of politics and just wanted to read and talk. It was okay, finally, to be a woman and to be smart, to win all the bridge games, realizing girls from better neighborhoods were even more scared than she was. After the election, her picture was in the student paper, and her father pinned it to the register on the deli counter, pointing it out to all his customers.

Everything went wrong when the Queens College Democratic Club decided that for its annual debate it would invite a woman to speak who had been in the French resistance during the war. She had escaped the Gestapo and come to America, where she thought it would be safe to say she was a Communist. Having risked her life

21

for more important things, she was hardened enough to be open about her politics. As president, my mother had to approve all activities, and she signed the papers to let the speaker come. It got to the dean, and the dean tried to get to my mother.

I have always imagined it in black and white, a bit scratched, the dialogue clipped and fuzzy. The dean, his hair slicked back, looking like Lionel Barrymore, tells my mother that of course he understands her desire to be fair, but true loyalty and the American spirit demand that she rescind the offer. In a gum-snappingly fast voice, my mother tells him her father read her the Constitution as a bedtime story every night, and it might be kid's stuff to some people, but she for one believes every word. Or maybe she is just very calm and looks him straight in the face and says no. The dean flares his nostrils and leans back in his chair, pulling on his tie. *Don't make me use force, my dear,* he says, or something along those lines. My mother is wearing jeans with the cuffs rolled up, bobby socks, and oxfords; her shirt has a Peter Pan collar. Or maybe she is dressed like Katharine Hepburn in the courtroom, complete with gloves and hat. Maybe she says, *For as long as I'm in office, I am the president, and I have a responsibility to those who elected me,* or maybe she gets up and shakes his hand with great dignity. At which point, the dean tells her that despite her perfect grade-point average, unless she agrees to a public recantation, he will see to it she never receives a degree from Queens College.

My mother did not graduate. The Queens College newspaper wrote an impassioned defense of her case, and the article in the college paper came to the attention of *The New York Times.* It was 1954. Joe McCarthy was reaching the end of his power as the unelected leader of the country. He had enough poison left in him to enter the mind of the dean of Queens College and turn him into Lionel Barrymore. But his light had been dimmed low enough so that the *Times* could take up the defense of my mother, using her case as an example of how things had gone too far, how it was time to return to reason. That is how she ended up in an editorial with her picture, which got pinned up in the deli too.

Once, my mother told me she had thought about going to law school but could not face the application process. Maybe it was the thought of the missing degree. Maybe the dean had put an end to her political ambitions forever. After her nongraduation, she went back to her parents' apartment and started working at the import-export company.

Many years later, my mother met Eleanor Roosevelt. By then she had become a reporter in New York, and she had been sent to cover a speech at the UN. A small group of journalists sat close to the stage. Afterward, Eleanor had looked up with that impeccable good breeding of hers and said, *I'm going uptown, does anyone need a lift?* My mother's office was across town in the Time Life Building, but she said, *Yes, I do.*

It was a long ride uptown because it was raining. I do not know what they said but I love this story, because Eleanor was everything I always imagined my mother to be when I was growing up: political, brave, compassionate, clever, East Coast. At many points in my life, I have felt far from the Eleanor ideal. Once, I have come to realize, so did my mother.

She had forgotten she had no money with her, and she had to walk all the way back to midtown in the rain, but it was worth it, every step.

DEMETER AND PERSEPHONE

Women need their mother's stories, but just at the moment in our lives when we should listen the most, we find ourselves enemies, staring across deep trenches where the bodies of our comrades have fallen before us, and we think we are alone, fighting a new battle. Just down the line, a little bit over the horizon, Persephone and Demeter are having it out. Persephone wants to be with her lover, the dark god in the leather jacket. Demeter is warning her about diseases, and Persephone says, *You just don't understand me, Mom; we're in love.* Demeter thinks of the corn that needs to be nudged along, so she says, *Okay, fine, go ahead, make your own mistakes.* Which of course Persephone does. Nothing underground works out the way Persephone expected (does it ever?), and she tires of trying to fix up Hades—cleaning the river Styx and renovating the thrones. She misses her friends the nymphs and the days spent by the river helping her mother make the wheat grow or gossiping over suppliants needing a favor.

Some say that Persephone was kidnapped, pillaged, and stolen and that Demeter begged the gods to make an arrangement; that, being a quiet and unassuming goddess, she tied her hair in a kerchief and made the rounds: *Effendi, please, my daughter—can't you do something?* The men met, the uncles and the cousins; they negotiated and sent ambassadors, traded favors, worked out a deal. They say because these gods were so clever, we have winter while Persephone is with her husband, god of the underworld, and spring when she returns to be with her mother.

Anyone who has ever been a daughter, or had one, knows what really happened between Demeter and Persephone. Persephone had her years of living underground, where she was convinced she could succeed without her mother's advice. After all, her mother was just a goddess of the earth, but Persephone would be co-ruler of the dead; she would show her mother she knew a thing or two about life and mortality and would do it so much more elegantly than Demeter, with her upper lip covered in sweat, one hand on the corn husks, the other digging through roots. How old-fashioned—all that dirt and fertility. How much more civilized and modern the cool, pale ranks of shades, dressed fashionably in black, drained of passion and blood. Hades might be a little taciturn, a bit quiet, but in time her husband would surely learn to communicate. Theirs would be a model marriage among the immortals—none of the usual affairs and carrying on.

Later, she can see what folly that was. It takes a long time for Persephone to recognize how much her story matches Demeter's, how they are really the same after all. It is only years after running away, when Persephone's heart is truly broken and she knows there is no way her husband the god will ever change, that she has the courage to come back up for air and ask her mother how she managed everything in her youth, juggling her celestial lovers and the work in the fields. I see Demeter with her sleeves rolled up, as she is interrupted by her daughter's return. Part of her thinks, *No, it is too late to come back; things can never be the way they were.* And they can't. The days when Persephone would play in her mother's garden without a thought of anyone else in the world are gone forever. But they come to a new understanding. Demeter can see Persephone's scars, see that she has been deceived by others and by her own dreams and that she knows, finally, how to listen. Spring is the talk that finally takes place between them, each bloom a phrase of laughter, each shade of green the promise of their peace.

We have come to Greece on a family vacation. I am sixteen years old, and my mother and I are fighting about my virginity. Like two hags in the market struggling over the same piece of rotten fruit, we cannot agree on its value. Having decided that my virginity is as worthless to me as my own body, I have already made several attempts to give it away. I would like to trade it for the world of masculine knowledge, something tough as leather that will bend but not break. I feel I have gone ripe long ago, and I want the inside story.

Once it is gone, you'll look at every man as a potential lover for the rest of your life. You don't know what a burden that is, she tells me, and I hear, *Stay where you are, don't leave me.*

The rest of the family seems to think everything is fine. Our fights have always had an epic dimension to them, and the onlookers have stopped keeping score. The real battle is taking place in another world; in our dreams, between our silences. Under every word we say to each other there is a faint clash of arms, the scrape of armor. It is just another family vacation.

We are in Europe for the first time in our lives and we have landed in Greece only briefly, on the last leg of a Christmas tour, almost as an afterthought. Greece for us is what it is for so many outsiders—the edge of Europe, the back alley, faintly seedy and litter-strewn. My sister and brother and I know almost nothing about what happened to our mother here and barely recognize any connection to our surroundings. To us, being Greek has only meant visits to our mother's relatives in New York, forced and reluctant in the summer while the world beat somewhere outside: a few hours in stuffy rooms on Long Island, polyester furniture, women with big doughy arms feeding us oily meats and tooth-numbingly sweet desserts. As for Athens and our Greek relatives, we are even less impressed. The city coughs out cold winter smog. The cousins are worse than the New York relatives, larger and more friendly, with even less to say. The younger ones smile too frequently, displaying bad teeth, an unforgivable offense to a young American from a middle-class family with expensive orthodonture. The oldest ones wear dark colors and move slowly. We cannot quite believe that all these people are related to our mother, who wants to extend our stay. She is the only one of us having a good time. One of the cousins, named Fanny, has frizzy black hair and a large gold-capped tooth. When we go to her house, Fanny offers my mother a beer in an old-fashioned brown bottle, and they laugh together until we are sick with jealousy.

We spend most of the trip in Athens, where we stay in an acceptably modern hotel, the best part of which is the indoor pool. Close to a training ground, a group of Olympic athletes use it to loosen their muscles after working out. My sister and I have escaped our family and are lying on deck chairs, drinking Cokes. We watch the long bodies move in the water, their indifferent heads turning with each stroke, not looking at us, and it makes our hearts pound harder. One of them actually stares at me when he climbs out, and I see that he is tall and wiry. He finds us later in the lobby, where we are lingering, nervous and obvious. He invites us to have coffee with him. My sister bravely agrees to come along, but it is clear when he invites a friend that he wants to talk to me; he is looking at me; he wants me. His dark eyes reflect tiny pools of light. He tells me he is a high jumper. His English is mellifluous and slow, and when he feels frustrated at not finding a word he needs, he rubs the backs of his fingers along my arm and I nod to show him I know just what he means. We make a date for late the next day.

My sister has spilled the beans. I can tell by the way everyone looks at me when we meet for breakfast. The waiter brings the toast that reminds us of congealed bread crumbs, and the butter scrapes along the surface in the silence. I put honey on my knife and spread it over the butter and take a loud bite. My mother says she thought we might like to go to Delphi, the belly button of the universe.

I am cool. I crunch on my toast and casually inquire how long the trip will take. My mother tells me we will be back in time for dinner, and I agree to go. I call the high jumper from the lobby phone and change the time from eight to ten o'clock. In the car, I make a special effort to be nice to everyone, including my sister, who looks smug.

We get to the ferry by three. I note the time for everyone's benefit, but no one suggests turning around. I wonder aloud whether we will really make it back by dinnertime. My mother is the general; she is running the expedition, and she says nothing about turning back. I try sulking, but she has already put on her armor. She blithely drives the car onto the ferry as if it is not already getting dark, as if we can still see the ruins and be back in time.

The site is signposted: 30 kilometers up the mountain. We start to drive as the sun goes down, the road growing more windy and more precarious. When I put my hand against the glass, it feels like ice. We are all wearing the jeans and cotton sweaters an Athens winter requires. Inside, the car fogs up with the heat rubbing off the struggle between our wills. Even my father has become quiet, and my mother asks him to turn on the radio, where he finds only static, up and down the frequencies, before turning it off.

We arrive at the site and find it closed. My mother suggests staying overnight to see it in the morning. But this time it is not enough to sulk. This time I start to cry and yell, *You knew all along this was going to happen; you manipulated this whole situation*, and, under the noise of my voice, *You bitch*. Then, *You promised we would go back*.

To prove she will not stoop to a public battle with me, she just laughs slightly and says, *Yes, I did. Let's go, then.* Everyone else feels their day has been ruined by me, and they push their resentment toward me on the drive back, but I feel calm, triumphant; I imagine myself kissing the high jumper, his snaking arms wrapped around my back.

Then we are driving through snow, and the car begins to slip on the road. My mother slows down. The atmosphere changes in the car. We are all looking out, peering into the darkness. The road is still climbing, and the snow is beginning to pile up on the bushes along the shoulder. We can see from the blackness on our right that the road is built on a cliff's edge and it hugs the side of the mountain. Now we all feel scared.

We see the headlights coming toward us from a long way away. It is not hard to figure out a truck has slipped over to our side of the road and is sliding toward us along the ice. I think of signs on highways back home that display brake failure, the cartoon cutouts of the truck sending puffs of smoke down the triangle of the road. My mother yells at us to get out and tells my father to take the wheel, to pull the car over safely to the side of the road.

We scramble across ice to the snowbanks on the other side. My father inches the car back to the shoulder, and everyone closes their eyes except me. I watch as the truck careens past the car and still have my eyes open to see my father step out the other side.

Now we are on a mountain in the snow without our car. My mother embraces my father. We are all safe. In the face of disaster, we have pulled together. I let the high jumper go. In my imagination, he puts his jacket back on and walks into the pool and under the water; the last thing to disappear are his pouting red lips.

We see lights in the distance and stumble toward them. We discover we have gotten stuck next to a ski resort, and we are not the only ones. They give us the last room. For as long as we can, we stay to drink hot chocolate and watch Germans in neon ski suits toast

29

one another in the lobby. Eventually, my brother and sister and I all fall asleep in one bed, head to foot, as we would at parties when we were small.

The next morning we find the car, missing a battery and our camera, but it starts again with some local help. *Probably the same people who stole the battery,* my mother says, and I laugh with her. She is conceding a battlement, letting me know I am half an adult; I am in on the joke.

We drive back to the ruins and spend an hour climbing up and down the amphitheater. I stand with my sister and brother at the top, while my father stands at the bottom, speaking to us in amplified whispers. We have fallen back into the right formation, and I find I am glad I missed the high jumper. I feel happy to be with my family, listening to my father's quiet voice. When we look down, we see the green cliffs of the mountain tapering off into distant fields and we understand why it was called the belly button of the universe.

The day has turned warm. The road shines, wet with melted snow. Before we get back in the car, we drink out of the spring where the ancient oracle was said to have gathered her wisdom. I see her between the crevices of the rock, near the ruined temples, a middle-aged woman with long hair and a black gown.

On the way back, we start down the hill again. A mile outside of Delphi, my mother changes her mind and says we will drive the other way, along the pass toward Athens. She does not want to go back the same way we came, although the new route may be longer. We reach Athens late that night to find a message waiting to call one of the cousins. They have all been worried about us, he says. There was a mudslide in late afternoon at the bottom of the hill and some cars were buried. If we had taken our original route, we might have been caught in a terrible disaster.

It is a pain and a pleasure, like an old loose tooth, the way my mother is always right. I feel her looking into our bones, reading our minds. She has a small jar full of incense; when she burns sage and myrrh, the smoke forms our names, tells her what she needs to know. In the temples outside her cave, there are large storehouses filled with olive oil and precious stones, gifts from all the people who have asked her for their future. She never shows her true face; her secrets are buried in a dark cave.

When I try to look at my own bones, they transmute themselves or run away. They refuse me completely. I only feel myself when someone else tells me I am there. When someone touches me I become visible. My bones settle down and my skin assembles itself. My mother is a large marble wall, nicked and rain-worn but still standing, through which I cannot see myself.

There was a turning point for Persephone when she began to wonder whether her mother had always been all-powerful and brave. It was not just that she controlled the weather, matched the wind to the rain. All daughters see their mothers like that—sun one day, cloud the next. Some say Persephone and Demeter were really the same goddess in different phases, that Demeter had done her time underground and knew all along both how to create and what has to die before creation can take place.

My mother had a best friend named Daphne. Daphne lived with her mother in the same apartment house, and her family came from the same part of Greece, Thessaly. The peninsula of Greece pushes itself out into the water like a fist, scattering islands all around it. In the palm of that fist is Thessaly, with long plains and harsh mountains. Guidebooks mention the fertility of the land, washed by rivers coming off the surrounding mountains. Daphne's family were from the plains, wealthy farmers, rich off beet plantations. Daphne looked like a daughter of the fields—her hair as golden as wheat, her eyes the blue reflection of a river when it comes out into the sun, open and bright, her cheeks the sugar red of beets. My mother's family came from the mountains, and her family had a mountain people's sense of hunger, a mountain people's expectation of loss. Perhaps that is why, although my mother has eyes as green as new leaves, lips as generous as mountain fruit, and cheekbones sloping like cliff sides, she never believed she was beautiful. People who come from the mountains cannot afford beautiful daughters, and no one in America would have told her that dark curls have power and a gap in the teeth is an ancient sign of strong women.

Daphne's father had sent his wife and baby daughter to New York just before the war. He had seen trouble ahead and decided they would be safer with his relatives in America. His family knew my mother's family; they all belonged to the same Thessalian community, refugees from the villages of the mountains and the plains. When the Depression passed, they ended up living in the same apartment house, one on top of the other.

In New York, in the beginning, Daphne and my mother did not care about their common origins or about Greece at all. They were New York girls, with New York ambitions and the new world's way of bucking old-world rules. They longed for the same things, loved the same movies and the same books, and wanted Manhattan with the same logic of inevitable destiny. Still, underneath this new-world similarity were the old-world differences: Daphne always believed things would go up, and my mother was afraid to look in case they went down.

They met when my mother was fourteen and Daphne was twelve. The war had ended, and my mother's parents were able to settle into one apartment without having to move on for not paying the rent. My grandmother planted a garden in a lot out back, where she grew giant dahlias, fresh herbs, and tomatoes. My mother's father had started to make money again, and he soon had enough saved to open his own deli. When they were not in school, the kids worked behind the counter; my mother learned how to keep a knife sharp and to cut fast. She told me her father kept a kosher section for his Jewish customers and instructed his kids to slice lox *so thin I can read the paper through it.*

Daphne lived alone above them with her mother, who wore dark widow's clothing and a heavy cross around her neck. Daphne had long tresses that she wore parted on the side, and her short rayon dresses fell on her body with the smooth lines of a woman twice her age. She was also sharp, smart, and curious. One afternoon, she climbed down the fire escape from her apartment into the garden where my mother was reading and asked her if she could borrow a book. Soon, they both learned to climb the fire escape into each other's rooms, and they shared books and cigarettes and dreams about boys until two years after my mother started college, when Daphne's father sent her a husband.

Every year, Daphne's mother sent her husband a photograph of his daughter. The year Daphne was sixteen, her father reminded her mother that he had not forgotten about her by sending over a young business acquaintance with a marriage proposal.

Daphne's mother prayed every night on her knees that her daughter would be kept with her, that she would not be sent back to Greece. The civil war had ended and strong laws made the country safe for business. Her future son-in-law was not yet thirty, but he already had a fortune, and when he walked down the gangplank of the steamer in Manhattan, she noticed his hair did not move in the breeze and his suit had no lines in it at all. She had to stop herself from making a cross over her heart in a gesture of supplication to God.

Daphne had told her best friend, my mother, about her prospective husband. Maybe she felt envy that my mother had new friends and a new life in college. When my mother became the youngest in her class—a freshman at only sixteen—she measured herself up, mop-headed and gap-toothed. Hopelessly unprepared to meet the sophisticated postwar coeds in their matching sweater sets and coiffures, she turned to Daphne, who told her what to wear and how to carry her bag and books. Maybe Daphne just wanted to prove to my mother that she could push further ahead into womanhood, skip college altogether, and become that sophisticated thing, a woman pursued by a man. Although younger, Daphne had always been the leader. She was the first one to steal lipstick for them both, and she showed my mother how to apply it in thick ruby lines. Daphne told my mother that as a New York American woman, she could wrap a Greek country bumpkin around her finger. She had every intention of enjoying the whole experience.

In the year before my mother started college, they had one summer together, a summer I see as clearly as I see the dry heat and chlorine reflections of California. I can feel the heat rising off the asphalt of their crowded streets, the expectation that sits in your limbs when you are ripe, urging you on like a kind of thirst. At night, Daphne's mother went to sleep before the light had faded, and they would climb up on the roof of the apartment house and smoke cigarettes together, sitting in beach chairs, looking out at the lights of Manhattan as they flickered on one by one. During the day, they took the train out to Jones Beach, and in the twilight of the dressing room they would tape letters across each other's back. These emerged later as pale messages across their tan skin: words of enticement, like *Hey, sailor*, or provocation, like *Yankees are the best*, or declarations, like *Smoke Camels*. When they went home at night, their skin burned under their sweaters with the power of all the caressing eyes that had turned on them.

Once, when they had stayed on the roof long enough for the stars to come out, they looked up together into the sky and dared each other to stare for as long as they could. Daphne broke first and tried to make a joke out of it by worrying how she would look at her own funeral, how would she know? And they made a vow to each other that wherever they were in the world when they died, the other one would come to make sure her lipstick was straight and her mascara on right.

(What does this story tell me other than how Greek they were, how in the midst of summer, their bodies bursting with life, they were looking for the other side, planning their deaths? Or that they worried how the world would think of them, would judge them even at the end. This is what I also hear: there was a vow between them that would have to take a terrible earthquake, a disaster, to undo.)

Daphne's future husband was twelve years older than she was. On the first night, after their first dinner, Daphne told my mother she thought he was all right for such an old guy. She sat on my mother's bed and tried on makeup from their secret collection, and my mother could tell from the way she looked at herself in the mirror: Daphne would go out with him again. As the summer continued, my mother saw less and less of her.

He took her out to dinner and into Manhattan to the shows. Sometimes, he would tip the doorman a little extra and they would go to clubs, where Daphne was singularly under age and more beautiful and fresh than any of the other women. She began to have bags under her eyes, and on the few afternoons she came down to the garden in jeans and sneakers, with her hair tied back, she had secrets she could not share.

At night, my mother and her family could hear Daphne's mother praying. When her daughter was dropped off by her husband-to-be, Daphne's mother would smile at him and take her daughter by the hand, but her grip was hard and her nails bit into Daphne's palm. When the door was closed, my mother would hear women's voices raised to screams, doors slam, and the sound of footsteps rushing back and forth on the floorboards above. Finally, Daphne's mother wrote an angry letter to her husband in Greece, and two weeks later, the husband-to-be came in his suit and tie to say good-bye, kissing the mother on the back of her hand and pressing himself up against Daphne's cheek for one last, lingering kiss.

Daphne told my mother this with her face buried in the pillow of

35

my mother's bed, her cheeks streaked with tears, her hair gone wild and long again. He was forbidden to see her until she was eighteen, and the engagement was canceled until then. Daphne would finish school; her mother had extracted a promise from her father that they would reconsider the matter once more at that point, but not before.

I don't know what she said to him, but I'm going to get her back for this, I swear. Daphne told my mother that she had been allowed five minutes alone with him with her mother breathing outside the door, but he had taken her into his arms for the last time and promised he would wait for her. *He's never coming back, I know it. Two years is forever. He'll forget all about me.* My mother tried to tell her if it was real he would wait.

She must have been relieved that Daphne would be there for a little longer. Although she was making new friends, she had missed their summer life together, and the thought of Daphne in Greece sent a cold pain through my mother's heart. Daphne now talked about *going to Europe* with her husband. She never said *Greece*, because he had promised her they would be part of the new European elite, that the borders would fall and they would be at home in Paris and London and Milan as much as Athens. My mother heard the names of the cities of the world and thought she would never leave New York; she would never leave her family or her friends. She had let Daphne travel ahead into a country she wanted to know nothing about.

After the broken engagement, Daphne stopped wearing girl's clothing. She went to school for the next two years in the heels and stockings of a married woman, and she told everyone she was engaged. She wrote long letters to her beau, and occasionally he wrote back to her. Carrying these with her in her purse for weeks, she showed them off in the cafeteria as proof of her romantic real life outside of school.

When Daphne turned eighteen, her mother received a letter

from the intended, asking again for her hand in marriage. A week later, she received another letter from Daphne's father in Greece, saying he had had enough of her nonsense and, whether she liked it or not, the marriage was going through. These letters came in September as my mother was beginning her last year of college. She and Daphne had drifted a little apart, and she could afford to be excited for her.

Daphne climbed up the fire escape to my mother's room, holding both letters. She jumped on the bed and bounced up and down. *I'm getting out, I'm getting out, I'm getting away from her*, she said. They would be married in January, on the first of the year, and Daphne's husband would move them to an apartment in Queens, where he needed to work on a few business deals.

A year later, Daphne was married and my mother was working as a secretary and living with the curtains closed.

At night and on weekends, my mother went out of the house only to help her father in the deli. She was careless about her appearance. She did not wash her hair often enough, and her skin grew pale from lack of sunlight. She did not want to see her friends from school; they all seemed busy getting engaged or starting the brief careers they would undertake before getting married. My mother found herself unable to picture either engagement or a career. She found it hard to imagine life would ever be any different from the way it was turning out to be for the rest of the days of her life.

And then Daphne's husband got into a fight with Daphne's mother, because she was spending too much time at her old home and not enough time taking care of her new home. His business was concluded. It was time to move to Greece. He had bought them an apartment earlier in the year, and now all he needed was a car.

They decided to take the boat to London, buy the car there, drive across the continent to Venice, and then take the ferry to Greece. It would be a second honeymoon. Daphne told my mother her plans one night when she came over for coffee. She was complaining again about how hard it was to balance loyalty to parents with loyalty to one's spouse when she noticed my mother sitting across from her, pale as the curtains she kept closed over her windows, pale as someone who was about to fade away.

Daphne looked at her. For the first time in two years she was once again sure that she would get what she wanted, and she was able to think about someone else. My mother was her best friend, her only friend really, and after six months of marriage she had begun to realize she might need a friend again. The low bulb on the table by the bed provided the only light, and Daphne could see ashtrays full of cigarettes piled up in the dim reaches of the room. *And you're coming with me*, she said. *I want you to see Europe with me*.

My mother had spent the afternoon ironing her brothers' shirts, which they claimed they needed for a truly "collegiate" look. She had asked them if they wanted her to iron their underwear too and they had said, *Sure, thanks, why not*, and so she had, with all the power of her arm going into each stroke. Daphne's marriage and her stories about Europe were no different from a story in a magazine to her. When Daphne said *come with me* she said *sure*.

Daphne insisted they go immediately to her father's deli to ask his permission. My mother was almost twenty-one, but she was still a Greek daughter. They stood in front of the counter while my grandfather wrapped slices of turkey breast for one of his customers, his belly just beginning to go round under his apron. Daphne told my grandfather that my mother would be chaperoned; they would make sure, *kyrie*, that nothing would happen to her. She would be back by October. Then she said my mother would help her settle in, and my mother's father, who was no fool, let himself be convinced. He looked at his daughter, pale and unhappy in front of him. He looked at Daphne, with her shoulder pads, expensive hair, and the air of a married woman. He gave his approval. Daphne let out a shriek and gave them both a hug. My mother said, *Thanks, Pop*, and told Daphne she would stay in the deli and do some work. Daphne whispered, *Aren't you excited?* and the way my mother said *yes* did not convince either of them.

But by August, she found herself intimately included in the travel plans, down to the trunks of clothing Daphne bought (always remembering to get something for her friend), to the placement of their cabin on the *Queen Mary*, to the type of car Daphne's husband thought they should buy. And when the luxury liner was set to sail out of the harbor, my mother found herself on the deck watching the towers of the city slip by and grow small in the distance. Only then, in the growing reality of the wide Atlantic, did she let herself feel anything.

Here I am, the egg standing up and looking at the chicken. What kind of daughter imagines these things about her mother? Not a Greek daughter, not a good Greek daughter.

ATHENA, DAUGHTER
OF ZEUS

Athena is the goddess who wants to pretend there are no other goddesses. She wants us to think of her as an exception, her body trussed in heavy armor, eyes peering over her glasses, down her elegant nose. Wise, just, unemotional.

Throughout the ages, Athena has been rewarded for her good behavior. Zeus allowed her to carry his shield; hardened warriors, men with stubble and wounds, called her name before any other. The round marble pillars, the hefty Caryatids with their wide breasts and enormous arms, the world's most perfect temple, perched on a hill above the city that carried her name, surrounded her glorious statue. In war, she created balance. In peace, she created math. No god ever linked his name with hers; no mortal ever caught her eye, willingly sacrificing his life for a chance to kiss a goddess. I imagine her at the end of a long day. Her sisters have been gossiping, talking about the relationship between this prince and that princess, between this god and that mortal; they sit around a table, grow tipsy on ambrosia, laugh. Athena walks past them without looking down. She enters her own quarters, where she lays her sword neatly by the bed and takes out a book. She tells herself her life is much better than theirs, that history will reward her, and it does.

I worry about Athena. Some say her real problem is not having a mother; being born from the head of Zeus, she never had a chance to love women and spent her days among men, those who raised her. There is another explanation. Athena was a new addition to Olympus, too young, growing up at a time when goddesses were giving way to gods. As a young goddess, she sat between the legs of her elders and observed. She saw the way Zeus could do whatever he wanted, change himself into a bull or a shower of coins and make love to unwitting princesses. She saw Hera chasing after him, cleaning up his messes. Reduced to a jealous wife, Hera seemed like a nag. Athena never thought to ask Hera about her life as a single goddess. Indoors, she started to feel suffocated, trapped. Little by little, she drifted outside, leaning against the columns, watching the male activity. She charmed the gods, convinced them to teach her discus throwing, how to hoist a javelin. She tried on their battle gear and liked the way it felt against her skin, heavy and safe. One day, she found herself in the Olympian fields, sweating from her run, surrounded by gods discussing the latest mortal woman who had caught their eye. The worst part: Athena laughed.

Somehow Athena convinced herself the things that happened to other goddesses would never happen to her. As long as she kept her mind on war and games, on law and math, she would be the favorite of Zeus and men. When Zeus circulated the rumor that she had arrived in the world fully formed, born from his own body, it made things easier for everyone. In all the stories and all the myths, in her singleness and rigid impartiality, Athena's hidden loneliness escapes, like a piece of hair coming out of a bun.

At some point in our lives, all women sail with Athena. With her, we look at the islands ruled by women and pull our ships away from the landfall. From a distance, we sniff the air, heavy with flowers. We turn to the salt spray and think we are more brave.

When we reach our destination, it is easier to imagine no other women have been there before. We will be safe from the mistakes of our predecessors, we think, as long as we pretend that the footprints we see in the sand are ours alone.

The second time I go to Greece, it is as if I have discovered a new country. I am filled with the possessive love of all explorers. What do I know? I am nineteen.

I am there for a college language program, which I have entered in the interest of perfecting my Greek. In the months before I started the program, I read the modern Greek poets in their original language. The square-shaped architecture of the writing echoed thousands of years. Greece has become a place of faded marble and lemon-tongued lovers, a land filled with the light created when sun strikes water. I have a hard time believing I was so naive only three years ago.

I am going to visit my northern cousins before starting the program. It is early summer, and I have taken a bus from Athens to Larissa, proud of the fact I could negotiate the ride. On the way up, I have gazed out the window almost continuously, watching the plains turn into mountains, the mountains into sea. Where a glimpse of amethyst water sparkles between the flat brown, my heart pounds.

Larissa does not appear on any tourist maps; it is a town of farmers and traders and always has been. The only story about Larissa from ancient times involves a group of centaurs raiding the wedding of the king's daughter. In the myth, the Lapids live in Larissa, merchants and salesmen even then. Like rabbits in a warren, they dart out to buy and sell, burrow to gather and hoard. In the mountains above them roam wild horse/men, burnished chests over four fast legs. I picture the scene. The table has been laid with a feast, the women lined up on either side, crowns of flowers fresh in their hair. Flies land on the food and they feel bored. When the sound of hooves shakes the earth, they straighten up. Carried away by the whooping centaurs, I imagine they feel relief—saved from life among shopkeepers to live off wild grapes and honey, riding the backs of their long-haired lovers.

Too far from Thessaloniki, an hour from the sea, Larissa still sits in the plains looking longingly at the mountains. As we pull into the terminal, the squat apartment houses, the tiny streets lined with shops, even the harvest haze, all seem glamorous, exotic.

I remember *some* of the cousins vaguely from my first visit. When I step out of the bus at the station, they move toward me in a tribe, and they look real to me for the first time. There are two men, Costas and Yiorgos, brothers who tell me they remember my mother, and their four daughters, all around my age. The brothers have married well. One woman has a movie-star face, blond and angular, but wears the rolled-up sleeves and old skirts of a hardworking house-wife; the other is round and dark and embraces me warmly. Their daughters look like all four mixed up—tall and thin, short and round, blond and brown, pretty and earthy.

We wait for my luggage while a group of priests who have also stepped off the bus take their bags and boxes out one by one. The oldest have beards down to their waists, and the youngest carry the heavy loads; one holds a cage of chickens he has brought with him. In the shelter between buses, children play a game with a ball while their mothers sit on the bench and gossip.

Costas and Yiorgos have apartments half a mile from each other, along a side road that the girls cross, back and forth, living in each other's places. In between the apartments lie their businesses: Yior-gos's garage, Costas's small and fragrant grocery. Both brothers have the large bellies and relaxed smiles of prosperous Greek men. When we arrive at the first apartment I take out the gifts my mother has advised me to buy: whiskey and perfume. The girls look at me encouragingly and I try my Greek; to my surprise the words seem to fly between us like tiny sparks, easy and alive.

It takes me a while to tell the girls apart, because their names sound so much alike. Two were named after the same grandmother, one of my grandfather's sisters who stayed in Greece. She was called Chrisoula, and there is a Soula and a Chrisoula. There is also a Koula and a Despina, nicknamed Despinoula. In the end, I just call them the four Soulas.

It is decided that, as a young woman, I will spend my time with them, and the other cousins will have to settle for short visits. The Soulas take me into a side bedroom and into their confidence. We all pretend the generations in America have evaporated, and we gossip over our few shared interests: the presents I brought them, our families, men. They take out jewelry boxes and open closets. If I express admiration, they give me whatever it is we are looking at: earrings, bracelets.

Later, one of them whispers to shut the door. The atmosphere grows tense and excited. One of the Soulas pulls a pack of cigarettes out from under the bed, and we all take one, solemnly smoking as if each cigarette were defiance and freedom. Another Soula looks out the window, keeping her eye out for her parents, who have gone home to get food to share in the dinner. If we hear footsteps nearing, we stamp out the cigarettes and throw them under the bed. The smoky air, the dim lights, and the heady perfume of the women crowded in together have the erotic enchantment of a harem. When they finger the bracelets along my arms and blow into my ear how pretty I have become, goose bumps shiver along my skin.

One of the cousins tells me she wants to take me to visit a friend of hers who has a house by the sea. The two of us rise at dawn and get on a bus. Fog blankets the city, and when it lifts we find ourselves surrounded by fields filled with thick green vegetables. Soon we enter a steep gorge, and the bus drives between two mossy rock faces, the road following a stream. We idle behind cars pulling up next to a shrine, a favorite spot for marriages. A little church has been built into the rock. Legend says that this is the spot where

Daphne was turned into a tree to escape Apollo. I take a deep breath, and the air smells like fresh earth and diesel.

When we come out on the other side of the gorge, the sun is pushing back the clouds. We pass a series of tiny farms built into the hillside and reach a village built at the far end of a wide bay, the end of the line. From there we hike along the beach to the house, pebbles settling under our shoes.

My cousin's friend has thick hair and a kind, open face. Her name is Antigone, she tells me in English. She has lived in America and says she is pleased to meet me. Antigone's house is made almost entirely of wood, with big windows facing the water. The sea is still a lilac gray from the clouds and last night's storm. We drink coffee, smoke cigarettes, and play cards for hours. In the afternoon, we walk to the village and buy fresh vegetables for dinner. Antigone shows me some of her paintings. We talk about books we have both read. She suggests we all explore the next bay.

A late-afternoon light has appeared, and the water evaporating off the foliage turns it a vivid green. Behind the bay, mountains reach into the sky. The sea has calmed to a deep blue, and we sweat from the humidity lacing the air. By the time we get back to her house, the sun has dipped behind the peaks. We are still hot from our walk; the water looks cool and inviting. When we enter it, the mountain's shadow hides the sand below me—like swimming in the dark. The two girls swim out confidently, deep into the bay. I am in strange water and hang close to the shore, feeling foolish, unable to let myself float blindly.

At night, we make dinner. Antigone tells me she is expecting her boyfriend to come by after work with a few friends. After the first star appears, we hear wheels crunching along the beach. A small van parks outside the door; three men in their late twenties, buoyant with their release from a day in a hot office, tumble out of the car holding up bottles of wine. They start picking at the food and flirting with us. We uncork the wine. By the time we get through the first two bottles, I know which one I will sleep with that night.

My lover has a droopy mustache and the deep almond-shaped eyes of a Byzantine saint. He says he will dance for me if I come with him to buy more cigarettes. We climb into his tiny white van, and every word we say to each other seems to have another meaning attached to it, tiny erotic offspring clinging to the fur of our words. Before we go back into the house we kiss, and he bites my lips. When we step in, my eyes become glazed. The others fade into a background hush. The women turn into a chorus, and he and I are on stage, our masks firmly sealed to our faces.

He is the first man I have ever seen dance like this. We put music on, the mournful wail of bouzouki, and one of his friends kneels in front of him. He snaps his fingers and sways back and forth. The music builds; the dance seems to be a battle against gravity. He dips his body, until he almost falls, and rises again. He is wearing jeans and an expensive-looking cotton shirt, which he pulls out of his pants so the flaps sway with him. His kneeling friend claps harder, and he whirls faster and faster, jumping into the air and slamming back down again, throwing his leg up against his thigh and slapping it with a clean, wooden sound. At last, the music dies and he has proven himself; he can fight the air.

At midnight, we all get into his van and drive down to another beach. He puts Bob Marley on, and we all take off our clothes and jump in the water. This time I swim into the dark. When we come out, we run up and down the beach to dry off.

When the sun comes out again, my face is burning with the scratch of his beard, and my lips are sore from kisses. I feel my body. I am safe.

The language program is having its first week in Crete, and I take the bus to the ferry by myself. I use my Greek to buy my ticket, and I hear another woman whose accent sounds like mine. She wears a white sundress and sneakers. I ask her if she is American.

She attends a rival college near mine, where she studies classics. By the end of the first hour, we have become fast friends. We flirt with the captain, who stops at our dinner table. When he invites us up to the wheelhouse, she looks alarmed but I agree. Barely five feet tall, like a banana dictator in his white uniform, the captain lets us steer the ship. He gives us some *chipro*, bootlegged mountain ouzo, and then asks us if we would both like to go to bed with him. *I can do it for hours*, he says, *no problem for two*.

We run out together, laughing and screaming, and lock ourselves into the cabin, where we stay awake until dawn, talking. We emerge in time to see the famous harbor of Iráklion, and I tell her about Kazantzakis, currently my favorite writer.

At the language program, I decide that the United States is a land of idiots and children. The American instructors meet with us in the lobby and inform us we will be taking our first *site-seeing trip* at noon. It is an insane hour; even the bees are sleeping. They tell us to remember *our friend, the hat*, who will protect us from *our enemy, the sun*. As if a hat would be enough to make it easy to stride uphill in the heat. They seem to feel they have the right to explore when and where they choose.

On the second day, we take a tour of Minoan palaces. We stroll through Knossos, reconstructed and painted by Arthur Evans, English archaeologist, who believed that, as a member of an earlier empire, he knew best what the palace once looked like. We take a bus across the island to Phaestos, a much more satisfactory rubble heap. On the way back we stop at the foot of Mount Ida, birthplace of Zeus.

On the bus I fall asleep, and when I step out into the cooler air, the currents along my bare skin feel like the brush of fingers. We are greeted by a guide dressed like a farmer, who has the short stocky

47

body of a mountain gnome. He takes us through orchards belonging to his family to a place where the fields open. A small temple stands in a clearing surrounded by looming mountains.

On the walk back, the line becomes more anarchic, and I work my way toward the back, where the farmer lingers behind us. His skin glows from the sun or the fading light, and his hair is white, the color of marble. I tell him I am Greek-American, and he points ahead to something he wants to show me. We stop under a grove of trees, their green almost silver in the dusk. He pulls down a branch of brown pods and breaks one open. Inside sits a cushiony almond. It tastes milky and only slightly bitter.

At the bus, he waits with me while everyone else gets in. My friend from the boat eyes me suspiciously. The farmer bears a striking resemblance to our sea captain, but I have decided he is authentic, a true poet. He must be harmless. Pointing up the hill to a smattering of tiny buildings in the distance, he tells me, *This is my village. You must come and meet my family, eat some real Greek food.* He wants to ask me a question about America, whether I like it better than Greece. Before I can answer, he puts one hand on my arm and another over his heart. *America has many things*, he says, *but it is empty, here*, and he pounds on his chest.

On the bus back to the hotel, I sit apart from the other Americans, including my friend. Later, I give her another chance and ask if she would like to wake up at dawn with me to see the sun rise over Kazantzakis's tomb. She turns me down.

The hill to the grave is steep, next morning, and the day has only begun to warm. At the park opening, a sign reads that there is a charge after eight, but I push my way through a gap in the fence and find my way alone. They have placed a giant black cross over the tomb, which reads I HOPE FOR NOTHING, I FEAR NOTHING, I AM FREE.

The rising sun behind the cross makes it appear to burn against the sky. I breathe in the roses and the early air. Down below me, the first boats have begun to come into the harbor.

Someone else is in the park. An old man under the rosebushes gets up and brushes off his suit. He takes out a pack of cigarettes for breakfast and offers me one. I walk over and take it. This is what Zorba would have done. We smoke together, as if we were sharing a cup of coffee, silently. He puts his hand on my knee. We are absolutely alone and far above the city. I let him keep his hand there while I finish my cigarette, trying to seem natural. He has begun to rub his hand up and down my thigh. I finish the cigarette and stand up. This time, I squeeze through the fence without looking back.

The rest of the program is scheduled to take place on Poros, a tiny island I have read about in the worn copy of *The Colossus of Maroussi* that one of my uncles has given me. In it, Henry Miller describes the passage into Poros harbor. He delights over the lemon groves on one side and the streets of the town on the other, like sailing on land—to go through the narrow strait is to remember passing through the womb. His book has become my constitution; I want to journey with Miller forever, starting in Greece to remake the world. With Miller, or Kazantzakis. When Miller describes the erotic flanks of Greek women, made more powerful by the weight of the burdens they carry, I skim.

The only teacher on the program I feel anything for is Kyria Zikou, the one Greek. An elderly and distant member of what was once the royal family, her aristocratic face perches on top of a tiny body twisted by childhood polio. She makes us memorize folk songs and gossips about the past. I skip all my other classes and spend hours reading in the groves or swimming. The rest of the time I inhabit the phone shop, making expensive long-distance calls to my Larissa lover. He tells me he is coming to visit.

When my lover arrives, we sneak out across the harbor to the town. I feel sophisticated and desirable sitting across from him as he explains about the bouzouki music playing in the restaurant. *The singer is the last of the great Rembetis*, he says. He tells me about *rembetiko*, the music of the refugees from Smyrna. His mustache is so Greek, I think, so fierce. I imagine him in 1922, smoking hashish and wailing for his lost land. We drink a toast to the Rembetis, and another to music, and another to sex. We drink ouzo and wine and eat octopus swimming in lemon and olive oil. When we get to the hotel, the room is spinning and I have to rush to the toilet to throw up.

The next day they tell me at the language program that if I choose to leave again, they will have to drop me from the program in order to keep their reputation. I pack my bags. Their most famous client was the girl who married the King of Jordan, and I can see I am far from the ambassadorial ideal. I kiss Kyria Zikou good-bye and tell my American friend I will write to her. Kyria Zikou reaches out a little sparrow claw hand and grabs my own. *You're doing the right thing, darling. I would too if I could.*

In a few hours, I am on a bus by myself, traveling through unknown country, heading back toward Thessaly, and I am happier than I ever have been before in my life. For the next month, I will live with my cousins in a tent on the beach under the shadow of a mountain. In a large group of women, we will gather under a green canvas, waking up only to swim and eat and sleep again. Although I will only see my lover once or twice, everything has an undercurrent, the air-borne electricity that makes Thessalian peaches twice as round and sweet as any others. When I return to America at the end of the summer, my mother will smile at the pictures and keep silent.

What she does not tell me is that she was on that sand before me. Like Athena, my mother thought she was safe, as if she were beginning again, free of whatever gripped her own mother still, powerful enough to jump over oceans. She was an American, and Greece was a country she thought she could both love and leave. How do I know this? Because I can imagine her arriving, in full armor.

To find this story, I have to do the opposite of fading in. There is a picture of my mother standing in her father's village, her face shiny and tanned, a bundle of twigs hitched on her back; she is smiling ecstatically. The picture has the yellowed tint of old photographs, monochromatic and strange. If I let my blood warm it up like a current passed underneath the tray in a photographer's darkroom, the scene comes into color, taking on the heated hues of summer mountains outlined against an ancient sea, wet deep greens and blues.

Sometime during her first month in Greece, the month that was supposed to be her entire trip but which became a year, my mother went to visit her parents' relatives. I imagine her leaving Athens on an old freight train, entering a land of emptiness broken only by villages. The villages had been there during hundreds of years of occupation, protective and strong, their social codes passed mother to daughter in a feat of Darwinian survival, an entire language and religion saved from a conquering power that did its best to wipe them out. Then Independence, and what had been so fiercely preserved under occupation was eroded by the most common of fatalities: freedom, poverty, and ambition for change.

The first century after Greece won its freedom, the country was torn up by war after war, and the result was a hunger so strong it caused families to round up children and send them off to places unimaginably far away: America, Australia. The villages had been decimated, but when my mother was there they still existed—in any family, like ours, four might leave but three remained to farm the soft land and herd the sheep over the hard. By the time I arrived, the villages had disappeared, leaving a clear imprint that looked like the past but was not, like a photograph.

What is a village? In exchange for adhering to an elaborate set of unspoken and spoken rules, each member gains the loyalty of the group and protection from a hostile world. Because the world is dangerous, even the next village is suspect, and after years of intermarriage, the village itself has become one family, with a family's blood ties and offerings. To walk into a village that can claim you is to see your own face replicated again and again. When the Greeks were forced off the land into their great diaspora, everywhere they went they re-formed into villages, fragmented but still clear in outline. Sometimes a few communities from the same mountain would have to band together, which is how my grandparents met.

When my grandparents came to America, they settled close to their kin; in the wide streets of Queens they were only shouting distance from their sisters and brothers. My uncle says Queens was a good place to grow up, that from its broad boulevards you could always see a stretch of sky. But to be a daughter of the village was to be a vessel into which social codes were battered, come will or resistance—codes about everything: not to pass salt hand from hand, how to cure the evil eye, how to make meals out of weeds, how to kiss a priest (on his hand), what was acceptable for women (nothing), what was acceptable for men (everything).

My mother grew up in a village in the shadow of New York. To gain protection in the new land, they kept to the old rules. When it was time for her uncle to marry, he returned to his village to arrange a match. He was forty, the protector of his clan. According to the stories, he let it be known he was looking for a *nifi*, a bride. He was standing in the square one day when a villager nudged him. *Here is a nifi for you.* He looked at a girl getting water from the well, small, only seventeen. In his mind she was still a baby, as she had been the last time he saw her. She looked up at him, and it was a love match. Although no one talks about the dowry, there must have been one. Her mother cried for days because she knew her daughter's marriage would carry her into a land from which she would never return.

So when my mother went to her cousins, she was both an insider and an outsider. She probably wore heels Daphne lent her, and a new fur coat that she tried not to get dirty as she gathered it up against her, leaning on the metal walls of the old granary train, the dust and feathers of farms floating in the air. She might have smoked a cigarette and looked out the window at the passing fields and thought that it was far from New York and strange, monotonous, and beautiful.

Standing in the frame of the train, she passed her luggage to a group of young men and women who immediately recognized her, as she did them: cousins. Conscious of her New York role, just before stepping off the train she tucked her coat around her shoulders and tossed the cigarette to the ground like a declaration. They would have glanced at the cigarette, the men thinking her fierce and feeling proud, and the women thinking, *Not now, not now, when will it be now?*

She was the part of them they had sent away, and they were glad to see she was as different from them as she was the same. She had enough of them in her to wonder what they would say as she took out a new cigarette, and enough of the new world to take it out anyway. She looked out from underneath her dark curls, looked down to light up, and looked up again. There were smiles in their eyes, but they said nothing. She regarded them closely, their hair as curly as hers, their eyes blue, green, and brown, filled with light like hers. She breathed deeply, took out another cigarette, held it out to them, and smiled. One of the male cousins grabbed it and took a puff, and the women shook their heads, laughing. Quickly as it took for the paper to burn down to its stub, they were trading names, and she knew them all, the stories of their mothers and fathers. She met the sons of the sister who, as a child, had gazed at my mother's father in awe, fifteen years between them. He was back from the Balkan wars in a uniform more clean than any shepherd's rags, and when he kissed her good-bye she knew he was going farther than a war. My mother also met the son of the brother who had gone with my grandfather as far as the ship's docks and been scared and run away.

Athena in her heart, my mother felt distant enough from all of them to be safe. She did not recognize the danger, the pull of the past. Time can only move forward, and the gods have never looked kindly on those who interfere with natural laws.

—

RHEA ☉ ON THE WATER

There are many accounts of how and why the world began. Some say that first there was an old, old god who had many children. Fearing his offspring would overtake him, the old god swallowed them all. One son fell out of the corner of his mouth and was saved. He grew up to become Zeus, who fought his father, rescued his brothers and sisters, and found them a home on Olympus, where they proceeded to interfere with, bully, rescue, and aid humankind. Like their origins in patricide and betrayal, the stories after the birth of the gods are full of war and terrible family tragedies, one after another. Mistakes made by one generation are visited on the next—rape and murder, stupidity and misjudgment, women at the mercy of terrible men.

There is another story, which you can find if you look in the right books or if you ask your imagination. In this story, a liquid blackness engulfs the universe in silence. The world does not know it exists because if feels nothing. Out of the quiet something stirs—the first feeling: longing. Longing takes on the shape of a woman who has as many names as there are languages. The Greeks called her Rhea. Because Rhea feels lonely, she creates time. In order to make it pass, she divides night from day and earth from water. Once there is water and light to animate it, Rhea creates waves. She moves her body as if it were a language, as if she could speak with it; her legs stamp and splash and her arms reach up, back, and forward. Out of her dancing comes the first wind, air heaving up troughs. The wind is the only other moving thing that exists. The wind dances with Rhea; it enters her body and plays across her skin. Rhea and the wind fall in love; where they roll across the land they create green, when they fill each other they create living creatures. The wind was always only a wind, and those who told the story recognized that longing remained. Later storytellers were uncomfortable with this idea. Perpetual desire was a formula for chaos, so that is what they called her—seductress and thief, the one who threatens to throw us back into the dark. Instead of Rhea we have Eve, who steals and lies, or Hera, the nag. The beginning of a story tells so much.

I cashed in my ticket and decided to stay. I heard that part many times. And I also knew the ending. Between the beginning and the end of the story, something happened that changed the course of my mother's life and the channel of the story of the women in our family. Beyond that simple sentence, there are other origins, fracturing out from the source, like tiny lines of water in dry earth. What happens in the beginning leads to the ending; one story to many and back again.

I have met Daphne's husband—he is a portly millionaire who suffers from poor health, a man both generous and polite. A kind of dullness in his eyes suggests a life of mild dictatorship, but he has none of the sinister charm he needs for this account. Since it all happened such a long time ago, I will have to imagine the key role he played.

In the beginning, of course, Daphne would hardly have noticed her honeymoon was over. Athens was close enough to other cities on their European tour; it had restaurants and clubs and people their age enjoying themselves, and she and my mother could have easily lived the lives of two Athenian socialites, with the food and the wine and the attention such women always expect.

In the morning, they would breakfast together on the patio. While they ate, various one-man enterprises visited them, selling fruits, breads, dresses, cheeses. While they sipped their coffee, the fishmonger took out his scales and priced their daily choice by weight, water dripping onto the concrete. There were large pots of flowers carefully tended by gardeners, and a maid who brought them trays of toast and honey. Maybe they were joined by the husband. Maybe they talked about last night's party or a new club. Maybe, at the end of the meal, my mother would look out across the patio to the sea and breathe in the air of the neighborhood, the air of newness—plaster and paint, jasmine and steaming coffee. While she looked away, Daphne's husband would kiss his wife on the lips before going off to work, and then he would kiss my mother also, on the cheek, like a proper brother-in-law. Daphne would tell the maid what they would like for lunch, and my mother might have felt proud of her for being so queenly and self-assured.

She and Daphne would pour themselves another cup of coffee and read in the sunlight while the day warmed up. When it grew too hot or too late and the bees were lighting on the food they had left, the sticky jam on the edges of the plate, the melting butter, the bread crumbs, they would go inside to rest and change.

They would have gone to the beach. The bays near their home in those days must have been pristine, green-blue and clean, and while the maid prepared their lunch, they could swim all morning, browning their bodies in the sun, tiring themselves out for their afternoon nap.

At night, there would have been parties, of course, in apartments in neighborhoods like theirs, with views of the lights below. They frequented clubs where the waiters spoke French and the women displayed plenty of décolletage. And my mother had escorts, handsome well-educated young men who welcomed her into their set because, as the daughter of an American who spoke their language as fluently and with as much good-humored irony as they did, she was a catch, desirable and exotic. They were mostly one generation away from the villages themselves. And Daphne would have been the perfect foil, with her husband in the ranks of the rising class of young men.

My mother put on Daphne's clothes, which she shared generously, and drove with Daphne in her husband's car. She slept in a room overlooking the sea, with clean white sheets that reflected the sun. She must have felt she would never be ordinary again, never let herself be shut out of anything.

Perhaps the first month of heat and wealth made her decide to stay. She had been to the village and met her relatives, but living in Athens with Daphne, dipping her feet into the cool waters of being one of a handful who mean anything in a country still made up mostly of villages, made her decide to cash in her ticket and write her father a letter explaining that she was going to remain longer than she had originally planned.

Or maybe it was not quite like that.

Maybe Daphne's husband never hired a maid and let it be known from the very beginning he expected her to prove she was not a spoiled American girl. Or maybe he hired a maid, but his family were shocked to see that Daphne did not know how to clean or cook and so, embarrassed, he asked her to do more to help around the house.

Or maybe the husband did not start it at all. Maybe on the first day they went down to the beach, New York style, wearing straw hats and carrying books to read, they found a group of fishermen on the sand repairing their nets, who did not even bother to whistle at them, nothing so friendly as that, but hissed instead, like snakes, air through clenched teeth, willing them to go back inside, shaming them into the house.

And when Daphne later complained, her husband just said, *You should know better than that, Daphne*, and *Don't you girls have enough to do here at home? It's not as if you're alone all day.*

In this version, my mother helped Daphne as much as she could. Unwilling to spoil her daughter's hands, Daphne's mother had always done the housework. My mother knew how to organize a house because she had done it for years, done it to help her own mother more and more. She understood exactly how to respond to need. My mother helped because she could not imagine letting someone else clean up after her. She trailed Daphne through the house as she discarded her nightgown, her robe, falling on the bed, naked and bored. *Daphne*, she whispered to her, *get hold of yourself.*

In this version, Daphne would have needed my mother very much. Daphne was in love with her husband; she was barely nineteen years old and she was afraid of him, more than she let my mother see. They went out at night, but he watched her jealously, and every so often he would snap at her: *Be more careful. Keep your eyes to yourself.* Always with them, my mother danced at the parties and sipped on her freedom, like a glass of scratchy champagne, a little more deeply every night. She wondered what would become of her.

Perhaps my mother decided to stay in Athens because she did not want to go back, because she had nothing to go back for and she was afraid—afraid of what her life would be like.

There is another possibility. I remember her trip north to her cousins. If I ask my cells, hidden in the body, which connects me most to her, they will tell me it was the land that convinced her to stay. She found something there. Between Athens and the north, between Daphne and her cousins, there was something my mother had come to Greece to discover. What was it?

There is really only one way to find out, and that is to go back to the story and enter it myself.

The third time I go to Greece, I arrive by taxi at 5 A.M. The sky is the color of cigarette ash, and there is no sign of light returning. I am holding the address of my Athenian cousins, which I have kept with me all summer, folded and re-folded. Hidden in my passport, safe under the mattress of a dozen small but pristine beds in different whitewashed rooms, the paper has become salty and brown with suntan oil. Now I clutch it in my palm as proof of a decision I am still not sure I have made.

The taxi driver takes me through forty minutes of a dark city and pulls to a stop. On the horizon I can see a milky white leaking out around the edges; the outline of office buildings forms a tunnel down the street. No lights. The sidewalks are empty. I know I have been taken here to be murdered or raped. I can hear the driver's fingers, sliding along the dashboard. Then he pronounces the name of the street I have given him and turns to look at me for the first time since I've gotten into the cab. I take this as the signal that we have arrived.

Nobody lives here, I tell him. *This is not the right street*. He pronounces the name again, more clearly this time, as if I have not heard him yet. *No*, I say again. *This isn't right*.

We begin a shouting match. He is angry when I tell him he has made a mistake. He yells back the name at me, as if volume is all it will take to convince me, but I am used to Greek men by now. I consider myself to be an American woman and not easily put off by shouting. Nothing in the world will persuade me to get out of the cab into the dark streets with my backpack and my vulnerability. I shout the name back at him, throwing it at him that it is his mistake, I am right and he is wrong. This is unacceptable to him.

He changes his tack and now shouts something I cannot understand. Finally he turns away from me and starts rummaging through

the front of his cab. I wonder if he has a knife. I consider opening
the door and making a run for it. Then he holds up a battered paperback and makes an elaborate pantomime of opening the book to the
correct page. He hands it over to me.

In the dim light of the cab, I can see the name of the street that I
want, listed so many times the word covers half a page, with different codes for different parts of the city. Once again, I am confronted
with the Greek tendency to use the same name over and over again.

Finally, we agree that he will drop me off at a hotel.

It is the first day of a general strike, and I have had to bribe the
taxi driver ten times the normal fare to take me from the airport to
the center of the city. In London, I had to squeeze onto the last seat
of the last flight available after Olympic Airways closed its offices,
landing just before the Athens air traffic controllers stopped work
and joined the rest of the country. If I believed in Fate, I would
think that someone was gently suggesting I turn back. I have spent
the whole summer since graduation traveling the Greek islands, trying to see a clear path in front of me and failing. Hoping the northern climate would clear my vision, I went as far as England. In the
end, I have ignored all warning signs and come back to Greece.

When I arrive at the hotel, I carry my own bags from the taxi
into the lobby. The two clerks in matching red uniforms hardly raise
their sleepy eyes to look at me. On the lobby couch, I gather my
things around me, turn my back to the clerks, and burst into tears.

I have completed my education; I have no concrete plans for the
future. I am twenty-one and I have made a decision. I have moved
to Greece forever. I am never going back to America.

THE EVIL EYE

There are many ways to discover if someone has given you the evil eye. Remember, the eyes of the world are vigilant, *ta matia tou kosmou*: weighing you up, watching your every step. If you take a wrong one or go too far, someone can give you a look you can feel; it zaps through your skin and enters your marrow. Sometimes you fall sick, and no one can explain why. Sometimes you stroll along, feeling the power of your own body and the sun on your skin, and when you stare at a young man who looks too long, you stumble, trip, lose a heel. The Greeks say *kapios se matiase*—someone eyed you, someone gave you the eye—and it is not meant the way it sounds in English; it is not that you have drawn their attention but that they have entered you, violated your anonymity, made you fall.

Sometimes it is enough to take preventive measures; spit the words out quickly if you suddenly say you are feeling great, *Everything's going my way*. Before the gods overhear and spoil your hubris, say *Ptu-ptu*. If you are full of gloom, never speak it in case another god, on the other side of the fence, decides to grant you your unhappiness. Women—and it has always and only ever been women—

who know the ancient formulas can cure you of the evil eye. My mother knows how to do it; she learned it from her mother, who learned it from her mother, who was the village healer, the one who drew power from herbs and incantations. Not knowing how long the recipe can retain its power, my mother has never passed on the cure to her daughters, though we practice prevention, spitting out the wrong words and watching our step. Instead, she has taught us how to roll grape leaves.

The recipe for rolling grape leaves shows that the women in my family know how to transform an unswallowable hide into a nourishing delight. If you look at a grapevine growing in the field, you might think of the fruit ripening in the sun: it is available and easy; with a little stomping and nothing else but time, it can be turned into wine. Unless you had been told the recipe, you would never think of stuffing and eating the leaves.

If you soak grape leaves in salt water, a brine that tastes like the sea, and let enough time go by, you can pack them in a jar and send them—a green bounty—to the hands of waiting women around the world. When you unpack the leaves, jammed together in rolls, the first thing you have to do is put them in hot water, not boiling, to clean and separate them. When you pluck them apart, using your fingers to separate a leaf stuck to the others, more delicate than paper, your skin burns with the heat. After a few hours your fingers are puffy with salt and water and your joints ache. You know that it will take hours to roll the leaves, but you also know the pleasure waiting at the end, and so you gather your courage and continue.

What drives you to decide to make dolmades, a dish that requires hours and disappears in minutes? Like the power of a curse lifted—anyone who has ever tasted it is subject to an occasional greed and hunger that nothing else can satisfy. The effort and determination add flavor to the simple ingredients: rice, onions, mint, grape leaves, rolled, covered, doused with lemon water, cooked from beneath.

Each one swallowed creates the need for another, an anxiety that there will not be enough. Since hours have been spent by not one cook but many, there is nothing to stop you from eating until you feel your stomach might burst.

One other thing: no one ever makes dolmades alone if she can help it. The lessons in patience are among the first a mother teaches her children: how to unroll the green leaves when young fingers make them too fat or too thin, how to select the right ones and cover up tears or holes, how to use a teaspoon to measure the half-cooked rice. You must never lose your patience and overstuff your spoon. Never try to empty the bowl more quickly, because then the dolmades will be too fat and will burst in the heat of cooking. There are hundreds to be rolled. In learning to measure carefully, each generation learns that the price certain tasks exact may never be known. This is what they also learn: curing bitterness is possible, but it takes both strength and time.

Going to the Seashore

First come the stories of the gods and the heroes. Then come the
family dramas. The most famous revolves around the members of
the house of Atreus. You only have to pass one table full of *cafenion*
philosophers, shouting at each other over nothing, to know Greeks
love drama. This one has everything—the interference of the gods,
the stupidity of humankind, a lot of blood. It begins the usual way:
Zeus leers at the wrong woman. To make love to Leda he has to
become a swan, and she gives birth to two daughters encased in a
hard shell. Perhaps because they were born out of an egg, they both
marry unsuitable husbands. Bored with Menelaus, Helen falls in
love with a visiting prince and causes all that trouble. Clytemnestra,
another great beauty, does not fare much better. When her husband,
Agamemnon, is stranded on the shore, unable to launch his ships in
the still air, he asks her if he can sacrifice their daughter, Iphigenia,
to the wind. *Sure*, she says, *why not?* We all want to stop her; we
know things can only get worse. The ships sail to Troy, packed with
sweaty troops who clamber out to be slaughtered. Many battles and
losses later, Agamemnon returns from the war with Cassandra, a

stolen princess and his prize. Clytemnestra cracks. In a bathtub, just as he starts to relax, she kills him with an ax. Her son feels compelled to kill her, and the whole cycle of blood threatens to run again until Athena intervenes.

Even this drama can be seen in a different light. Clytemnestra and Helen came from a long line of powerful queens. Only a few generations before, they would have thought the taking of new lovers to be perfectly natural; some say that queens not only ruled but killed off their husbands once a year for more virile replacements. Out of this tradition storm Menelaus and Agamemnon, barrel-chested and impatient. Instead of realizing transitions can be rocky, instead of giving the enormous change its due, they lose their tempers, vow revenge. What would have happened if they had just left Helen in Troy? As for Clytemnestra, perhaps her anger arose from the first mistake of Agamemnon, the sacrifice of their daughter.

Although I can imagine the three male playwrights (who so enjoyed laying on layers of blood in the versions that have survived) jumping up and down in their togas, yelling at me that I am wrong, I see a happy ending. A mother who has been robbed of her power and had her daughter slaughtered here takes revenge; why not celebrate? There are even rumors that the truth has been lost, that in the old version, her son, Orestes, does not murder his mother; he is grateful to take the kingship granted to him by a priestess. They discover his sister, Iphigenia, not killed at all but rescued, ruling happily on some island, a priestess doling out advice and helping women with potions and childbirth. Only Agamemnon falls into the fate he deserves. Even Cassandra might receive a better ending. After all, she was a woman who was granted the gift of foresight by Apollo, in exchange for which she promised to sleep with him. When she changed her mind, he spit in her mouth and said no one would ever believe her truths. A prophetess who spurned a god might have been able to slip away from Agamemnon before the ax fell. Why not imagine her hiding in the hills, growing gray, hair wild, telling stories to herself? Sometimes, from her cave, she shakes her fist at Apollo and cheers for Clytemnestra, her daughters, and her son.

When *Never on Sunday* had its American debut, my mother, who was still a reporter, and her brothers, respectable and well connected, were invited to the premiere. Both prominent, and good Greeks, they invited my grandfather, their father. The movie stars the beautiful Melina Mercouri, who is not only blond, slim-waisted, and wide-hipped but will go on to become the Minister of Culture while I am in Greece, fighting the English for the return of the misnamed Elgin marbles. Melina plays a kind-hearted prostitute who enraptures a French pencil pusher—played by her husband in real life, Jules Dassin, who directed the movie—and generally has a good time down by the docks. In the movie's Piraeus, the water is pristine, before island steamers and pollution. The prostitutes and deckhands work hard, but they also jump into the sea when they are hot, and at night they gather in their local taverna to dance and argue, sing and make love. The most beautiful scene involves Melina comforting a sailor far from home. She puts her arm around him and sings, *Poso me lipis palicari, pame mia volta sto phengari*, one of the most famous lines in modern Greek songs. Its poetry fades on translation: going for a walk under the moon, the longing for old friends.

It was the first movie about Greece to have a big New York American premiere, and my mother and brothers were very proud. When the lights went up at the end they turned to my grandfather. He was already standing up with his hat on his head. As they shrunk into their seats, he spat with fury. *Ptuuh! This is the filth they bring to America to show what our country is like?*

He had a point. Not only were the prostitutes and sailors enjoying their simple life by the water, they were also incredibly naive—a European cliché about the wisdom of Mediterranean folk. But what

I love about the film is the way Melina retells the Greek tragedies. They all start out the same way—the official story of mistaken identity or tempting the gods. Always Melina adds a new ending, a happy one. Just as things look like they are taking a turn for the worse, just as the ax is going to fall, the son kill his father, the mother find out she has slept with her son, Melina says her famous line: *And then they all go to the seashore*. Instead of blood and retribution, the stories end by the beach, maybe with a swim and a glass of retsina.

As an American, I have always expected happy endings. As the daughter of Greek and Jewish ancestors, I am also suspicious of happiness that comes too easily, as if it can only be deserved if hard won.

I traveled throughout Greece in the summer, when the entire country seems to be in a good mood. I landed, though, at the turn toward winter, when another side of the country starts to reveal itself: a fatalistic expectation of disaster, as if the gods are still around, as if houses, people, and countries still can be cursed. Perhaps, in moving to Greece, I was following a dark line in my blood; perhaps I craved it, wanted its bite, wanted it to bite me. Maybe after two generations in America, I was seeking it out in order to bite back, to swallow bitterness in order to turn it into sweet. To find my own adventure, I had to be pursued by one story before being rescued by another.

A month after moving to Greece, I am living in the Pensione Angelika. I lasted almost the full three weeks of the strike at my cousin's apartment. It was in a building owned by his father, who had lived with my grandparents in New York while getting a degree from Columbia. When he returned, he had become so eligible he was able to marry an heiress with many fields. He sold some of them and built an apartment in Athens, one floor for him and a floor for each of his sons, Stavros and Aristotle. Many apartment houses in

Athens are like this, new floors added for each generation, the last left unfinished to avoid taxes. You can see them topped with kinky lines of wire, like hair.

Stavros was heavy, with a large jaw. Aristotle was slight, a schoolteacher. Stavros married a woman to match him—a Greek-American waitress he met while visiting our New York relatives. Meropi had swift hands and a wide, gap-toothed smile and ran their small apartment like a general. With only one sink and a kettle full of boiling water, she laundered and cooked and clucked at her two small daughters. Their grandfather, my great-uncle, was living with them, and she managed him also, but he was scholarly and quiet and not too demanding, as Greek men go. The other brother, Aristotle, married a woman named Didi, who was very thin and plucked her eyebrows. Didi worked in an office and gave him sons and money. They lived in a house in the suburbs with floors so polished they were dangerous.

These two brothers had stopped speaking to each other. It often happens in Greek families. Though each side had its own version of what started it off—Meropi working too hard, Didi not doing enough—maybe it was as simple as the choice to break away from the past, to live in the suburbs instead of the family apartment, to climb up instead of down. The scent of their feud hung around the house every day, an absence in the upstairs apartment.

On my previous visits, I was a stranger, an American. Greeks have two congruent and conflicting laws of hospitality: *philoxenia*, love of a stranger, side by side with suspicion of those in your clan but outside your immediate family. A people who are hardest on themselves can afford to love others, never knowing whether a stranger might be a god, but always sure with their own kin whom to blame, who cost the most blood. It seems to take so little to push an insider outside; a feud can happen in a moment. As an American, a stranger, I was offered everything, denied nothing, forgiven for all my odd behavior. Now I had announced I was moving to Greece.

In the beginning, Stavros and Meropi took me in as they would any visitor from afar. As a potential new Greek, a returning daughter, I had to learn their rules. The first was that women never venture far from home. The second was that, far from being filled with the wisdom of the ages, Greece is a country on the verge of political chaos, and has been for a long time. In Greece, political parties are like feuding families; when one gets in, it feels the need to sweep every office clean of its predecessors, from messengers to ministers. The businessmen who rely on contracts and handouts go with them. When one party is in, half the country starves and half thrives. The Socialists had new policies but had not changed the system. Now the whole country had gone on strike, and Athens felt like a ghost town.

During the day, I would try to help Meropi, but I kept bumping into myself in the small apartment. The buses and taxis were also striking, so I would step out on short trips into the city and read the American newspaper, but when I returned, Meropi looked worried. Since I could not get far on foot and they were two neighborhoods from the center, my circumference grew smaller and smaller. At night, we would watch the news. Stavros told me he was a member of the local conservatives. As the situation got worse, he took the bad news with a kind of glee. *The tanks are going to roll*, he would say. *There will be fire in the streets*. And there was—a few cars were overturned after a demonstration and torched, and I only missed it by a block. After that Meropi insisted on coming with me, which made going out even more difficult.

Meropi and Stavros were very patient with the fact that I had no real plan or aim. In any Greek family, the solution to all problems is to give an opinion, a piece of advice. They gave me advice about how to find a job, how to dress, who to talk to, how to behave with taxi drivers—never talk to *them* since many had been spies under the dictatorship—what to eat, and where to go. Words piled up like stones. At night, as I tried to sleep on a bed in the living room, I felt them on my chest, pressing down on me.

One day, I asked for advice about a place to live. Both answered with relief—and who can blame them? They were skeptical about finding an apartment, because housing was very tight, but thought in the interim I could try a *pensione*. When I said good-bye, I hugged them gratefully and even kissed their two daughters. The children were sorry to see me go, because I was a source of great amusement for my awful Greek, even worse than theirs.

That is how I have come here. Angelika's is not my first *pensione*. Before I knocked on her door, I had been living at Mikeli's. Mikeli was an aging architect with artistic pretensions, who liked to hang his own paintings on the wall and talk to the guests about them. After I had been there a week, he must have decided I was going to stay for a while; he knocked on my door with a bottle of wine and two glasses. I told him I was not feeling well and had to push him out of the room. He had a bloodhound face, jowly and sad. He looked back at me like a dog I had sent out into the rain. The next day, I walked two blocks to Angelika's and moved in that afternoon.

Both *pensiones* are in Koukaki, a neighborhood where even the *pensione* owners like to think of themselves as bohemian. Koukaki encircles Philopapou Hill, a garden perched on a small peak, a park once owned by a philanthropist who stocked it with native Mediterranean plants. Like a hoopskirt, the streets slope down the hill in ever expanding loops. The higher the street, the more intimate, filled with walled gardens spilling greenery. At the bottom of the skirt, streets widen, lined with shops that serve the neighborhood. The style of the houses contrasts with the bland blocks of most Athens apartment buildings; tall and old, painted in fading pastels, they exude a sleepy, Parisian air, with their shuttered windows and shallow balconies lined in plants. In Koukaki, Athenian doctors and teachers and artists live side by side with permanent foreigners. Two blocks higher than Mikeli's, Angelika's rises on a steep hill, the entrance a block above the back. I wonder if sleeping on an angle contributes to the way the inhabitants live.

Angelika rents to European and American models who have come to Athens on their last luck. An illegal under-the-table trade flourishes. Too old, too fat, or too drunk for Paris and Milan, the models support a business still taboo to Greeks. The building is three stories high, the top floor towers too steeply and the bottom sinks too low; the middle floor, where I have my room, seems calm and grounded. During the early hours of the day the building rests, quiet and dark, curtains closed. In the afternoon, the rooms fill with the sounds of hungry footsteps drumrolling up and down the stairs, doors slamming, pots of water boiling in the kitchen for coffee, the television turned to dubbed American sitcoms. Everyone rushes to the shower before the hot water runs out. It always does, leading to loud curses in English, French, or German. The models, both male and female, live alone or in couples or somewhere in an ever-changing geography in between. Those who find work rise early, miraculously cured of hangovers, energetic and suddenly professional. On one shoot, they can make enough in a day to last for weeks.

Although this is not what I had in mind when I told myself I was moving to Greece to discover my roots, I am enormously relieved to have found my room—despite the eccentric house rules. Angelika's father, who had owned the house, was a painter. Although she lives in the suburbs with her lawyer husband, she likes to honor his spirit by selecting tenants carefully. Her clientele live by their art; no one complains when she stints on the heat. On the day I knocked, Angelika, who never rents to ordinary citizens, had just kicked a model out for nonpayment and decided to change her policy. When I told her I was a Greek American and offered her cash, she took me into the room and assured me she would clean it up immediately. I looked at the high ceilings and the tall windows filled with light and said, *Of course*.

After only a few days in my new home I find myself in the middle of a small household war. My housemates are having a feud, which seems to have arisen out of a dispute over sex but has quickly become a war over food. The beautiful Isabella, a tall and regal-looking brown-skinned American, heads one faction. The evil Marta, a petite German with an aggressive haircut and bad teeth, heads the other.

It all began the first week I moved in. Marta was sleeping with Yves, a blue-eyed black-haired Parisian who likes to read the paper in the morning in the kitchen but otherwise ignores everyone else. One day Marta was living in Yves's room; the next day she was living in the top flat. Two nights later, Isabella could be seen straddling Yves in the living room, kissing him over and over as he tried to watch television.

I was surprised that they had become lovers, because the first and only thing Yves had said to me when I introduced myself was that American women could never be sexy, since they put no thought into it. *Like wearing those horrible things, what are they called, tights? No European woman would dare wear something so ugly, so unappealing.* I tried to argue the importance of convenience and comfort, but he had retreated behind his paper and picked up his coffee as if to say, *The matter is closed.* Soon after he and Isabella started sleeping together, he warmed up, as if conceding American women might have some charm. This was my first evidence of Isabella's amazing power over men, even pretty French egoists with flexible sexual orientation. It made me admire her from afar.

Marta decided Isabella had become her enemy forever. Not only had she seemed to succeed where Marta failed, but Yves had become such a nice person. Marta has not taken a direct approach at gaining her revenge, however. She sabotages Isabella's food.

We have one common refrigerator, with designated shelf space, and cupboards. Buying supplies requires that you go to at least three different shops—the bread and dairy shop, the produce stand, and a general store. I am still in love with the small-scale democracy of the street market. There is nothing slovenly about the service; proprietors hustle their products with pride, each a king or queen of goods. By the second visit, we have had a chat and they know my name. People are delighted when I tell them I have moved to Greece; they encourage my language and forgive me my mistakes. (It is only as time passes that I find myself accepted as a native daughter, asked to pay a daughter's price. For now we are still in love with each other—the local Greeks and the Greek-American girl.) I spend whole mornings lingering. Even the post office employees offer me coffee when I get my mail. The models, however, see anything that drags them into daylight as a chore. Squabbles over shopping escalate quickly.

Marta raids the refrigerator at night. She takes Isabella's yogurt, her slim rye crackers, her cubed American cheese with cows printed on the front. Does she eat them or hoard them? No one knows. No one has seen her do it, but Isabella has accused her publicly more than once.

Today the house creaks with added tension. Marta hides in her room while Isabella and Yves fight loudly enough for each floor to hear. Isabella wants Yves to take her out, to go to clubs, to dance until night has turned over into morning. Habitually broke like all the other models, Yves refuses. Isabella curses him and calls him useless and a bad lover—without frills or imagination. Now she has come into the kitchen and flung open the fridge.

Her yogurt carton has been left on the shelf, but mutilated, half empty, torn. Isabella yells that she has had it with the Greedy Cow, and we know who she means. She slams the refrigerator deliberately and bounds upstairs. There is a big catwalk show today, and this morning the house is half empty. A few remain: a closeted Canadian former child star, the Swedish couple who live in the basement but never come out, an Irish girl who is still asleep, myself, and Yves. When he hears Isabella going up the stairs, Yves comes out of his room and tells her to back down. The Canadian grabs his arm and tells him to let her be. We know we are about to witness a drama.

Isabella goes into Marta's room. We hear them screaming at each other. Isabella is tearing the room apart, and Marta is trying to stop her. Then we know Isabella has found the hidden store, all the food Marta squirreled away: under the mattress, in the pillowcase. Marta is weeping. We hear a smack. Marta screams and cries but does not come out. Isabella climbs back down to the kitchen, ignoring Yves and the rest of us, and starts to put away her food calmly.

Later, I am walking back from the post office and I see Isabella on the other side of the street. Naturally, I am a little nervous as I watch her cross over to stop me.

Aren't you American? When I say yes, she lets out a torrent of abuse against the Greeks, the French, the Germans, and Europeans in general. She tells me to come with her to her favorite souvlaki stand and asks if I have found my way there yet. When I say no, she looks at me with great pity and then flings her arm around me, as if that settled something.

She wants to know my opinion of the fight, if I thought she was too mean to Marta. I look at this woman capable of punching another woman. I say I can see why she lost her temper. She laughs and says temper has always been a problem for her. She tells me that after she divorced her husband for cocaine addiction and womanizing, she was tempted to do something really cruel to him or to pay for someone to do it for her. She confined herself to putting sugar in his gas tank, and she never regretted it. I wait a few moments and then ask, *Why sugar in the gas tank?* She asks me where I am from, and when I say California, she stops in the street and gives me a hug. *Me too.*

She tells me she grew up in San Francisco and that her mother was black and her father was Armenian. I say she must feel at home in Greece, and she just looks at me and rolls her eyes. Isabella has skin like cinnamon, and she is wearing sweat pants and a T-shirt with a big print of a puppy on it. Without makeup she looks young, and her smile is sincere in a way that I miss.

We are walking toward the Plaka. As we cross the main boulevard, two men in a black Porsche pull up and roll down their window. *I thought angels were white until I saw you,* one man says, and Isabella gives him the finger, which he seems to enjoy. After smirking at us, he drives off.

I can't wait to get back home! I tell her I understand just how she feels, and at that moment and to my surprise I do, her voice and style so familiar I am aching with nostalgia. Still, I look around, as if the old lady in black sweeping the sidewalk across the street could hear, understand English, and bar me from the true Greece beckoning from the corners of my imagination. She tells me she has broken up with Yves. *He never wanted to give me head.* I just look at her. *Honey, if you don't sip from the cup, you don't get served at all.* The idea that you could discard a perfectly beautiful young man, one who seemed disease free and basically gentle, because he does not perform your preferred sex act seems novel. She asks me if I want to go dancing with her later. I imagine her, dressed in full regalia, parting the crowd as I follow. Even now I would give a great deal to see Isabella enter a room full of men and watch them fall powerless in front of her.

At the souvlaki stand, she smiles at the man behind the counter and orders two specials in a sweet-toned, American-accented Greek. She hands mine to me carefully—warm and greasy, wrapped in slippery white paper. Sitting on the curb next to the stand, we can look up to see the Acropolis. She has never been, and I suggest we go now. She says she wants to dress for it and bring her camera; we agree on a plan for later in the week. With the silence of two old friends, we eat our souvlaki wrapped in warm bread, spilling tomatoes and pickles, spicy yogurt sauce.

We walk back past the sleepy, shuttered houses of Koukaki. It is four o'clock. The shops have closed until six. The laundry on the roofs of the neighborhood snaps gently back and forth as if the breeze were turning over in a white bed. As we pass a small *cafenion*, the old men do not look up at us but talk to one another. From the open doors of the shop comes an air of thick ground Turkish coffee, the clatter of porcelain cups. The women in our neighborhood have painted old olive oil cans red and blue and set them on the stairs of their houses with bushes of basil, and they have lined the walls of their garden with jasmine vines. Turning the corner to Angelika's, we see the cats of the neighborhood asleep, on the walls of the gardens, under the cars. Isabella invites me to her room to take a nap.

In Isabella's room, the windows are open. When we lie down, the scents of the neighborhood drift in on the wind. This is the aroma of Koukaki: basil and coffee, fresh bread and vegetables almost on the turn, diesel trucks, and, below it all, the faint aroma of cats. I curl up next to her.

In *pensiones*, no one has a plan beyond the next morning or the afternoon. I can step out of Greek and step back into it. Hovering over a deep sea, I dip but do not dive. It no longer matters why I have come to Greece. It has become impossible to imagine what I would be doing if I were not here, in this house, lying next to Isabella, watching the light grow dim.

As I fall asleep I feel warmth emanating from her body, the glow coming from her steady breathing, the shine of someone who can throw herself into the unknown and ride it like a roller coaster without fear of falling off. I do not know where she got her courage, but I synchronize my breath with hers in hope that I will breathe it in.

Next Door to Olympus

The ancient Greeks were a practical people, and they gave their gods a real home in a real place. Mount Olympus is still there, though the gods are gone; you can see its snowy peaks—you can even ski them. Olympus has a neighbor rarely mentioned. It may have never been home to the gods, this other mountain, Ossa, but it has its own history and a secret name. The two mountains face each other, separated only by a gorge called Tempi.

On either side of the gorge is a sheer face of dark granite; below rushes the water Alexander crossed to conquer the world. Across a rickety footbridge, you can reach the shrine my cousins showed me, the cave where couples flock to get married. Although a saint moved in when Daphne left, the sense of sacredness remains unchanged. An interesting choice to bless young couples, Daphne wanted to hunt in the fields forever, always a nymph, never a goddess. One day, out in the woods, she was spotted by Apollo. Daphne knew that once a god looks at you it is only a matter of time before you are dead or immortal or pregnant with the hero of someone else's story. She ran from him, but, being a god, he was about to catch up when she called on Demeter, who turned her into a tree. Is being a tree preferable to being loved by a god? At least she was rooted to the earth, could feel the rush of water from the river where she sat and dreamed. Apollo has no temples, seers, or worshipers these days, but Daphne is still around, her name part of the woods. To me, the Greek word for roses has also always had her name in it— *triandaphilla*, thirty daphnes, blooming and well protected.

When you go to the Vale of Tempi and drive through its flanks, you can sometimes hear a rolling drum, like thunder. They say the sound is the two mountains battling. Some say Ossa was fighting Olympus for being condemned to be forever in second place: not as high, not as snowy white—the place where the gods stopped to wipe their feet before going home to the goddesses. Maybe Ossa is fighting Olympus for a different reason. Maybe Ossa is the home of the story that hides behind the story: Daphne, not Apollo.

Ossa has a different name for the Greeks: Kysavos. Kysavos is the mountain that shook both my grandparents off its flanks, sending them flying into the new world. My grandfather came from a village high on the mountain, a rocky, tough outpost clinging vertically to the land. The buildings are made out of red jagged stone, piled without mortar, link by link. In the houses, families sleep in one room, with the animals kept below them for warmth, the year's harvest drying in sloping attics above. The villagers are mostly shepherds grazing off the land, which taught them to be wily and sharp. My grandmother came from Retsiani, a name that rolls around in the mouth like a cherry. Retsiani is closer to the plains, and its people are farmers. The same river runs through both villages, but up near my grandfather's village it is a sharp, steep torrent. By the time it gets to Retsiani, it has widened and grown shallow and safe. Next to the river, plane trees surround a broad square.

My mother would not have gone to the villages right away. All trains stop in Larissa, where she went first. Helped with money sent from America to start businesses, her cousins had already started coming down off the mountain to find enterprise in Larissa's small squares. They were all near her in age, young and childless and ambitious; the ones who were shy, who liked the quiet of the earth, had stayed behind to work the fields and tend the flocks. Anxious to show their sophistication, the Larissa cousins would have fed her long meals and asked about her family, about whom they knew a surprising amount. They would have been especially interested in her brothers. After raising their glasses they would toast her name and her luck in finding a husband, and my mother would have just smiled: after all, isn't that what she has been escaping?

Eventually, someone would have said that she had to go to the mountains, to see the villages. One of the aunts would have gently led her aside and offered to lend her more suitable clothing. She would have borrowed a man's old gray sweater, loose wool pants, and boots, and they would have ridden up in a pickup truck the next time a villager came down to bring watermelons to market, or eggs, or baskets of cherries piled loosely on top of one another. In the back of the truck, surrounded by an aroma of straw and fresh earth, they would have bounced painfully along the dirt road leading up to Ayia, the market town at the foot of the mountain.

The route to Ayia leads first through low beet fields, then up through hills fragrant with fruit orchards and goats tied in little yards. Ayia is the only town on the mountain, holy, with a handful of churches and one big square with an open-air vegetable market. It would have been the first year in a long time that there were goods to put out on the stands, the harvest beginning to return to the health of peace.

Families in those days were large, so large her cousins remain nameless for the most part, the links in a chain that stretches back through time. Someone's aunt or uncle or third cousin in Ayia would have taken her in, fed her dinner, made her lie down and rest for the journey the following day. I imagine that when she woke up, she saw the river that starts in the deep heart of the mountain above her, spread among boulders and trees and rocks, a gentle shallow stream, shimmering toward the sea. She would have walked out onto the large square, filled with people selling goods out of stalls, piles of fruit and vegetables and chickens in wire baskets, baked bread in rings, the women calling out to her in a language she knew before she knew English.

Another cousin took her to Retsiani, her mother's village. There were no roads on the mountain then, just donkey tracks. Her cousin must have gotten the donkeys and helped my mother on; they would have left early, before the heat, in the first hours of the day. Swaying slowly up the track, listening to her cousin chide the donkeys in a village patois, time changed rhythm. Instead of the speed she always felt, she entered continuity. It was the same unchanged path her own mother, my grandmother, had trodden. Its outlines must have been etched in my mother's dreams, because it all looked so familiar.

I imagine she saw what I saw: a dream village, perched on the gentlest slopes of the mountain, protected by the river and open to a view of the sea. The trees are generous and old, safe from the fiercer weather farther up. Instead of the sharp pine, wide-brimmed nut trees grow; the orchards around the village are rich with fruit. The houses, white with red roofs, spread themselves along the cobbled streets, leaving plenty of room for yards and light. Grape arbors straddle wooden tables where neighbors gather and chat.

Like a spring under a shadow, the village was the source—one way her own mother's life might have turned out. Whatever the water whispered to her, she kept it to herself. Is it wrong for me to imagine that, looking at the village, she began to wonder what it had been like to leave it, what had moved my grandmother, what she had had to leave behind?

There is another photograph of my mother that I have seen, hugging a tiny old woman with long white braids, all dressed in black. The woman has lost her teeth and she is frail as a bird, dwarfed by my mother's healthy new-world arms. Delight shines in both their faces. She is the woman I always imagined was my grandmother's mother—still alive, living in the complex of houses that was run by her only son. He was a farmer, not yet married, who had dreamed about his sisters in America almost every night of his life. The old woman who turned her cheek to be kissed by my mother looked like a piece of fruit left on the vine to go dry, puckered by the decisions she had made, for her own children and so many others. Because I do not remember when I found out that my grandmother's mother was the village healer, when I saw this picture I imagined the small whitewashed house behind them hung with dried herbs, the aromatic scent of remedies. Later, I found out that the woman in the photograph was my grandfather's mother, and not my grandmother's after all. *No, she died before I got there*; it is this kind of casual aside that changes the whole story.

When my mother arrived in Retsiani, maybe this is what she found: not her mother's mother but what was missing in her own mother, a silence that had always been hidden. A mother sends away three daughters: eighteen, sixteen, and fourteen. She would have packed them up tightly because they had a long way to go. She had already given them knowledge—how to ward off curses, how to measure the earth's moods, how to lay hands on a body and feel pain, how to soothe it. Taking her secrets with her, she never told my mother what it meant never to see your own future blossom.

By the time my mother got to her mother's village, the one son who was left, the son who stayed to work the fields, lived in the small house. He was still a young uncle, maybe too young to host her, a girl on her own from America.

In the house across the street lived the son of my grandmother's first cousin, with three daughters close to my mother's age: the Kalidis girls. Their mother came from a village near the sea, and each girl exhibited a different shade of sun and water, light and green. Unlike the other village girls, they desired education and read more than schoolbooks. Talking among themselves, they had formed their own philosophy. Their father had loved their mother, who died when the girls were young, and because they reminded him of her, he never tried to control them. Careful, they never broke any rules and helped their father keep house and gather harvests. The Kalidis girls ordered books for themselves from the town shop, eventually writing to publishers in Athens and Thessaloniki. When my mother saw their books, surrounded by girls sitting comfortably, legs on the ground, she felt at home. She asked her uncle if she could live with them.

She was supposed to have stayed a few days. Each day blended into the next one until she no longer knew how long she had been there. In the mornings, she would follow her cousins to the river, where they would climb on top of the rocks and read to one another. In the afternoon, she would help her cousins around the house. In the evenings, they would dress and stroll into the square, each of them arm in arm, protected from the hint of impropriety by their numbers and their familiarity. Once, when the moon was full, they dressed in black and stole out of the streets into the forest, where they climbed three ridges to get to an abandoned Roman aqueduct. They crept along the broken stone until they were at the center, looking over the precipice. After the dark of the forest, the moon made the air look like day, and she could see the outlines of her cousins' faces. They confessed that they did not want to marry local boys; they wanted the city. She told them about New York.

She had not taken a shower since she came, rinsing off sometimes with a bucket behind the house; her hair had not been washed and she had worn the same clothes every day. Yet she felt comfortable, relaxed. When she sat next to the Kalidis girls, shelling walnuts for their father, my mother would lift her hand to her face and smell the earth rising off her skin. Hearing herself laugh about a character in a book they had all read, or commenting on the

83

villagers' histories and quirks, my mother remembered her own mother talking to her sisters in the cramped kitchens of New York. Did she ever wonder if this was a life that might have been hers, if this was a life her own mother had left behind, one she could take back from where fate had hidden it?

Her cousins finally persuaded her to go up to Nivolyani, her father's village. They told her they would hire a donkey for her, but it was expensive and she would have to go alone. She had to carry a loaf of bread with her to bribe the wild dogs, who still wandered the forests between villages. When they put her on the donkey and pointed her in the direction of the next village, she had to trust that the animal knew the way, that when it clopped on the edge of the path, without looking down, it was being sensible, not suicidal. To keep her mind off the drop, she looked ahead, to the wild forests, to the peak of the mountain hidden in the clouds.

The donkey climbed the mountain clinging to the edge of the path, and my mother did not look down. She hugged her loaf, waiting for the dogs, wondering what the village would look like. When she saw it in the distance she had to look very carefully to make it out. Only the roofs stood out against the brown and gray of the wild peaks; the houses looked as if they had been carved out of stone, with their slaty walls and wooden beams.

I imagine her coming into the village. Everyone would have looked at her face and known her immediately, shouting at each other as they helped her down. They made up a bed for her in the house where my grandfather was born, blankets laid on straw mattresses. As she fell asleep, she breathed in the scents of her father's childhood: the sharpness of goat skin, ripening cheese, soft wood, and musky earth from the onions piled overhead. It must have been a mix she could almost recognize, something that was strange and familiar all at once.

Just above my grandfather's village was the source of the river, a spring with a tiny church built next to it, where her ancestors' bones had been hung in embroidered bags. In my imagination, my mother goes to the spring. She leans against the rocks and hears the wild wind pushing against the walls and in the trees. She thinks to herself, *I can live in Greece, I can stay here forever.* When she closes her eyes she can see the smiles of the Kalidis girls, picture Daphne holding a cigarette. They represent a new kind of Greek woman— following the rules but not getting trapped by them.

But here is another mystery about my mother's year in Greece. When I went back there without her, I knew nothing about the Kalidis girls, had never heard of them. The numbers she gave me, the addresses she had managed to keep, only told one side of the story; they were all her father's cousins, so many I never thought about my grandmother's relatives. As for Daphne, her name was never mentioned, her address never delivered. Even the story of the aqueduct came out differently.

Many years later, I overheard a conversation between my mother and one of her American cousins, Zoe. Zoe was the only daughter of her mother's oldest sister, so cherished as a child that her father never let her have any suitors. He could not prevent a new-world story; one day at the library Zoe asked for a book, and the librarian fell in love with her. He was short, grumpy, and Jewish but deeply romantic and passionate. When he found her number he called, and her father answered: *Who is it?* The librarian answered, *A friend of Zoe's.* Her father replied, *Zoe has no friends but her mother and her father,* and he slammed down the phone. This is a story we heard many times and always loved—how her father took her to Greece to get her away from the librarian, how he spent his life savings to follow and eventually win her.

But another detail emerged in this conversation. Zoe explained to my mother that she also went to the aqueduct when she was in the village, but this time she had been invited by a man, a local suitor who had lured her with tales of Roman ruins. She had to run back in the moonlight to the village to escape him. And my mother laughed, saying, *The same thing happened to me—it was probably the same man*. You can see how stories fall between gaps: how it could be the lecherous stranger or it could be the beautiful cousins, how I could have missed one story altogether. But I know it happened. My mother was lured by many different mythical creatures on her voyage, and some of them were hideous and others beautiful. I know because of what happened to her later, not just because of what happened to me.

HEROES

In the tales of ancient Greek heroes, dangerous creatures often take the form of women, snake-headed or scaly-clawed, greedy and fond of human flesh. Hercules with his overdeveloped arm muscles, his massive thighs, pumped on hormones, strides through the legends, wiping out monsters with long eyelashes. When he defeats a scheming priestess and rescues a helpless princess, I want to tear back the stories and find out what was really going on. When Jason and the Argonauts stop on their journey at the island of Lemnos and are invited to father a new generation, since the women living there have killed off all the men, I don't want to follow them any farther. I want to stay on the island; I want to know why the women did it, what government they created, what it was like living there.

The real temptation, the real danger, resides not in the challenges but in the heroes themselves. Look at the story of Theseus and Ariadne. Ariadne was a princess living in her mother's palace on Crete. Bare-breasted priestesses who wrapped snakes around their arms were still well respected; in the shaded courtyards, everyone she passed greeted her with the proper awe due the daughter next in line to the throne. Grapes hung from the archways. When she was a girl, all she had to do was wait for them to be ripe enough and then reach up to pluck a few. Because her father, the king, had tempted a god and her mother had been cursed, her brother was half beast and unable to help rule. They kept him locked in a maze, where he snorted out bad breath. One day Theseus arrived from Athens, determined to kill the Minotaur. Ariadne must have known he was trouble from the minute he stepped off the ship—in a short thigh-revealing skirt, blond locks a bit too long—flexing his muscles. She was smart and sensible; it was her cool head that thought of using thread to get through the maze; Theseus would never have pulled it off without her. It is clear from the stories that she must have been deeply lost, because after she helped him kill her brother, after an earthquake threatened to split the island in two, she abandoned her throne and her position and fled with him in his waiting ship.

I imagine what must have happened when they got to the island. Theseus would have raised himself off the bunk where they were making love and told her that he wanted her to come with him to explore. He might have been a little rough in bed, a little blood-thirsty, but he would have focused his entire attention on her while she lay under him, and she would never have guessed what he had planned. After their swim, he would have given her one last kiss when she fell asleep on the sand, the water cool between her toes. By the time she woke up the ship was already pulling away, and it would have taken her a moment to realize she was alone with a trunk beside her containing a loaf of bread and a jug of water. The worst part for Ariadne, screaming at him as he leaned over the rail-ing, hand waving, would be that Theseus refused to see himself as anything less than brave, a hero. While trembling with fear, he shouted back at her that he was sorry; he respected her as the daugh-ter of a king but she had to understand that he was busy, too young for commitment; he had too many adventures ahead. The last thing she would have heard before the ship grew too distant was, *Anyway, you're better off without me*. If it were not for the thought of all she had given up, the heat of the island, and the few supplies he had left her, she would have thought he was right.

If you look at what happened to Ariadne, you will realize that you need to be on guard against heroes with their flashing swords. You never know when you might be quietly weaving on the roof of the castle, enjoying the feel of the sun on your skin, when you will look out on the horizon and see his ship, pulling into your bay.

After she spent some time in the villages, my mother returned to Athens and her life found a pattern. She would spend a few weeks with Daphne and her husband in the city, where she soon found herself part of a circle of interesting young Greeks, Americans, and Europeans, most of whom spoke English and French. Daphne became involved with her husband's business, and she and my mother became comfortable housemates. My mother would wake up in the morning and Daphne would already be gone, or they would find each other in the afternoon, and their conversation centered around what they would wear to go out that evening or Daphne's retelling of stories about bolts of cloth, distributors, and corrupt officials. When my mother woke up with too throbbing a hangover, when her eyes felt stung by too much smoke, she would tell Daphne she needed to visit her relatives and would get on the train to Larissa. She would hardly wait in the town before catching a ride on a truck going into the villages, her face turned to the mountains. Breathed in deeply, the scent that greeted her changed with the seasons: the musty damp of autumn, the woolen sting of winter.

In the villages, she settled into another rhythm; everyone had a role, was expected to work hard. In the fall she helped bring in the harvest. In winter she sorted onions and garlic and nuts in the attic and slept with the farm animals below her to keep her warm. In spring, she went out again into the forest, gathering wild greens for the *pitas* the Kalidis girls contributed to the local festivals. After a few weeks of carrying wood on her back or buckets of water, never having a shower and letting the dust cake in her hair, she would kiss them all good-bye and go back to Athens, where Daphne would share her perfume and the clothes her husband bought her, increasingly more expensive and flattering. In Athens, she could enjoy long silent days, reading on the porch and waiting for Daphne, and crowded nights, snatching conversations above the smoke and din. When she grew lonely, she would go back to the mountains again.

While my mother shuttled back and forth between village and city, sure she was following her own rhythm, her extended circle made plans. Letters sent airmail to her parents assured them that it was only a matter of time before their daughter settled down. Someone would find her a husband. Protected by her uncles and cousins, she would have been valued like a daughter. Like Ariadne on the island, she would not have noticed the trap until the ship had almost receded.

The story about what happened to her when she went to the taverna reveals how easily women step into danger. Steeped in village lore as she was, she was still a New York American. When a group of her male cousins stopped by the Kalidis house and said they were going to a special dive deep in the mountains where the *chipro* burned like fire and old men sang songs with tears in their eyes, she did not notice the other girls refusing and thought it would be all right. The cousins cheered as she said she would come with them.

In the room full of men, she drank until her head swam and smoked cigarettes handed to her one after another. I can see her in the smoky room, and I know how much she loves a crowd, how she lights up a party. The temperature rises with all the bodies and drink. My mother joins in the singing, her feet stamping the wooden floor and the crowd clapping. When they tumble out after midnight, moonlight floods the river, and the cousins laugh at my mother as she dips her head in the water. She feels heat running through her body, feels her heart lifting with the bouzouki still on the air. They march home singing in a big crowd, helping one another to walk without falling over. For my mother, it would have been like being with her brothers; she felt tough and alive.

By the time she got back to the village, the lights in her mother's house were still on. Seeing them, she felt cool all of a sudden and shivered. As the male cousins shuffled off quietly, she stepped in the door alone. There, she found her uncle waiting, his face pink with rage. Rumors had passed all night from one wall to the next until they reached his ears. What he told her that night or what she told him has fallen off the end of the story: that she would have to move back with him or learn to behave, that she was going to destroy the reputation of the family, of her mother and her mother's mother. It was only one story, the taverna story, so I think she probably never went back again. It is possible that his rage softened her up for what came next.

Courtship, she might have thought in the beginning, was a convenient way to get out of the house. It did not take her long to gather suitors. For her two lives, she was pursued by two men. One was a local professional, a dentist who had been educated in Italy before the war and who had had an unimpressive military career before setting up his practice in Ayia. He was introduced to her by her cousins. At their first meeting, he was probably brought in by someone, introduced in a big crowd. After the meal, they found a way to sit him next to her, and she tried to talk to him in polite phrases while feeling all eyes on her. He had been hearing about my mother from the day she arrived and would have longed for the status she could bring him. In person, he might have found her even more alluring than he imagined, even a bit frightening. To my mother, the dentist was a way to pass the time, to flirt and tease. He was a bridge into a future she rolled around casually on her tongue, a future she might choose to swallow: the wife of a local professional, one step ahead of her mother but not too far.

Her other suitor was Athenian, a lawyer. He was the one to worry about, the one who almost caught her and kept her, the one who would have brought me into the world in Greece instead of Los Angeles. And because he is the one she never talks about, never laughs about, he is the one I have to watch out for. He is the one I can find only through my own experience. The live body of the story has to be fished out of the dark waters of the memory that has been swept clean at birth.

When I called my mother from London to tell her I was moving to Athens, her voice came through across the Atlantic: *Just don't marry a Greek man. That's all I ask. Don't come back with one.*

Did I need my mother's warning? Greek myths tell you that sex can make you forget your name, can maroon you on an island, can spawn wars and disaster. Today modern Greeks still fight against what the sun lifts out of their blood. Some men use their reputation as lovers to ply the tourist trade on the islands; they even have a name, *kamakis*, after the spear used to catch fish. Women are considered so dangerous that in church they are told to cover their arms and legs, lest they tempt the eyes of men away from God. Virginity might make men feel safe, but it gives a false sense of security; there are doctors in Greece who earn their living sewing up hymens before marriage. What you fight hardest against, what you need to gather most forces to resist, is always going to be more powerful than you expect.

Isabella has invited me to go with her to Glyphada, to an American bar. She is dating a basketball player, and that is where he likes to go.

Glyphada has changed since it was an exclusive Athenian sub-urb by the sea, the spot where Daphne had her first house. Its name comes from the swamp that was cleared to make way for the first apartments and resorts, the brackish bad water that still comes back when the weather turns and stinks up the bays and beaches.

Eventually, Greece became a member of NATO, and to prove its new status the government invited the Americans to build a base there. The sleepy town filled with soldiers. Entrepreneurs came to open bars and discos and pizza houses, all the things they imagined soldiers would enjoy. After the bars came the expatriates, to drink themselves into mindlessness listening to music they remembered from hazy sessions at home. The basketball players, part soldier, part expatriate, part drunken reveler, have staked Glyphada as their own.

The bars are staffed by seemingly identical petite British women, most of whom came over on holiday and decided to stay. Escaping a depressed English economy and rainy, bleak towns, they find jobs under the table with lovers turned boss. The bar owners keep them on slave wages, with the threat of deportation if they complain. Few Greeks come to Glyphada, only a few prowlers looking for a fast drachma or an inebriated bedmate.

Every once in a while, there are bombs.

Isabella has dressed in her most casual attire, jeans, sweatshirt, little makeup. The basketball player favors cotton and sneakers, and she has decided to look sporty and American. We take a taxi and arrive after ten. Isabella says we are going to Bobby's. On the way she tells me the bar was bombed by a left-wing fringe group a few months ago, blasting away half the bar and breaking all the bottles. Bobby repaired and reopened in a month. Although a few anonymous threats have recently circulated, she says it is like light-ning striking twice. Bobby's now enjoys a reputation as Glyphada's safest bar.

When I enter I feel at home and displaced at the same time. The neon-draped walls, heavy rock music, and sawdust on the floor take me back to a part of my country I have never experienced. Budweiser posters show well-muscled crew-cut men playing volleyball with frosted air-brushed girls. A cacophony of voices rises over the bar; no one speaks Greek.

The faces have a green tint to them, as if they have spent too much time underground. I spot the basketball players easily. A tall, animated pack, their bright cotton T-shirts contrast with the dinginess of everyone else. Isabella shouts *Yo!* She has put on her cowgirl charm—all pastels and fresh-scrubbed skin. Shaggy brown hair hiding half his face, her swain makes room for her and invites me to sit down.

I suppose I know right away. He is talking to Isabella and her boyfriend, and he barely glances at me to introduce himself, but Steve Paleologis, Greek-American basketball player, star of the second string, flushed and cruel, is just what I want and just what I will have. When he gets up to buy a round, he lopes across the floor graceful as a predator, dirty blond hair cut short, Bruce Springsteen T-shirt thrown over blue jeans.

Taller even than his fellow players, he makes the other men in the room shrink. When he sits down next to me, I can feel the heat from his thighs cutting through denim to mine. His angular face frames large eyes, burning and dark. Lips that might be considered too full for a man part over his teeth, white and sharp. When I see his arms, stretched out across the table holding a beer, and his large calloused palms, I am lost.

He invites me to come with him to another bar. He has bought me a beer, and I have laughed at his jokes. That seems to be enough. When I kiss Isabella twice to say good-bye, she gives me a squeeze of reassurance. He is the friend of her friend, and she thinks that makes him safe.

We go to a pizza joint where the waiter speaks Greek, and Steve orders something so quickly I cannot make it out. The waiter laughs.

Steve has a fluency and a familiarity with the language that I cannot imagine I will ever have. He tells me his parents both came over to Boston in their early twenties, just before they had him. Although his accent and his gestures are pure urban New England, he grew up in a Greek community. He was an altar boy and learned Greek street slang. When I tell him about my own background, he smiles and pulls my hair behind my head. His fingers feel rough against my neck. He leans his lips against my ears mid-sentence. *You have great eyes*, he murmurs. A shiver runs down my back. *I don't need compliments*, I tell him, and I suppose he believes me, because that is the last he ever gives me. When he invites me to his apartment, I agree without any hesitation.

It is just up the block and we decide to walk. In the dark streets, he puts his arm around my shoulder and pulls me to him. His kiss buries me. He is tall enough to block out my view of the night, of the stars, of the streetlamps above me. All I feel is the weight of his head pressing down on me, and the warm, surprising softness of his lips. His tongue slides into my mouth and feels right there. His skin smells like soap.

At his apartment house, we skip his room and go straight to the roof. The stars hover close to our heads. Beyond the edge of the suburbs and the last lights, the sandy yellow hills glow in the dark. The breeze against my bare thighs almost feels too cool, but then I forget about feeling cold, I forget about the mattress burning into my knees as they rub back and forth. I don't even wonder why there is a mattress on the roof, already waiting.

In the morning he walks me back to the center of town to get a taxi. The bars are all closed; the chairs turned up on the tables look like a crowd, waiting for the next shift. While we are waiting he tells me to say something in Greek. My tongue sticks to the top of my palate; I stumble over the words. He corrects me, the smoothness of his language running over mine. When the taxi pulls away from the curb, I look back and think I can see him waving. The interior fills with the sound of waves lapping at the shore of a desert island, the last ripple of a ship disappearing over the horizon.

Looking out the window, I run my hand over my thighs, secretly, to feel the bruises. I think, *How strange, these are my thighs, how strange*.

ECHO AND NARCISSUS

As everyone knows, Narcissus was a beautiful youth, so beautiful that everyone fell in love with him, men and women. He used to wander around the ancient world in a little toga and show his worshipers just how satisfied he was with himself by ignoring them completely. What he wanted, more than anything else, was someone worthy of his love. He had developed his high opinion of himself from his mother, a nymph who had been raped by a minor god and took her revenge through her son. Every day she called him gorgeous, better than the gods, and he believed her. By the time he had hair on his thighs, even the gods would not do for him. He needed someone he felt was his equal to truly love, but until he saw his own face in still water, he remained untouched by desire.

Echo was a nymph who must have had a good life before she entered the story. She grew up by a stream, under a tree, watching the sky rise blue day after day. Maybe because she talked too much, enjoyed telling secrets given only to her, she ran into trouble with a powerful god. In the quiet of a meadow, enjoying his own thoughts, he overheard Echo chattering with her companions, and the rise and fall of her voice in the air irritated him. Deciding nymphs like Echo were better seen, not heard, he took away her voice, rolled over, and went back to sleep. Now she could only repeat what others said to her. Imagine her frustration. Wherever she went, when she got on buses or met someone new, they could only see the woman of limited vocabulary—like a child, reflecting themselves. Inside her, the voice that had once been her way of forming the world was trapped and stunted. Maybe her cousins among the immortals thought they could find her a good husband, that being such a mirror, someone would want to marry her.

Unfortunately for Echo, instead of a man content to hear his words repeated back to him, she found Narcissus. She saw him leaning over a pool of still water and fell in love with the shape of his back, the glossy curl of his hair. She thought if only she could get his attention it would be some reward for all she had suffered. But just at the moment Echo spotted him, Narcissus finally discovered the perfect partner. In the water's reflection, he saw the world's most beautiful being. Narcissus fell in love with himself. To the mirror in the water, he spoke tender words, carried back to him on Echo's voice. He never looked up at her, never knew she was there. Putting his hand in the water, Narcissus saw himself disappear. When he realized he could not possess the only being he ever really wanted, he threw himself in and died.

As for Echo, her voice lingers still. She runs beside us when we walk, taking our heart's worst fears and bouncing them back to us. Because we think her voice arises from inside us, because her tones match our own, we dismiss her. If only we realized that every day her story repeats itself. Men fall in love with themselves, angry at potential lovers who can never touch them at their core. Women lose their ability to speak anything other than what is spoken to them. What must she feel as she watches us heading toward the river, about to disappear?

Isabella is angry with me. We have risen late, as usual, and I have come into the kitchen to find her peeling an orange and looking in whatever direction is opposite mine. She eats the orange segment by segment and does not offer me a piece. I can feel the Black Russians from the night before like pinpricks of light in the disco of my brain, throbbing to a bad Euro-pop beat. Outside, the day looks warm for November; the breeze coming in the open windows feels soft.

I make strong tea, the color of mud, and sit down next to her. Steam comes off the mug; Isabella cools off. After a few sips I am ready to say good morning. She wants to know why I am still seeing Steve.

It has been three weeks, and by now I should know better. The beginning was bliss. I saw him every night for a week, taxiing back and forth to Glyphada, making love in every room—noisy, wet, satisfying sex that made his roommate grumble when he caught me tiptoeing out in the morning. I found that there was not an inch of his body I did not want to lick, not a crevice I would not explore. His arms were long, and his skin flushed rosy red. He had stamina. When I put my hand on his chest to hold myself up, the muscles lying flat along his bones were taut and hard.

In the second week, I realized the inconvenience of a lover without a telephone. He became more difficult to find, calling me an hour after I had come back from where I said I would meet him, apologizing the first time and not offering any excuse the next two times after that. Isabella found out he stood me up the third time it happened and went from the benign delight of having a friend dating a friend to the anger of a woman watching an animal trying to cross a busy road. She yelled at me to stop, but I was dodging cars and could only see the other side. The first step in her strategy was to break up with her own basketball player, to show me how it might

99

be done. The second step was to take me out with her on the town, getting men, big and little, to buy us both drinks, and hoping the effect of alcohol and attention will distract me. She has stopped just short of telling me I have lost my mind, but I can tell today she wants to.

When the phone rings, I run to answer it. If it is Steve, I say I will meet him. If he wants to meet after the bars close, I say I will take a double-charging night taxi and see him at three in the morning. Isabella watches me as the speeding car nears.

Today, I want peace. Isabella is the only friend I have, and I need her. I tell her I think we should go to the beach.

Isabella decides this is a sign of health. After dragging me upstairs to her room, she pulls a multicolored straw bag out from under the bed and tells me to find the sunblock. Personally, she does not want to get a tan. My *skin*, she says, *is dark enough*. I tell her she is beautiful in every shade.

We change into bathing suits and T-shirts and wide-brimmed hats and fill our bags with books and magazines. As we stop on the bus, I imagine we are driving toward the postcard version of Greece, pastel clothes hanging on a line, a whitewashed dome against a vibrant blue sea. Athens passes by, identical blocks of apartment complexes erected under the dictators. The newest buildings already look old, white walls gone gray, the pavements speckled with peeling plaster and paint. As we move south toward the sea, every neighborhood looks the same.

We want to go to Voula, to the last suburb, the end of the city where the sea turns clean. Isabella takes out a copy of the more superior of the two American newspapers, the *Athens Star*. Along with a good international news synopsis and investigative local stories, it has an excellent horoscope. The picture of the astrologer over the column shows a middle-aged man in a toupee, smiling with the happiness of knowing our fortunes. Isabella reads hers and then she reads mine.

Listen to this: You have been seeing the world through rose-colored glasses, but today you will have the wool ripped from your eyes.

I imagine the little man in the photo winking at me as he types the word "ripped."

The bus is an express for Voula, but it makes the mistake of stopping in Glyphada, a fact I try to ignore as we get closer and closer to Steve's neighborhood. Isabella is aware of the danger, and she is doing her best to help me by passing me a magazine and telling me not to look out the window. Maybe I look too unhappy or maybe she has decided a swift end is the best way to put me out of my misery, but when I suggest getting off at Glyphada, *because it's getting so late*, I only have to promise twice that we will go straight to the beach before Isabella gives in.

We march toward Steve's apartment. I have found I have a will as strong as Isabella's, a force inside me that matches hers. She runs along beside me with an expression on her face as if she is watching a horror movie, the ax about to fall. *What's wrong with asking him to come to the beach?* My question is rhetorical, and she does not bother to reply. Somewhere in my body I am imagining him inside me, but I push the images out of my mind. His roommate buzzes us up and my legs are trembling as we get on the elevator.

Steve's roommate opens the door a tiny crack and looks at us— *Hang on a second; let me tell him you're here*—and then he closes the door again. We wait in the hallway for ten minutes and Isabella looks at her watch. *Don't you think we should go?* But I have a purpose; I will not be dissuaded. Steve is inside.

Finally, his roommate invites us into the living room. Steve is nowhere to be seen. *Wait here*, he says, and disappears into Steve's bedroom. We can hear two male voices. Underneath, like a smooth current going the wrong way in a turbulent sea, runs the clear sound of a woman's voice, only a few words. We sit in the living room for five minutes. When Isabella gets up to walk out again, I follow her.

In the street, she hugs me for a long time.

The beach is empty. Isabella spreads her towel back from the water and lies down. She says, *I don't want to say I told you so but I did tell you so*. And I say, *Yeah, well, at least it's decided now. I'll never have to see him again.*

The sand is not white at all. It looks dingy, pocked with the detritus of a summer of packed-in bodies, vying for the sun. Paper, empty containers of suntan oil, and plastic bottle caps wait to be blown away by the winter winds. The sea flattens out like a blue plate, solid, not clear and shimmering, the light too low in the sky to shine through the water. I want to swim anyway and Isabella waves me on. She relaxes back into the sand, relieved that the worst is over, the accident has happened.

I wade out to where the water comes up to my chest and slide in. I push out into the distance, but I am afraid to let myself go where I cannot see the bottom. Instead, I crawl back and forth, parallel to the shore, keeping one eye on Isabella and another on the horizon. For a while I look out to the west, a world inhabited by people I know. Then I turn around and look at the beach, and wonder in a distant way what will happen next. I kick back and forth until my arms ache, feeling myself get stronger without any risk of drowning.

When the tall body in shorts steps past the volleyball net, I know who he is. He sits down next to Isabella, who turns over in disgust, and I drop my legs. They hit the sand and I walk in, moving away from the water to feel myself drown.

His sheets are damp and smell like sex. When we make love, I imagine the body of another woman twisting on the bed, her skin on my tongue like a lemon, squeezing behind my eyes, making me cry chest-heaving sobs, tears pouring out of me like sweat as I come.

ARCHAEOLOGY

Olive trees grow in the least hospitable places; perched on hills overlooking the sea, battered by wind, no rain for months, they turn crooked and crouched. They build up layer upon layer of wood, never getting too tall, bending but surviving. Each year they produce a crop of olives, small black fruits that need to be soaked in salt water before they can be eaten. When squeezed, they deliver a liquid, golden and rich—a blessing to everything it touches. Olive trees rise out of soil that appears solid but can easily break. Thin and dry, it yields secrets like promises.

For hundreds of years, Greek farmers and shepherds ambled over the past, ignoring bits of marble, a broken column, a disembodied arm nudged by the herds. Not bothering to dig, they closed their ears to the stories the pieces told them, listening instead to the cicadas' saw, the sky's hot sigh. Still, buried stories have restless spirits. Written down by monks who scratched them out to each other, page by page, time censored some of their fire but not all of it. Eventually the stories landed in the imagination of boys from another part of Europe, one that felt too quiet and tame. Confusing mythology with history, when the boys grew up they invented archaeology and plundered the world.

On Crete at the turn of the century, Arthur Evans discovered the palace of Knossos and then rebuilt it exactly the way he imagined it had been, complete with indoor plumbing and painted walls.

In Turkey, J. T. Woods searched out the temple of Artemis, one of the ancient world's seven wonders, by following donkey tracks in a field. While he worked, never shaving his beard, hardly removing his jacket, the farmers he hired made bets as they sat in the shade. One day, he broke his hip and had to ask his wife to take over. While he was carried in a basket, she dug. Together, they found the right pile of rubble under the earth, the fluted columns and intricately carved foundations. Destruction had scattered the marble so far afield that matching blocks were discovered holding up the arches of Roman aqueducts. Instead of trying to fix the past, they let the temple keep its ruins, like a ravaged woman her last rag, and returned home together, hand in hand.

With his scraggly beard and tattered *Odyssey*, Heinrich Schliemann set the trend for all future mad Europeans. Dreaming in gloomy Germany about the glories of Homer, he burned to recover Troy. He had to dig under seven layers of rubble on the Turkish coast to find a city that fit the shapes of the stories winding their way through his brain. Everything he found provided evidence: a battered gold face—Agamemnon's; a shield—Hector's. Schliemann's greatest treasure was his Greek wife, half his age and the daughter of an Athenian. In her quiet demeanor he thought he saw ideal womanhood, the glories of a vanished age. His letters home extol her charm, how hard she worked in his shadow, how much more beautiful she was than the ambitious women back home.

When Schliemann dreamed of his wife, he saw her as one of the legendary heroines of the War of Independence, who jumped off a cliff as the Turks approached, choosing death over dishonor. Diners from New York to Wyoming display posters of a famous nineteenth-century romantic painting depicting this scene. It shows a group of women in traditional costume, white loose sleeves and tight-knit embroidered wool vests, caps fringed in gold coins, edged at the cliff as the army ranges in the distance. Eyes turned to heaven, they hold hands as they dance toward the precipice. What did Schliemann's wife dream? Heart beating, palms sweaty, a big German hand plucking her away?

If you pick up a fragment, you have to re-create the way it fits with everything else around it. On the surface, you can observe the heroines with strong arms, roping in children, wiping off counters—one way of looking at Greek women. All up and down the Levant, men sit together and talk. The women work hard and say little. When they get old, they have worn off their beauty—dressed in black, faces like leather, their hands rocky and gnarled. If you looked only at the surface you might imagine the men have strength the women lack. Fitting the piece more carefully, you can see that Mediterranean women match their olive trees. Stunted trees create hard wood, black fruit turns to gold. Women who have been treated like children most of their lives—first by their fathers, then by husbands and sons—take revenge. As their men become more child-like, they toughen up. The older they grow, the stronger Greek women become, muscles like iron, sometimes with the hint of a beard. Fattened on the bad habits of power, their men become vain, petulant, and weak.

In another story, Schliemann's wife tells her husband that she thinks the women should have turned to fight, that they should have done anything but jump. She follows him into the fields in her long black dress and pushes up her sleeves, grabs a brush. When they find the seventh layer of Troy, the burnt marble, evidence of war, she suggests they look further. She finds the statues of the goddess and the wide-hipped flasks still full of grain, finds both sides of the story. Curling her body against his as they go to sleep, Schliemann's wife enters his dreams, her arms wrapped in bracelets, her face shining like lost gold. To uncover all the layers, you must be willing to dig far enough.

Before I went to Greece, the stories of the women in my family had shattered in pieces. Behind the stories my mother occasionally tossed out, the fields where I discovered history, hid the stories of my grandmother. She was like a fragment of marble in a field, something I passed every day, someone I thought I understood, having been named after her. She was always there: mother of my mother, dead before I was born, the one who came from Greece, who started the new-world story. I never questioned why my grandmother seemed to exist in silence, why I knew her only in such tiny fragments. If my mother's story was broken, my grandmother's was in even smaller, more jagged shards.

To find her, I look in the fields. Picking up what looks like a memory from my childhood, I brush across the surface, blow off the dirt. Underneath, the black brush strokes emerge, a picture of a woman who lived in America from age sixteen until she died and never received citizenship. Every year, when her papers needed to be stamped, she sent one of her children to the post office in fear that the authorities would come to take her away. I turn over a memory. When I tap against its mud-encrusted side, it makes a hollow sound.

My sister has stolen a piece of candy from the corner store. We are in Laguna Beach for the summer, a place nestled between the chaparral-covered hills of Southern California and a calm bay of water. The sixties are over; the town still resounds with rainbows and noisy festivals full of artists and hippies. Only five, my sister is tuned to the anarchic spirit of the times. When she sees the blue gum ball, wrapped and glorious, she knows enough to bury it quietly in her pocket and say nothing. Somehow, my mother the psychic discovers this and is furious. Even my sister, small and willful though she is, seems worried. According to my mother, it is a great calamity, a disaster, and we are all forced to march back to the store, while my mother holds my sister's small arm in her fist, dragging her along. With great ceremony, my sister apologizes and gives the man the money for the candy, long gone. We troop back to the shingle-covered house on the hill above the beach where we live. As the sound of traffic fades, calm takes over. My mother stops us and makes us turn to her. We hear for the first but not the last time: *This is what my mother always used to say: First you take a piece of candy, then you steal an egg, and before you know it you are an ax murderer.* As my mother speaks, she takes on a thick Greek accent, as if she is a medium or an oracle. The word murderer sounds just like this: *moorrrdurrrer*. When we tell the story over and over to each other again as we grow up, sometimes seriously, sometimes as a family joke, we always use the same voice. It is how I hear her in my head, tangled and full of doom, in a language that is not her own.

The sun beats down on the hard soil, and even the cicadas hush. Pushing my hat back against my neck, I bend down. Something glints under a bush. I pull it out. It is a story from my mother's brother, the one who was drafted during the Korean War. He told me that when he left for the army, his mother put her arms around him and whispered, *Na yirises nikitis*—return victorious—old words echoing from mothers to sons. Wanting to discover more, I take the rag from my pocket and begin to polish the gold.

It is a sunny Saturday morning. My uncle is a teenager, and he wants to go to the movies—Joan Crawford in a melodrama. He strides down the sticky sidewalks of Queens, wearing jeans and a light cotton checked shirt. Just before he reaches the marquee, a cloud covers the sun and lets go a big piss of rain. He ducks into the dark theater, soaking wet. Air-conditioning has chilled the air; that and Joan's overacting give him the shivers. By the time he leaves two hours later, he is shaking and feverish.

He gets back to the house and tries to duck into his room before his mother, my grandmother, spots him. He knows he's got a cold, but how can he explain to her the mechanics of rain and air-conditioning, the evil effects of bad acting? She comes out of the kitchen and puts her hand on his brow. A few hours ago, she sent a son out of her house, healthy and strong. He has returned, burning and shaking and weak. She tells him it is the evil eye and pulls him into the kitchen.

His father comes home for lunch from the deli and finds his wife heating olive oil on the stove and his son moaning on a chair in the middle of the floor. He suggests calling a doctor but does not push it; women have their own realm of magic, and he does not want to interfere.

My grandmother makes the cross of olive oil on my uncle's fore-head and says an incantatory prayer. She circles his chair, perform-ing rituals she learned from her own mother and grandmother. The earth is blocked by concrete foundation, floor, and carpeting. She tries to draw it up into the room, like breath. Feeling her son shiver-ing under her palm, my grandmother tries to cure him of Hollywood and the dangers of the dark country around them, dangers she is helpless to prevent.

Sometimes an archaeologist can dig for years, unrewarded. The rows of wheat hide the ancient tracks that lead to the temple; a shep-herd's hut sits on top of the king's burial ground. Luck plays a role— the farmer finds a piece of gold; the rock that appeared to be only a rock takes on a new shape. When the evening light outlines the stone as if for the first time, the archaeologist realizes it is the base of a temple, laid on its side. Such moments keep whole teams digging for years until the ground finally delivers treasures.

Two generations later, I am driving alone with my mother on our way to New York, and she decides she wants to visit her mother's grave. We are traveling together from Boston between my first and second year of college, and the road takes us near her old neighborhood. Driving slowly on the crowded, pale-boned Long Island Expressway, she tells me a story about her mother. *She asked me to come to dinner the week before she died. I had just started seeing your father, and I decided not to go.* I feel guilty, as if I were the one who missed the chance to see my mother one last time. We get off at the exit for Flushing and find ourselves driving past Kissena Park. My mother tells me that when they were growing up, they would hire rowboats to float out on the small lake. One of her uncles always followed behind in his own rented craft, unwilling to let the children who collectively belonged to all of them drift too far away.

With a few wrong turns, we find the graveyard, grass pools studded with stones bearing immigrant names: Polish, Greek, German, Italian. My mother thinks she remembers the right corner.

Under a crab-apple tree, we find the line of stones, laid flat in the ground—no ostentatious markers, just a name and two dates— the sisters and their husbands. With borrowed buckets and a roll of paper towels purchased at a corner store, we set to work, pulling out weeds, washing the dirt out of the lettering. When we get to her mother's name, my own mother leans over, letting the water pour over the stone again and again. The sun catches in the water as it washes over the marble, and my mother leans over, her face tender and open. She caresses the grass, rubbing it down. *I used to rub her back,* she tells me. *The knots were like rocks.* Sparrows in the trees around us fall silent as a cloud passes overhead. I pull a dandelion out of the ground and ask her what I have always wanted to know. How did she die, my grandmother—too young, long before I was born? *Officially, she had a heart attack.* My mother looks at me. *But her heart had already been broken. She died of a broken heart.*

We leave the graveyard and drive to Queens Boulevard, where her parents used to have their deli. Walking down the block, she points at the storefronts, identifying the businesses that used to be there: Mrs. De Souza's carpet shop, Mr. Levi's tobacco and candy store. The deli has been turned into an Italian restaurant and we seat ourselves, staring at the menu. I try to imagine the nicked counter and the jars of pickles, the way my mother had to learn at an early age how to cut meat thinly with a sharp knife. My grandfather stands next to the brass cash register, leaning on one arm. My grandmother hides in the back, where she can find a blue sky inside herself as she wraps feta in wax paper and lets the English words wash over her.

Too full of pizza, we go back to the car. Just before we get in, my mother stands in front of the open door. The sky is hazy, a New York sky, yellowed at the edges. Grass grows out of the broken sidewalk, and the concrete of the streets cracks in spiderweb lines. In the distance, we can see the first tall buildings, the offices of midtown Manhattan. In the streets leading off from the boulevard, the houses look compact, neat, covered in aluminum siding, painted white and green. *What was it about your mother's life, Mom, why was it so hard?*

My mother looks at me across the car and says, *She was like you or me but more so. And she lived at a time. . . .* My mother shrugs. I peer down the block. I can feel the life in the houses, the small kitchens, the streets that crawl around and under the neighborhoods, blocking the women in. Looking at the fractured ground, I try to pick out the face of my grandmother, whose living face I have never seen. Without the story, she evades me, a piece of pottery that does not fit. We get back in the car and drive the rest of the way in silence.

I do not ask my mother, *What do you mean, like us? What do you mean?*

Medea's Longing

Framed by the wilderness of the surrounding mountains, Larissa sweats in the plains, dusty and sedentary. Like a promise, the peaks rise in the distance, garlanded in gorges and wild onions, goats and streams. According to tradition, those remote recesses hide witches—practitioners of magic, black and white. With one eye closed, the witches appear crooked and ugly, black and cursed. With the other eye open, they reveal themselves as healers, close to the earth. Passing their secrets, mothers to daughters, Thessaly's daughters engender suspicion from fathers and sons.

Although technically from farther north, Medea ranks as the most famous Thessalian witch. She married Jason, who launched his quest from the base of its mountains, and her name evokes the rocks and water, mists and storms of the wild north. Medea was born where the earth falls off the maps, daughter of a king who had the one thing in the world Jason wanted: the Golden Fleece. Told by his corrupt uncle he had to obtain the Fleece before being given power, Jason gathered the beefiest and best heroes from all of Greece to help him search out its magical qualities and become a real man.

When he reached the edge of the world, his prize in sight, he encountered Medea's father, who did not want to give the Fleece to some Greeks from the south. Without Medea, Jason had no chance. How did she fall for Jason? After all, she knew powerful spells and was not afraid of blood. Medea fell in love with Jason as many had before her: because he was a guy on a quest.

I picture Medea when she first sees Jason. He shines beside the quiet northerners who have always bowed their heads to her. He ripples with singleminded determination, eyes gleaming with his mission. Imagine how attractive that is to Medea, who has been worrying lately about how to balance all her roles—career and family, performing rituals as a king's daughter while needing to gather herbs under a full moon. When he comes to her, dripping in sweat, and says, *Only you can help me, Medea, only you can understand*, her heart stops. Fresh bruises shadowing his brown skin, Jason pours out his heart; he tells Medea about losing his birthright, how he needs the Fleece to become the king he knows he can be. She smooths the hair off his brow and kisses him to give him courage. In her own gold-encrusted room, wearing lavender-scented robes, Medea feels powerful and calm. Only after she uses her mother's magic to steal the Fleece from her own father, only after she kills her brother to help her lover, does Medea lose her edge. Watching the waves retreat back to the disappearing shore, it hits her. Medea has to follow Jason, wherever he goes.

When he takes her south, not to Thessaly but to Corinth, Medea's troubles begin. Jason promised her they would rule together in the mountains, but after Medea helps him take revenge on his uncle, he decides greater fortune awaits him elsewhere. In the flat fly-infested plains, he seems more interested in local politicking, deal-making. Without the benefits of daily battle, Jason has put on weight, is getting heavy about the hips. His quest shrinks to his plans to make a match with the daughter of a local potentate, dowry-rich in cattle and land. He parades the much younger princess in front of her, and Medea feels as wrung out as a rag. Too far from home, disillusioned with her husband, when Jason asks Medea to help him further his ambition by supporting his new marriage, she loses her temper. Never one to do anything by half, she murders the princess, kills her own children, ruins his career.

Like faded paint on stone, another story lies beneath the one of middle-aged love gone wrong, the story of a mountain daughter who loses her magic. Jason has taken Medea away from her family and her land to live surrounded by foreigners who do not speak her language. In the dry Corinthian ground, she cannot find the plants she needs. No one thinks of her as a powerful healer, royal and wise. She is just another foreign mother, another disposable woman who has nothing to say and no words with which to say it. In exile, she goes mad, but for a different reason. Medea despairs, consumed with longing not for her husband, Jason, whose best years have already passed, but for her homeland.

So does she kill her children and serve them to Jason at a feast? Does she poison his new girlfriend with a beautiful cloak? Medea becomes morose, turns in on herself. She loses interest in her children and gives them over to their father, never teaching them the language that she alone can speak. Without ever mentioning mountain crags and waterfalls, she destroys herself. Her children are left to wander the world without her, wondering about the pain that sometimes seizes them, the longing for something they have never known.

Like Medea, the women in my family have always begun their journeys by water. My grandmother grew up on the side of a mountain, but always over the horizon she could see a glimpse of blue. Before she left for America, my grandmother never went any closer to the sea than that glimpse. Five miles is as far away as five hundred when you have lived enclosed for your own protection for hundreds of years. If they had not both gone to New York, she might never have met my grandfather, although they grew up mere miles from each other. A quality of light that only comes from growing up with wide horizons must have resided in her dreams. Who knows why they sent her away? The Retsiani of my imagination looks prosperous, but it was not enough to sustain so many daughters, each needing a dowry. The youngest son could stay, but the girls were sent to follow their older brother, first to Larissa, which must have seemed like the end of the world, then to Athens, then to the port and down into the hold of the ship.

When my mother went back it was on the *Queen Mary*—a good cabin, and days looking down on the Atlantic as if it were a mirror. Did she think about how her mother had traveled, only one generation before? As for me, I flew Olympic Airlines. Skimming over the water, watching the land configure itself far below me, how could I imagine what it felt like for my grandmother, a girl of only sixteen, going down into that dark hull where she would not see the light for more than a month?

My grandmother lived in the deepest womb of an iron ship for weeks, never seeing the light but imagining how each day passing overhead was carrying her farther and farther from her land. In steerage, she woke to the smell and the rhythm of the cows, their shuddering skin a kind of companionship. Close to the bottom, only a thin wedge of metal separated her from the deeps. She traveled during the First World War, through the U-boat blockade, when German submarines patrolled the Atlantic, seeking out the soft underbelly of ships to drag down. Her fear and claustrophobia must have been passed on to me, because I can imagine her at night, floating in water vast as space. The darkness smothered the hold completely, the only air several stories above them, where unfamiliar people strolled the decks freely, wearing silk and fur. They could hear the hum of engines calling out to the U-boats, like a fox yapping down dogs. At any moment, she thinks, the torpedo can find them, and no light will catch them as they fall to the bottom.

I have been told about the icon, many times, because my mother still has it. My grandmother carried it in her arms from Greece to New York, and it brought her to safety, though it could not help her afterward. To this day, whenever we go on a long journey where we may encounter hostile waters, my mother makes us kiss the glass, framed by gold wrapped in vines made of silver. Despite sending her away, her mother must have loved her, because the icon was worth more than all their other possessions. Under the glass, the face of Jesus has a rosy tint, tiny Byzantine eyes solemn, looking out at the distance. Mary looks like a woman I would like to know, confident and kind. She has soft eyes that gaze directly out of the frame, deep into the eyes of the person leaning over her. For years, the face of Mary was the face of my grandmother.

She was the middle sister, which created all kinds of problems. At Ellis Island, the youngest one, skinny, red-cheeked, was mistaken for a consumptive instead of a beauty about to bloom. The authorities kept them in a tower they called the castle, *to kastingari*, while they ran a TB test. For years afterward, the sisters whispered the name at the same time they spit it out—*ptu!*—like a bad dream they never wanted to remember. Officials poked and prodded my fourteen-year-old aunt, threatening to send her back alone, while her sisters used every survival skill developed over centuries of placating ruthless overlords to convince them to release her. Finally, they let my aunt through, the sickliest-looking one who turned out to be the strongest. At last, the three women joined their older brother waiting for them in New York.

My grandfather had gone to high school in Ayia with their brother, although of course he had never known the sisters. Before they ever met, he would have felt close to the family, even without the bond of the river running through both villages. He knew about Retsiani girls with their green-eyed beauty. When he met the three sisters, he picked the middle one, falling hopelessly in love with my grandmother. This time, the trouble came from her older sister.

According to village tradition, the younger sisters must wait for the older sister to marry first. My mother's older sister waited a long time to marry—seven years. I never found out why. My grandparents loved each other in crowds, fingertips touching surreptitiously. My grandfather had finished high school, and he wrote letters in an elegant hand, at least one a day, sometimes two, through the seven long years. Was my great-aunt so beautiful that she felt she could afford to wait and choose? Was she ugly and unwanted? That part, the explanation, never made it into the story.

I found out once when I was trying to balance a plate on my arm, that my grandfather could carry trays of full glasses and not spill a drop. He learned this skill working as a busboy and then a waiter in the Ziegfeld Follies, on the roof of the Amsterdam Theater on 42nd Street in New York City. I picture him, efficient and sharp, not awed—you cannot intimidate a Greek who has come so far—as the gleaming dishes gather around him. The music and girls and money fog the air with the Vaseline glow of old films. Seeing the sweat that went into the glamour taught him how to plan ahead, how to hustle. In America, his fortunes dipped and rose. By the time he found a safe shore, his own business, the relatives who sent him away needed him again. He made enough after the war to support his whole village. For years he sent money—started a school, helped his nephews begin their businesses. As a man he could go back, which he did, twice, to enlist in two Balkan wars. I have seen a picture of him in his uniform, worldly wise.

Smart and strong, my grandfather landed feet first when fate shoved him. My mother told me that when he was in the army, his recruits were so backward and illiterate they did not know right from left. My grandfather made them hang an onion off their right ear and a clove of garlic off their left and taught them to march not to left and right but to garlic and onion. He was also handsome, worth the wait. What did the seven years cost my grandmother? In the photograph from their wedding, she is wearing an A-line 1920s lace dress, a long veil, and lace flowers in her hair. She is smiling; my grandfather looks stiff. Behind the sepia I can see they have already lost the bloom of their youth, and if I want to imagine my grandmother's face before she came to America I can only find her if I look into my own.

After my grandparents finally got married, they embarked on one last trip to Greece. On their honeymoon, they returned to the villages and hung their marital sheet out of the windows of their first homes. I can see it there, in the sunlight, the villagers gathering to notice that in America not all honor is lost. My grandmother's blood stains the white, a shadow in the brightness, flapping in the wind.

The only sister out of the three to survive to old age was the baby, the beauty who almost had to return. When I knew her, her cheeks were red with rouge, not passion, but she still carried herself with the confidence and charm of a very beautiful woman. She had good bones and wisps of dark hair, dyed. No matter how much my mother tried to trick her out of it by not giving her any warning, when we visited her, she would have a feast waiting for us, as if in that one afternoon she could feed us all the love we missed during the rest of the year. Although she was the closest reminder of my own grandmother, I chafed under that abundance, her long nails scratching when she pinched my cheeks. To me, her apartment smelled like old age—plastic-covered sofas and mothballs. When she died, I did not go to the funeral.

But my sister went with my mother and she told me this story. The Orthodox church does not spare its parishioners and extracts the maximum drama from each occasion. Not only is the body laid out for all to see, but everyone present views and then kisses the corpse. She held my mother, who was hysterical, sobbing, knowing what she was losing at this moment, what we all lost. My sister forced herself to approach the body and lean into the coffin. When

118

she kissed the cheek, the skin felt fake, like plastic, cold and hard. It was the last chance to look at our grandmother's face in one of its versions. My aunt came from the same womb that made her, but achieved a better ending. When my mother cried she mourned not only for her last remaining aunt but for what her mother could have been.

Once, when I was a teenager, we had a summer house and I decided it needed a garden. I was driving with my mother and we were looking at gardens we liked, gardens we did not like. My eyes hovered over the wildest ones, patches where colors clambered together in a happy crowd, competing for light, yards without any particular shape or plan except exuberant joy. *Those were the kind of gardens your grandmother liked*, my mother said. *Even when we were really poor, she tried to have a garden like that, hollyhocks and gladiolas, all together. She knew how to grow things, and she loved the earth.* It was the first happy story I had ever heard about my grandmother.

PANDORA'S JAR

Some say there was a time on earth before women. Ignorance reigned, and knowledge, the province of the gods, had to be stolen. Until Prometheus tricked Zeus into giving them fire, men ran from cave to cave, shivering and eating raw meat. For such a theft, the punishment seems unduly harsh—Prometheus was tied against a rock for all eternity, with an eagle tearing at his liver. Proving the arrival of women sharpened the wits of gods and men, Prometheus fooled Zeus into releasing him. In a fit of temper, Zeus decided to take revenge on Prometheus and his protégés, mankind. Purple with rage, acting in a hurry, Zeus created woman. He molded one out of earth and fire and gave her a big jar to carry. The first woman on earth woke up and opened the jar immediately. Out came all the plagues of the world, matching the moment when men crept in from the wild to live by the hearth with the moment they began to suffer: fear, anxiety, jealousy, possession, passion.

A kind of fool, silly and empty-headed, Pandora opened the jar because she was told not to. Her name means *universal gifts*—Zeus's little irony or a clue to her real role, even braver and more beneficent than Prometheus. With fire alone, men could cook but they could never grow. In the jar, pressing against the sides with so much friction Pandora could feel the heat burning her fingers, not plagues but stories waited to be released. The beginnings erupted first, spilling all the troubles, but when she turned over the jar to shake out the bottom, she found the ending: hope, the last plague. Hope makes us turn the page. After she emptied the jar, Pandora walked back into the world, calmly watching the stories she shook out finding their way into the hearts of untamed men, who ran in packs. As they spread like a mist into every corner, the men broke off from one another, fell in love, embarked on adventures, fought, and married. Pandora created civilization, with all its woes and treasures. Wise, she knew those who itched to return to the wild would slander and blame her.

Stealing knowledge can be dangerous. From Pandora's uncurling gifts, I have plucked my stories like a thief. Some have come to me a little ragged, with a few holes that needed to be pinched and folded in order for the final shape to hold its contents. Molding them in ways the storyteller may never have intended, I have refashioned them into morsels I can claim and swallow. Of the many acts village life forbids, stealing stories seems doubly dangerous: both for the theft and for the invasion. Like a mountain bandit I have crossed treacherous boundaries to plunder my treasure, used both tricks and honor. However reshaped or re-created, all of them are true—as true as memory, as true as what has to be told in whatever way.

My mother has a collection in an old wooden box of letters from my grandfather to my grandmother. The first one begins with their engagement. The last were written after they had been married twenty years, from his deli. He sent them home by messenger. They had seen each other at the table for breakfast; they would see each other again a few hours later for dinner, but he still needed to send her his love. They are moving, passionate letters. Their dry paper

121

rustlings release phrases of tenderness and delight. He calls her his darling love, tells her how much he misses her and how he cannot wait to see her again. The words in Greek sound even more lovely than in English: *Glyka, Glykoula*. Sweet, Little Sweet One, does not convey the taste in the mouth of baklava, thick with honey and nuts, or the sticky rind of melon marinated in sugar that the Greek words evoke. The word *little* cannot match the diminutive created in Greek by adding the lilting *ou*.

This is one of the things I know about my grandmother: that her husband loved her from the moment he set eyes on her until the day she died. And this, we have been told, almost every day of every one of our lives, is what every woman wants, what will make every woman happy.

I know my mother and her two brothers as they are now, as adults. I know my grandfather gave each of his children a letter before he died, telling them to stay close to one another, to take care of one another, and I know that although they have tried it has not been easy for them. One of my uncles, the younger one, was still living at home when his mother died. After years of unpredictable storms, a modern doctor committed her for a modern treatment. Returning home after two weeks of electroshock therapy, my grandmother felt like a forest razed by fire. Nothing in her stirred. My uncle said she returned home and meekly got into bed, where she stayed for weeks. At the time, none of them understood what was the matter with her. He said, *We thought the doctors knew what they were doing, and that she was recovering, gradually.* She got up to watch TV and lay down again when the program ended. She died like that.

My uncle said, *She was watching the news. She waved good night to Eisenhower, and then she fell.* He said the sound of her body hitting the floor shook the whole house. My mother was living in Manhattan, which might have been the other side of the world. She called the only man she knew with a reliable car, who happened also to be a doctor and would become my father, and they drove through every red light to get there. I have seen the houses of Queens—a small window, a little porch. I can imagine the darkened rooms that greeted her, the TV still flickering in an underwater light. When my mother rushed past my father, the heavy furniture muffled her sobs. She told me, *When we got there, your father and the other doctor gave each other one of those doctor looks, and I knew she was dead.*

Once I asked my mother, *What was it like to be in your family?* Something slammed down behind her eyes, and she waved her hand to push it away. *We never knew from one minute to the next what was going on.* I have heard about the hospitalizations, the trouble. What I never heard was an explanation.

At some point during her stay there, my mother must have decided that she would live in Greece forever. The dentist up in the plains never would have been a serious prospect. Her cousins shared in a lie that delighted everyone: she would marry the dentist and live in a large apartment in Larissa off one of the squares and go up to the village every holiday and on long summer weekends. He dated her in large groups of young men and women and never got closer than holding her hand. He did not even own a car, but he could borrow his brother's motorcycle. At least he had a profession and a full head of hair. We also know about him that he was short, not the kind of characteristic that would survive a story about passion. Everyone assumed they were engaged, although my mother never made him any promises.

The Athenian worries me. He made her practice deception, which already endows him with some power. At night, they would go out with proper chaperones, in groups. After giving her a lift home under the supervision of her companions, he would drop her at the top of the apartment. She would come in with the others and take off her shawl, decline a cup of coffee, claiming exhaustion. Then she would slip downstairs to the part of the house where she had a bedroom. Lying on her bed fully clothed, she listened to the house settling down, the creak on the stairs that told her everyone else had gone to bed, the sudden quiet dark. Heart beating, she would hop off the bed and slip her shoes back on. The bedroom had a window that opened onto a small balcony, built at street level. Sliding open the glass, she would step out into the night as if she had been reborn. He lurked at the bottom of the street, his lights off. She could see the glow of his cigarette in the dark. When she got into the car, he drifted downhill until he could safely turn his engine back on, and they would speed into the night.

For the long stretches of time between the beginning and the end of the story, there is little else about him. He was a lawyer and someone who knew Daphne's husband. This gives him a certain amount of status, a place in the structure of society above the dentist, above anyone she had met before. Trying to find him in the murky waters of my genes, why do I know he would have been handsome as well as cruel? He was tall and dressed well. Hair always in place, he had serious eyes and a firm jaw, yet he could smile suddenly with great charm. His car was black, a sports car with an open top. At night, racing back along the streets to Athens with the moon illuminating the waves, the air rushed down my mother's throat. She felt like opening herself to the world, felt like swallowing the sky and all its stars.

Although I have been back in Greece since September, I have yet to make the trip to Larissa. The Athenian cousins will have informed the Thessalian cousins of my arrival, but as a month turns into two I feel more and more embarrassed to call. Weeks go by, and I think now I really ought to go, but life with Isabella and the models seems to eat up every day, as if we are always half asleep. With Steve, sometimes, I try to speak Greek; around his friends he will often refuse to speak English. The words bump and swerve like rusty cars.

I still have only one small bag. I can get on a plane and be home by Thanksgiving, or I can go north and abandon English for a few weeks. I begin to pack.

It takes six hours to go from Athens to Larissa by bus. The autumnal landscape has a familiar shape, but the hills and plains are gold and brown instead of green and blue, the water choppy with whitecaps. My cousins kiss me as though I have never gone away and hide any surprise they feel at having me arrive so suddenly in the middle of their lives two years later. They give me the converted couch bed in the living room and trade hosting me for dinner. After a week, it is clear that this is no longer summer vacation. Everyone has to work. Even my aunt, who seems only to cook and clean, has errands that send her rushing in and out of the house. Of the four Soulas, two are still in school but two have jobs, one as a secretary, another as a piano teacher.

Again, I am cushioned by their generosity, brought into the rhythm of their lives as if I have always lived there. After dinner, the Soulas go out to the local square for long coffees with various friends. Antigone, the girl who invited us to her beach cabin, is teaching piano also, and we talk together easily, more easily than I would have imagined. I want to tell about my life in Athens, but it seems unreal even at this short distance, so we talk about books instead. She is reading Virginia Woolf and Pirandello. Her boyfriend owns a club. He is still best friends with my lover of the droopy mustache, who, she tells me, has started a computer business. More than in Athens, I can see myself staying; I can imagine how a life in Greece could happen. Why do I start to talk about getting back, as if I have something to go back to?

My cousins tell me the villagers will hold a festival in another week and ask me to stay until then. It is as easy to do one thing as the other.

On Wednesday, I go with the eldest Soula to her piano lesson in the small school near her house. She shows me her class and then tells me to wander off. In another room, I see Antigone, and I tap on the window. She is tutoring a student in a private lesson and comes out to hug me. Her boyfriend's friend, my lover, has been looking for me. Since he knew I was staying with my cousins, he was lying low. Later that night, they will all be meeting at a bar in the square. She asks me if I know the location, and I do.

That night, I plead exhaustion after dinner; my cousins worry and tell me to go to sleep early. By eleven, the house is dark. I have been lying in bed in my nightgown for over an hour, my heart pounding as from a run. While I stare at the ceiling, I imagine lines like invisible wires blocking my actions, preventing me from getting what I want. My veins pulse with excitement.

At midnight, I slip out of bed. The house has settled around me, into the rhythm of sleeping people. I have stashed jeans under the bed and I retrieve them, put them on. I push open the door and pad into the hallway in my socks, carrying my shoes. Behind me, I wedge a pen in the door to hold it open a crack for when I return. In the landing, I do the same for the outside door and put on my shoes.

The streets are empty and dark, but I know the way by heart to the square. I keep to the middle of the road in case someone tries to jump out from a doorway or pull me into an alley. What if some citizen sees me and tells my cousins, my hosts? I imagine them escorting me to the bus station, suitcase in hand, gruff silence as they send me away. Why risk it? Comfortable though I feel with my cousins, I sense an invisible fence, and that makes me want to climb over.

When I reach the square, the lights block out the night. I find them sitting at a table inside—Antigone, her boyfriend, and my lover from two summers ago. He looks the same, a bit more creased around his eyes, but still expansive and handsome. He smiles at me and offers a glass of wine from their half-empty bottle. I want someone to acknowledge the risk I have taken, my sense of trespass, but they act as if women in Greece meet lovers in the square after midnight every day. When the wine is finished, he proposes giving me a lift back. On the way, we stop at his apartment, which I have never seen. It is one small room next to his parents' house. We tiptoe through clothes strewn on the floor and fall back on a mattress that serves as his bed. Because he says we need to be quiet, the sex happens quickly and I find myself staring at the wall, where he has stacked hundreds of empty cigarette boxes in a pyramid. He still has the van, and he holds my hand on the ride back to my cousins' place, turning off the engine as we round the corner, kissing me quickly in the dark.

On the way up I am careful to pick up the pens. I fall asleep just as the sun comes out.

The festival takes place on a Saturday, and we drive up in two cars on Friday to clean out the house. No one has been there since August and the beds remain stripped, giving the place an empty appearance. We start by pulling out the sheets again, damp and cool from being stored in an unheated house for three months. The Soulas enjoy being together, find it easy to touch one another's hair, to hold hands. After we have cleaned and organized the house, we lie down on wool blankets. I read a book and they take out a pack of cards. We have put fuel in the stove, and the long room with its soft wooden floors warms up. Four heads bend forward; each face carries something identifiable in one of the others.

The next day we cook, starting early in the morning. The Soulas give me work to do, which I take as a sign of acceptance. We stand side by side in the kitchen, surrounded by leaves turning colors, the cold beginning to seep through in the wood; the scene feels familiar and cozy. The Soulas have put an old transistor radio on; they sing along and I try to follow. We use walnuts that have been stored under the house, onions, and cheese. The oil and the bread, we have brought with us. In the afternoon, we hike down to the square. The village is different as it creeps toward winter. A few leaves cling to the bare branches, and the red-tiled roofs seem to huddle together, thin lines of smoke curling above the bleak view. The valley below is lost in fog.

Everyone has brought a piece of wood. Inside the building that acts as a *cafenion* and community center, tables have been set up in a long row, already piled with food prepared by the village women. We add our dishes to the communal feast, platters of *pitas* and *kiftedes* and large bowls of salad. The Soulas join the men and boys outside, throwing wood onto a pile stacked high in the middle of the square. While the crowd builds, village matrons serve up the food. Young men in tight jeans and girls whose sweaters cling to their bodies eye each other. Urban relatives catch up with the ones who have stayed behind, men and women in separate circles, gossiping. When my cousins tell me to help myself, I wonder what to do. The women hand out plates and pile up dishes, too busy to do anything other than nod at me while I pick my way through the food. Wives prepare platters for their husbands; their children scurry between their legs, looking for extra handfuls, which the old widows distribute.

As soon as the sun sets, the crowd moves outdoors. The young men and women light the pyre, which soon catches and begins to burn. Forming a circle, the villagers cluster together, close and warm. As night comes on, we all turn inward, toward the firelight. When the flames grow, the men add heavier logs, building the pyre until it points up like a pyramid, toward the sky. The wind comes up, whipping ashes in bright cascades over our heads, and the air smells sweet, like smoke and autumn. Brushed by the wind, the sky overflows with stars.

From inside the community center, someone puts on a scratchy record, a traditional song. I recognize its rhythms and remember in my body the steps the Soulas taught me two summers before. Watching the movement of the circling feet, I join the line dancing around the pyre. Each of us feels the warmth coming off the flames in front of us, while the dark mountain blows at our backs.

This circle links a tribe of people, living and dying together from the time before memory. No one is in charge; no one has told them what to do. The priest of the village sits in a chair to the side, filo crumbs dotting his beard as he eats *pita* prepared for him by the women. He remains a spectator, part of a ritual older than priests and churches. Women run the festival, although men build the pyre. They know what to do because they have followed their mothers and grandmothers, who did the same.

For a moment I forget that I am not part of the circle. I feel safe and warm and a part of something old and solid. Then I remember: I am only the last leg of a long voyage. I do not form one of the tight links; I am part of the wind that moves over mountain and seas. I belong in the dark.

A Very Simple Recipe

To be a good cook requires you to be a bit of a poet and a bit of a liar. Living in modern American cities up and down both sides of the country, the women in my family save *spanakopita*, spinach pie, for common social occasions. Other Greek Americans put things like onions or pine nuts into their pie. We keep it simple: ten eggs, a pound of feta, two bunches of fresh spinach washed and chopped, mixed up together in a satisfyingly slimy concoction. Then we take paper-thin filo dough (bought in any supermarket) and layer it: eight pieces of dough, a third of the mix, six pieces of dough, another third, six more, the last third, and finally eight more on top. Simple and mathematical, the art and pleasure lies in the butter sprinkled between the dough layers. My mother likes to use two sticks of butter and a large dollop of olive oil. I use half that. She complains that my *pita* is dry, ungenerous, modern. I think hers is too rich. Sometimes we are making a pie together, grumbling over the layers, and a paper-thin piece of dough will stick or break. *This is what my mother would do*, she says, and finds a way to make the layers fit together. When the pie is baked, there is no sign of breakage or disorder.

Spanakopita is the recipe most easily learned and most easily shared. For years after I lived in Greece, *pita* accompanied me to potlucks or appeared as the centerpiece at dinner parties. When it emerges from the oven, I flip it over onto the platter and then remove the pan. The surface appears golden, shiny with butter— perfect. Picking up a square piece, the dinner guests observe the thin layers of dough, the way it flakes delicately off their fingers and melts in their mouths. They taste the earthy green of the spinach and the tang of the cheese, trying to guess the alchemy that created such a complex taste. I lean over the table and wait for the candlelight to gather their faces. Smiling without an explanation, I let them think I rolled the delicate-as-paper layers myself. Later, after the wine, a woman will corner me in the kitchen, the place at parties where truth makes itself comfortable. Amid the half-empty beer bottles and overflowing trash, she will confess that she bought her gua- camole ready-made. Picking up a potato chip, she wonders if she ought to have mashed avocados instead of finishing her article and going for a run. Then I always tell her how I bought the filo in the frozen section and how easily eggs and cheese can be layered into pie.

Justice sits on my shoulder, nudging me to admit I was show- ing off. She reminds me that priests have always used art to vex the uninitiated, making what should be effortless seem mysterious and difficult. Although *pitas* hit the tongue with a complex and mysteri- ous flavor, their basic ingredients come from the earth and can be found right under our noses. If we have had enough wine, I tell the woman the full story of the *pita*: how, in the past, women did break their backs forming the dough, but supermarkets have been invented to save us. She might think she can recover the original savor by breaking her soft skin on their hard rocks, but the flavor won by labor has been lost forever. In the kitchen, we open another beer and I write down the recipe. I always remind her to never try to recover complexity by adding onions or pine nuts. The simplest ingredients are the best and will give our bodies everything they need.

I do not tell her how I myself once ignored the lesson of *pita* almost until it was too late, until I could feel the eggs crashing on my forehead.

THE SONG OF
THE REMBETIS

The perfect Greek rebel is the klepht, a mountain bandit with a huge mustache, gleaming crescent-shape sword, and red wool vest. Solitary and individualistic, klephts follow a rigid code of honor, although they can fight, steal, and wield a knife. The first to rise up against the Turks, klephts are worshiped by Greeks to this day. Their songs follow wild lines, fierce and ecstatic—the songs of the countryside.

The rebels I love are the Rembetis. Hanging around dens in dark suits, with hooded looks and secret codes, they refuse to mix with polite society. Refugees from the east, Anatolia and the Black Sea, they remained Greek-speaking foreigners, exiles. When the Turks kicked them out during the genocides of the 1920s, they could only return to a land their ancestors had left generations before. For the Rembetis, Greece was never a real place but a memory, a hope. Even when they settled along the fringes, scroungers, Greece remained a dream. They congregated belowground, in basements down alleyways, smoking hashish and trading women. In their lyrics, they stab at the daylight world—criticizing corrupt leaders, the pashas who eat too much and have too many women. They demonstrate how to light a joint, how to tangle with women who break plates, how to bribe the right jailer. Under the words the music mourns, a melody that rises out of empty bellies, full of the bitter consolation of survival.

In the songs of the Rembetis, a stranger's hands are always knives, tears are always black tears. A woman is a little bird and other men are cats, stealing into your yard, eyeing her feathers. If you take their lyrics and try to translate them, they come out flat, uninspiring, like turning a smoky den full of wasted angels into a tacky neon-lit nightclub. What happens if you translate the songs altogether into a different gender? If a woman wanted to sing a *rembetiko* song, what would it be?

Two photographs frame my mother's year in Greece. In the mountain village, with a bundle of sticks on her back, she blends in with the background, the dusky black and white. More young and at peace than I have ever seen her, she grins like a little girl. In the other photograph, she leans back in a booth, between Daphne and two men. Her cheekbones are high, sucking on a cigarette, her lids low. The flash has caught her in the nightclub dark and she shines with glamour, the world spread in front of her like a red-draped table. Far from the slippery ambiguity of her childhood, she holds two baubles in her hand, tossing them from palm to palm at will: the city with its smoke and cigarettes and, when she tires of that, the closeness of the village, her women cousins, the mountain, and the sea. Weeks without a bath, and then the return to the city again, to Daphne's and perfume and pampering.

In the beginning, I imagine that her dangerous lover would have seen only the surface, a woman who knew the rules of both city and village. When they danced, his suit would be pressed, expensive wool, and the satin of the dress she borrowed from Daphne would slip against it easily. He would take out a cigarette and feel a proprietary thrill when she put it to her lips, leaving lipstick stains on the paper. Sometimes he would enter the front door as an invited guest, and he and Daphne's husband would sink into leather couches while Daphne and my mother served them plates of *mezedes* and frosted glasses of ouzo. Maybe he saw my mother as his little doll, his *kouklitsa*. He might have forgotten that in the words of the *rembetiko* songs he taught my mother to sing, little dolls sometimes turn suddenly and smash a plate against the wall. He might have forgotten or he might have imagined that when she spoke Greek with a charming accent, mingling the mountains and New York, her thoughts were as blunt and compliant as her words.

As a lawyer, he had a balance and logic that must have been very attractive. He had read the classics as a child and could recite Homer as easily as he spoke French. When my mother tried to argue about politics, he smoothed the silk across her back and said, *But darling, the Greeks invented democracy*. If she was lost for a word in Greek, he could offer her a dozen, explain their etymology, and lace the best through quotes. He had a degree from Cambridge, while my mother never managed to explain about American public education. As for her roots, he found them charming, told everyone she was his *americanida*, but whenever my mother tried to talk about her home— the streets, the scents, the characters—he knitted his eyebrows and changed the subject. He praised her hair, her eyes, her body, but as for her mind, he had so much to teach her. The first time he quoted a poem by Sikelianos, where Greece floats like the ghost of a murdered woman fleeing her conquerors, she tried to compare it to García Lorca. Spain, he said, was still a barbarian country compared to Greece.

Sometimes, late at night, they would take his car down to Piraeus. Leaving the empty new streets of the suburbs, they drove down into the maze of tiny alleys, sailor's bars, and *rembetiko* dens. Slowly, they cruised the unlit channels until they found a back street too narrow for even his tiny car. When they got out, the air

135

smelled like a port: damp wood, rope, and dead fish. My mother would take his arm to negotiate the cobblestones. She wore high heels and a tight skirt and had to lean against him, which he must have liked. The bars he favored would be hidden below street level, in an old cellar filled with smoke. Sometimes a woman would sing, two men playing bouzouki behind her; sometimes just a man and his strings.

Elbows crowded on a tiny table, her thigh next to his, my mother absorbed the sounds—the clash of bottles against glass, a woman's sharp laugh, the mournful songs of exile. When the thick tobacco haze stung her eyes, she would close them and listen. Her mind dragged back scenes she never described to her lover: two women trading words across a fire escape, the street closing in with sunset; a child running from a gang of other children, mouths open like dogs, falling, the scraped knee, turning to fight; the first time she hit someone. If she kept her eyes closed long enough, she could almost smell the time of day, early evening, onions frying in olive oil. Once, the din calmed to an expectant hush and my mother opened her eyes. A hoary old man perched on the stool, cradling his bouzouki like a lost lover. He commenced with a tender low beat, and his words all spoke of love for a mother far away. Tears filling his eyes, he sang to her to remember him in the land of strangers, to take comfort in the pain that would always connect them. My mother's lover mouthed the words to the popular song. My mother listened carefully, the lyrics already engraved on her heart.

To stay in Athens, I need to get an apartment and a job. My savings will not last forever; the *pensione* is more a hotel than a home.

I call every English-language organization in the city: magazines, newspapers, news bureaus, bookstores, schools. One of the schools tells me they might have something in a few months; a man at a news bureau says he will have dinner with me to talk about the work. No one else responds.

136

We meet at a restaurant near his office in Kolonaki, the plush neighborhood on the other side of the Plaka. Not a taverna, its tables are covered in cloth and the waiters all wear jackets. As we enter from a bright evening, the dim lights show only a few customers; one is a heavyset man with a stubbly face, crushing a cigarette in an ashtray. To my disappointment, he rises and introduces himself as Leo, the man I spoke to, a reporter for United Press International. He invites me to sit across from him and orders wine. When he rattles off the names of half a dozen *mezedes*, the waiter bows. Settling back into his seat, he lights another cigarette, holding it like a truck driver between thumb and second finger. Stabbing it forward to punctuate his words, he says, *Let me tell you about how to get into journalism in this country. Like everything else, you have to take the back route.*

Instead of explaining how I can get into journalism, he launches into the story of his own career: how he arrived from England, a green college graduate, son of an English mother and a Greek father. All doors slammed in his face. Eventually, he found work on a small English-language paper run by a crook. *The guy who runs the paper is an old pedophile, and I was young and good-looking. Hell, I needed the experience, but I never bent over.* He's laughing now, taking out another cigarette. He asks me if I smoke. Something tells me I should decline. *The paper only survives because the guy will print a story from anyone who pays him—Arabs, Kurds, terrorists. I got so worried about being bombed I had to quit.*

When I ask him if he means bribes, he looks at me like he cannot believe I am so naive. After working a few years for what he calls *that rag*, he was hired under the table to help out a group of reporters permanently stationed in Athens for UPI. Like characters in a Cavafy poem, they considered themselves exiled from the true cosmos: New York, London, Washington. Every summer, they would go off in search of more Pulitzer Prize–worthy stories, leaving Leo, only a little less inexperienced, in charge of the office. One year in

August, the most sluggish news month, a TWA plane was hijacked en route to Athens. Leo rushed to the airport. *And I covered that story, baby, better than any other reporter. I was so scared, I didn't even know how to work the machines—they were talking me through it from London as I filed the stories. But that was my break; now you see me.* The other reporters were fired and he became the chief, the only real reporter, the office manager. One of the old staffers, a man who made his name covering Onassis stories in the sixties, was retained out of what Leo calls pure charity. He blows smoke out of the side of his mouth and says he thinks he could use some help.

Now I lean forward, finally interested. He tells me he can hire me under the counter, not much money, but I can recycle any story I write for him and sell it to the *Star*. Ever since finding the fateful horoscope warning me about Steve, I read this paper every day, know the names of all the reporters. *Maybe even get a byline,* he says, inching his hand across the table and brushing it against mine. Thinking this may be some bizarre form of job offer, I leave my hand, which is a mistake. He changes the subject suddenly. *Let me ask you something a little bit more personal. Do you believe in sex between friends?*

I am not quite sure how to answer. Is it purely hypothetical? Did he think that my nodding encouragingly over his wine-soaked anecdotes was a sign of friendship? Instead of pursuing these questions, I croak out *fine*, anger beginning to warm my skin. When he offers to walk me home, the hope that he might return to the subject of hiring me keeps me from refusing. Instead, he whistles to himself along the way and smiles confidently. At my door, he leans over and asks if he can come in. His breath reeks of garlic and retsina.

The night before, Steve had me naked, down on my stomach in his living room, my hands held behind my back as he undid his belt. He was telling me what a sick whore I was and how much I loved sex, and at the time I believed him, at the time I did.

But something turns in me and I push against Leo's heavy chest.

No, absolutely not. You're drunk. Though I can't muster anything more biting than this, I actually laugh when he stumbles back in surprise, and more than the rejection, this seems to hurt. Once I am safely behind the door I am about to squeeze shut in his face I have the courage to say, *I hope I never see you again.*

Two weeks later he calls me with what I think is an apology and tells me he does not really have room for a reporter, but he thinks he can afford to hire me to organize the files. He says, in a much more sober and professional voice, *Look, I'm sorry about the other night. It'll never happen again.* I am willing to take the chance, and I tell him I'll remember to watch my back.

I am in a back room at UPI, sometime during my first week of work. It looks a mess, untouched for years, clippings in piles strewn across table, chairs, floor. I have been hired to create a filing system, with clear labels that make sense. It will take years. Coming into the main office for air, I find a woman whom Leo introduces as an editor of the *Star*. She looks only a few years older than I am, with curly auburn hair and a pretty face covered in freckles. Her name is Emily, and she shakes my hand in a new-world way, telling me she is Canadian. When they invite me to join them for lunch, I feel rescued.

Leo has invited me for a few meals since I started work, but I have avoided them. He has never referred to that night and seems to treat me with an entirely different attitude and voice, gruff but professional. He does not ask personal questions, nor has he shared anything personal, which is fine. During the first few days, he has stayed in the front room, talking on the phone or typing, and I have buried myself in the back with my clippings.

We go to a little *ouzeri* near the square. The room is shaped like a wine barrel, shelves lined with bottles of ouzo and wine. Garlic ropes hang from the ceiling, and the menu offers only the choicest *mezedes*: fat white beans; delicate greens with lemon; fried *haloumi*, tiny bite-size fishes. Leo orders a round of drinks and six plates of these delicacies, accompanied by two baskets of crusty bread. This is the kind of place, I think, I would never come to on my own.

Emily asks me about my background, and I tell her what I did not explain to Leo—my college degree, how I need to work and want to write. She mentions that the *Star* is always looking for good local features and invites me to submit some. Then she smiles and describes the features editor. *He's about your age, from California, went to Berkeley. His name is Sam, and he's really cute.* Leo's smoke blows right into my eyes, and I suddenly feel shy. When she says she will introduce us, I say that would be nice. I don't push it.

Although Leo does his best to monopolize the conversation with more stories of journalistic competition and capture, Emily keeps switching her attention back to me. She finds out where I live and exclaims that she loves Koukaki. Her own apartment is only a few blocks from Angelika's. Not only that, her neighbor is looking for a tenant for her studio apartment. I cannot believe my luck. I ask her for the address and tell her I will come by that afternoon. Emily's eyes look like clear green pools, nothing hiding in them. When she describes her own route into journalism, it lacks the color of Leo's stories but seems much more believable: a few jobs copyediting, the Athenian owner of the *Star*—desperate for any experience—giving them all impressive titles. *Really, I learn new things every day.* At the end of the lunch, she reminds me to call her about the apartment.

There are some flaws with our otherwise perfect neighborhood. At the very top of the hill, on the last street ringing the park, pine trees make the perfect cover for exhibitionists. Isabella and I have seen more than half a dozen, men in all kinds of outfits, from the traditional trench coat to a crumpled suit. At the bottom of the hill, the six-lane river of Syntagma flows on its way to the sea. The traffic makes a hum that drifts through the street layers, giving the whole neighborhood a constant low vibration. The sidewalks of Syntagma that mark the bottom end of Koukaki are the traditional hunting grounds of the city's transvestite community. Isabella and I have passed them so many times on our way to get taxis, we think we know them. Once, a tall man in a long black wig and leopard-skin dress came chasing after us, thinking Isabella was one of them, almost six feet tall as she is, red-sequined and red-lipped. When he got closer, he realized his mistake, and we dove into our waiting cab, sniggering.

The neighborhood has a problem with cats. Most Athenian neighborhoods have their share of strays. They are treated like vermin, not pets, and are chased off and abused. On every street, you find a gang in matted fur, sleeping under parked cars, pissing on the steps, ribby and begging. Koukaki residents feed their cats, and the population has exploded.

Still, I never consider living anywhere else. I know the name, history, and children's names of the milk seller and the produce stand owner down the block. On Wednesday mornings, the middle street hugging the hill becomes a market, stalls selling cheap vegetables and eggs and olives fresh off the farm. Like everywhere else in Athens, the neighborhood pockets quite a few *cafenia*, with their usual atmosphere of smoke and masculinity. But the Koukaki *cafenia* hold mostly harmless old men, who are too busy arguing with each other to look up and comment as you pass by. And the women are fierce and protective, sitting on their stoops and balconies, watching the street life.

When I climb up to Emily's address, I already know I want to live on that street. Almost at the top, the houses rise steeply, like steps. She invites me in for coffee. Her house has a small front, painted blue, but opens to a large enclosed backyard. Muddy prints from a child's hand pattern the walls, and the kitchen spills out into the other rooms—half an eaten apple on the reed mat of the living room, a cake tin on the couch, a box of crackers on the bedroom dresser. When she apologizes for her missing husband, out walking with their child, I am surprised, because she looks so young.

Across the street, an impressive modern house, all white walls and big glass windows, takes over three floors. Underneath, the owners have built a small studio, which Emily tells me the wife had been planning to use for her sculpture. Now they want to rent it. To let in the light, they installed floor-to-ceiling sliding glass doors that open onto the street. I ask Emily if she thinks it will be safe. She tells me everyone on the block watches out for each other. By the time I cross over to the studio, my heart is strumming like an old bouzouki.

I find a woman sitting at a table near the window, wearing a long white caftan, drinking tea with a young man about my age. She welcomes me in and introduces me to the man, Ari, who has also come to see the studio. We all sit down, and she offers me tea. She says she hopes she will make the right decision about her next tenant.

The bouzouki string snaps. Eleni and Ari seem to match somehow. Although she has a tall, thin frame and cropped white hair and he has a short, stocky body topped with curly black hair, their eyes both twinkle with the same unspoken joke. Each speaks in the same soothing tones, with different accents. Ari, a jewelry maker from Israel, wants the studio for his work. Eleni asks him about his materials; they seem ready to settle into a discussion about metals and blowtorches, stones and chisels.

I want to drink my tea quickly, rush back to the *pensione*, and cry. They want to keep me there, for some reason, and start asking me questions. When I describe my job, I blush. It doesn't seem like much when I picture it in my imagination, crouching over boxes of dead paper, all bought on the privilege of a blow job denied. They want to know more, why I have come. Eleni puts her hand on mine when I tell her my mother is Greek-American, and she does not offer any of the usual responses about finding my roots or congratulating me on coming home. She just peers at me and wonders if it isn't hard to be so far from home.

Ari and Eleni catch each other's eyes and a decision passes over my head between them.

Right, she says, *you shall have the place, don't you agree, Ari?*

He tells her that, yes, I plainly need it more than he does. He already has a home and was really just hoping to find a work studio. I tell them absolutely not, Ari was here first.

Women always come first, he says.

There, dear, don't argue anymore, it isn't polite. We've settled it. Now, would you both like to come upstairs and see my work?

Eleni lives on the three floors above the studio. What I took to be the front door leads into a plant-filled courtyard decorated by a large fountain. Ari and I follow her white dress floating up the stairway. She tells us we shall have the complete tour. *My husband is an engineer but always wanted to be an architect. He built this house exactly the way I wanted it, and my needs were very specific. Wasn't I generous to give him that opportunity?* She laughs.

The first room off the courtyard has concrete floors; clay faces and earth-colored bowls compete with a few half-painted canvases. Upstairs, one long room has been divided into living room, kitchen, and bedroom, with a corridor enclosed in glass connecting them all. We sit down on a white canvas-covered couch, surrounded by her art: paintings with Fauve pink-and-green faces, sculptures like stamping dancers. *I started to use the room downstairs for my sculpture*, she tells us, *but I must have gotten too old. Now I just want to paint.* Ari complements her healthy appearance. Over sixty, she swims in the sea every day, even in winter, and highly recommends it.

She was born in Koukaki. When she was a little girl, she and her sister lived just next door, in their parents' house. Their parents were very wealthy, and they traveled all over Europe as a family. During the war, her parents had to sell off everything but the house, and when it was over the shame killed them. Eleni married her engineer and moved into the house he built her, next to the shuttered building where she grew up. *My sister still lives there, but she does not come out much. She's not a very happy woman.*

I look at her elegant fingers, brown against her white dress, her survivor's face. I want to tell her everything about her is precious to me. I want to tell Ari that he can be my friend, that he can come to the house that should have been his any time. I want them both to know they are the first people I have found in Greece I wanted to claim as mine.

I move my things in that night and invite Ari over for dinner a week later. Isabella has my phone number. No one else, not even Steve, knows where I am.

This is my home, however much my heart tells me it is not for long.

If I were to take out my bouzouki and sit under the stars, roll a big joint, and tip my black hat, if I were to sing to the night sky, it would be a song of longing, of exile from a land I never even knew.

Platonic Love

You've heard this before. A wise old man in a toga sits on a marble bench overlooking the city. He eases a calloused foot out of a sandal, and his youngest disciple, a boy of fourteen, slides over to massage the instep. Athens spreads out below them, a bundle of white-washed classical houses lining clean cobbled streets that fork out from the Acropolis, just enough for a decent-size city-state. The day is probably warm but not hot; there were pine forests on the hills surrounding the city in those days, and the air was generally cooler, fresher. Not such a bad job for the old man, who likes to admire the sculpted bodies of his disciples as they sit around him, fresh-faced and rosy-cheeked. The air gives off the scent of masculine ease, spicy and salty.

He is talking about love. He tells the young men the story: long ago, human beings were creatures of four legs, four arms, one head, one heart. (His oldest disciple scribbles it all down on a mud tablet, letters like knife marks.) Then, one day, Zeus took a big lightning bolt and tore the creatures asunder. Ever since, they have been two people, two souls, wandering the world, looking for their mates. The young men nod.

The young men move off. Some of them will go to the sea, to swim together, and afterward lie on the sand, caressing each other's back. It seems to make sense to them, that sex and love and marriage are not the same thing at all. They will search the world for their second half, but not in the woman they marry. Women could not be the missing half, they think, since women belong to them, like a limb or a bowl. Not being equal, women cannot ease their loneliness.

Meanwhile, in the houses below, women who have only gone outdoors once in their lives, to move from the home of their father to the home of their husband, wonder how their mother is doing, in the next block over, and their sister, who lives forever apart, six houses away. They think about their husbands, wandering the city, voting in the market place, sending a slave home with fresh vegetables and their favorite fruit, and they are not ungrateful. But each of them wonders where her other half has gone, if it is wandering in the outer world, waiting for her to be joined together—not the masculine half of herself, but the part of herself that could have been, if she had been free.

At some point during her year in Greece, my mother must have felt she was beginning to lose her way. She had arrived without a job or hope for the future. Now she had prospects, better ones than her mother had been able to expect for herself, but wouldn't she have wondered if those really were the prospects she wanted? She would have looked back to how close she and Daphne had been in the beginning, how much she had wanted to stay with her and not be left behind. Now she had noticed how Daphne retreated into the distance, a bit more each month, into the land inhabited exclusively by married people. Daphne and her husband shared secrets she no longer felt able to tell my mother.

Sometime toward the end of winter, she took the bus down from the mountains. The seat back had an old metallic taste as she leaned her cheek against it. The women next to her twittered like sparrows, one voice rising over the other. Around their feet, they had stacked bags of vegetables, country produce they were taking to their relatives in Athens who still had trouble finding cheap good food. A handful of priests, their dark gowns swishing around their ankles like dresses, chattered together, the ones with long white beards staring sternly at the younger men, whose new black hair sprouted wildly on their faces. She thought about Daphne waiting in the city two or three hours away from her. Sharing an intimate pool of candlelight, Daphne would be slicing lamb for her husband while he regaled her with his latest business deal (*Don't tell her,* he would say, and they would hold the secret between them, a pledge of their life together). My mother tried to imagine the future, looking out the window into the dark. Out there, the plains of Thessaly stretched down to the sea, and night obscured the little villages without electricity.

Catching a glimpse of herself in the glass, she felt her two lovers inside her like pinpricks of light in a vast, dark field. For both of them, the soft and the hard, she had a clearly delineated role. To the dentist, she appeared on a horizon emptied by war and plagues like an early goddess, a gap-toothed American beauty who knew how to haul wood up the mountain and whistle. When he asked her when she would let him take care of her, release her from her village chores, she laughed at him. About to take offense at the insult, he would laugh too, and for a reward she would tousle his hair and call him *swell*. Though he drove to see her in the village on his new motorbike, when he pictured her after they were married it was always in the city, a house his mother had already picked out for them. He imagined her at their dinner parties, speaking her charming American Greek and impressing his friends. With the dentist she felt large, a buffalo, loud and full of breath.

With the lawyer, she became a nymph, childlike and petite. A head taller than her, he liked to lean her head on his shoulder when they danced. Her face resting under his chin, breathing in the scent of expensive cologne and feeling the scratch of his skin, my mother might have felt both right and wrong. Every day, she watched Daphne flirt with her husband as fiercely as if they had just met, saw him pull a wad of bills from his pocket and peel off some while Daphne thanked him. Still, any sign of a Daphne who might have gone back to the fire escape in Queens had vanished; hair always perfectly done, nails and two-piece satin suits, nothing distinguished her from any of the other young wives they met at clubs and dinner parties, sleek with money. Now my mother's arms held a man who would take her to Paris, to London, who would carry her over to a world more distant from her childhood than she could imagine. When she felt herself shrink next to him, like someone about to jump into cold water, she pushed back the feeling and peered instead into the blind uncertainty of her future. His water might be cold but it was lovely and clear, so when he mumbled into her hair, she snuggled closer to him. Whatever question he asked, she always answered yes.

That must be part of the explanation for why she agreed to marry him. Although my mother once told me that, in those days, *People got engaged all the time; it was like dating*, from the rest of the story, I know that the bond had more glue in it. I imagine her coming into the apartment she shared with Daphne, after the dinner where he handed her the ring. She would have been breathing a little too hard, as if after a swim, exhilarated, skin flushed. Daphne was alone for once, without her husband. When my mother told her the news, said they should share it with all their friends, Daphne's reaction felt like a sharp yank down. Daphne congratulated her, but her tone fell flat. The hug she gave her was small, her smile tight. This was the path they were supposed to take, Daphne leading the way. The wedding would mean they could stay together in Athens, and they spent some time envisioning their lives, how my mother would live close by, how they would travel together, entertain. Neither mentioned wedding plans and when Daphne said she had a headache and needed to sleep, my mother said of course. In her own bed in the dark, my mother pulled her cool sheets close to her body and shivered. She put Daphne's response out of her mind. Saying no to the lawyer, or even thinking it, was to stare off into vast night plains where she did not know anyone or anywhere to go.

Emily has introduced me to the features editor, and now I am dating Sam. It is the first time in my life I have ever dated, but this ritual seems to be it. We go out to tavernas together and eat slow, careful dinners, each one of us impressing the other with our ability to order in easy Greek. Not just order but in the correct Athenian way, casual as comrades. Most waiters in Athens are proud Communists. Tourists may find them rude, but good service can be obtained with the right political attitude.

Sam lives in a tiny studio in the Plaka. The room feels like a cave, but I like going there with him. He has draped the furniture in Indian fabric and put movie posters on the walls. We listen to tapes he brought with him from the States, swing music, Crosby, Stills, Nash and Young. When we talk about books, California, school gossip, our references bounce off each other easily; I know the college paper he edited, and we both sing the tunes to the same seventies sitcoms. He has told me about his experience falling in love with the shy daughter of an Athenian professor. He followed her around on her daily routine, which was easy since she worked as a translator at the *Star*. Finally, she invited him over for dinner with her family and her father asked him if he intended to propose. Men in their mid-twenties from California are genetically programmed not to

149

propose to anyone, let alone a girl with whom they have never had a private conversation. Nevertheless, he hesitated and even considered it, but in the end he had to say no. The father made his daughter quit her job and Sam never saw her again.

Sam seems so normal to me. We are like two birds from one flock, off track in another hemisphere but coming back again to the same point of departure. With guilty pleasure, sometimes we let our Zorba-like enthusiasm for all things Greek slip. We sit together at the taverna tables and whisper in English, sniggering at the other diners, whose passionate arguments we have learned amount to negligible disputes. When Sam walks me home, the men disappear from the shadows. At my door, he kisses me on the cheek. We never mention sex.

One day he takes me to a trendy taverna overlooking the Plaka. It used to be the house of a wealthy family; tables have been placed in the former drawing room and out on the wide balcony. The furniture and paintings remain as if the family has just stepped out for the night, and it feels like trespassing, being in someone else's house when they are not home. Sam picks a table outside. It is early December and not too cold, a rare evening. The tiny houses of the Plaka look like the fishermen's village the homesick islanders tried to make it seem like once, winding streets and round houses with windows painted blue.

So I decide to get drunk. I have trespassed one boundary. Now I want more. The waiter brings us wine in a brown ceramic jug. We order *mezedes*, beans dripping in herbs and olive oil, thick fingers of grape leaves stuffed with rice, slices of tomato and cucumber with slabs of feta, and baskets of hot white bread. The wine burns down into my core. I begin to tell Sam about Steve.

It starts as a joke. The sun setting behind my back outlines Sam's face in light, and his eyes crinkle at the corners as he listens. I caricature the basketball players, talk about their two-bit league, how none of them could make it in the States, the way they prance around Glyphada like NFL stars. Then I describe how I started dating Steve, how I was so smitten I actually waited around for him to call, a Greek man and his ego. And then I look up at the sky behind Sam, where the sunset has burned an orange line across the winter blue. My eyes tear, and the wine shoves me forward. *The worst part of it*, I tell him, as if I am about to share a punch line, *is when I found him sleeping with another woman*.

He nods at me in a sympathetic way, waiting for me to get to the big finish, how I stormed in and broke a plate over his head, how I told him I never wanted to see him again. I explain about leaving the apartment and going to the beach with Isabella. Sam makes a clicking sound with his teeth. I can see he would like to take my hand. *And then*, I tell him, *I went back again. I thought I would break it off there and then, but I didn't*. He has been leaning toward me across the table, his hand playing with the stem of his wineglass only inches from mine. Now he pulls back. He asks me why.

I wish I had an answer. I want Sam, the boy from my hometown, the boy with a job who gets up to go to work and, when he comes back, writes letters to his mother and listens to Benny Goodman, to understand what I have done, what I am doing. I imagine if he does then I will be able to understand it myself and, understanding it, will stop. This is naturally too much to ask, but I do.

He asks me again but I can only shrug. Croaking slightly, as if the words have caught in his throat, he wants to know if I am still seeing Steve. When I say I haven't, we both realize that I am not saying I won't. The first stars have appeared, and the food has grown cold. Sam asks for the bill and insists on paying it. He walks me home, but at the threshold he shakes my hand and does not come in. A wind has come up, and the thin cotton blouse I put on in the afternoon offers no protection. Even as I stand in the doorway shivering, I think it makes a kind of cheap ironic sense. Sam will not be calling on me again. And the first thing I want to do, more than anything else, is get out of my unheated room and wander the bars of Glyphada until I find Steve. So that is what I do.

The following Monday, I am returning from the office and I see a tall tanned boy with long blond hair trotting along the sidewalk across from me. He glances at me and I catch his eye before looking down. After two more corners, he is nipping at my heels like a puppy. I cross the street and he starts firing questions—where am I going? where do I live?—and at first I ignore him. Coaxing a monosyllable out of me, he weaves the answer into a conversation and soon has made me smile. I notice he has a very fine taut body, lovely hair, and smells nice. We end up at my house and I let him in.

We make love, satisfying, simple, face-to-face sex. He stays for three days. In the morning I go to work, and at night I come home. He has been in the army and come to Athens after spending the summer in the islands. I don't ask him what he has been doing since the weather got cold, but he tells me he is staying with friends. He is nineteen years old.

On Wednesday night he starts complaining about my not being home. He tells me he wants me to quit my job, that he can support me. He tells me he has taken the phone out of the wall because he does not want me to get any more phone calls.

Without a hint of fear, I plug the phone back in and tell him we should take a walk. When we get to the main boulevard, I call a taxi. He gets in beside me and I ask him which neighborhood he wants, because I am dropping him off and will never see him again. He wants to protest but the taxi driver is waiting. If I hesitate even the tiniest bit he will be all over me, so I wait in a small cloud of absolute calm. My mind separates from my body and floats above us as he gives the driver an address. I drop him off and take the taxi home again. The next day I change my locks.

I have discovered I am not afraid of anyone or anything except Steve, the missing half of myself. All my fear has been distilled into that one oversize man, and with him I am still so terrified I have only to hear his name and my hands shake. I seek him out again and again. It is like finding my balance in a world that is teetering around me, ready to collapse at any moment.

HISTORICAL TRUTHS

Once upon a time, there were two ancient Greek historians, Herodotus and Thucydides. Both of them are considered by Western culture to be among the first to try to capture the past, to tell what really happened. Thucydides recounts battles and makes a great effort to number the troops exactly, the precise movement through which mountain pass, the weight and size of shields. Never unwilling to rework the truth when it suits his angle, Herodotus gossips, molding each god or king into a familiar character. I picture Thucydides as a soldier, with a strong jaw and a shaved and grizzled head. Herodotus I see in a flowing robe, wearing many rings, enjoying a good glass of wine. We like to say that Herodotus may have started history, but Thucydides was the real historian, because he never sacrificed the events to the narrative. I leave him bending over his tablets, brows knit. To Herodotus, I blow a kiss across time for knowing what we are just beginning to discover: all stories are personal stories, all history the story of the storyteller's heart.

Americans and Greeks have entirely different attitudes toward history. Americans like to think of it as a loose-fitting but comfortable coat, tailor-made, something they can put on and take off. Greeks know they do not make or choose history but are chosen by it. Americans would never blame the past; they constantly forgive it in the name of the future. Greeks refuse to anticipate a future they consider to be justly claimed and already blighted by the past. If you go to Athens, you can spot the Acropolis from almost any corner, any hill. You only have to look at it to know that one slice of a marble column could crush you easily. If you are a tourist, you can enjoy gazing at the Acropolis and be reminded of how far back into time human endeavors go. If you are Greek, you feel it as a kind of pain, a heavy weight at the center of the universe pulling you down and back. Even after a munitions cache exploded inside, it still stands, beautiful, defiant. But Greeks live surrounded by a surfeit of beauty, and it does not seem to help much.

For Americans, history is a record that changes according to the needs of the present. Americans believe, if they can reimagine the past, the future will behave itself accordingly, like choosing the right road. The rest of the world sees us as adolescent, and that may be right. Adolescents can be lovely in their lack of knowledge about what comes next. We are like drunken teenagers in a speeding car, careening around corners, blind to the sharp curves.

We all come from elsewhere. When we arrive we pick up the narrative where someone else left off and make it our own. The one thing that binds us together is the one thing we refuse to understand: we refuse to understand consequences.

The letters arriving from home all say the same thing. My friends are getting jobs, finding their way in the world. I can hear the sound of the cables zinging all over America from as far away as Greece, the message pouring through telephones and fax machines and television antennas: Climb or fall off! Climb or fall off!

Leo tells me that a very important member of the American government is coming to Greece for high-level meetings on the NATO bases. A VIP reporter from the States is flying in for the occasion, but meanwhile UPI has asked him to cover a sidebar. Leo explains this is a big break for me, and he wants me to know he is being generous in giving me the assignment. His reasons become more clear when he delves into the details: the official has arranged a special visit to the Acropolis, which will be opened for his private viewing in the company of a deputy minister. To avoid crowds, events have been scheduled for dawn. Leo reminds me to set my alarm for 5 A.M. Although I know the story will be rewritten and sent out under his name, I thank him.

By the time I get to the Acropolis, the sun has pried open the sky by the tiniest fraction, leaking blue into black. Greek and American security types crawl over the marble. They have cordoned off the journalists into a huddle, controlled by an American woman in a trench coat holding a walkie-talkie. I try a side entrance and encounter a Greek policeman.

Wearing a crumpled gray suit, he looks like every Greek man who drives a taxi or runs a taverna or sits behind a desk down a long corridor of an unnamed bureaucracy. He wants to chat, and I do. He offers me a cigarette, and I ask him for a light. After a few deprecating remarks about the Americans and complimentary ones about the Greeks, I am up the hill. Joining a pack of privileged invited members of the press, I flash the card proclaiming that the reader is obligated to do everything possible to assist me. Like tame hounds, we scramble behind the stiff American official as he strolls past the columns, nodding proprietarily. Unsmiling American ex-football players in dark glasses and expensive trench coats line up against the marble columns. They look like male Caryatids, worshipers with earphones.

I go back to the office and write two short paragraphs. They hide the story I want to tell, epic pages about an arrogant American official with a bulbous nose and domed head who commands a world monument for his own private viewing, like a man hires a woman.

Underneath the regimented sentences revealing who-what-why-when-where slink other, more ragged phrases, poems of unsmiling men with shaded eyes, dawn cracking like an egg. Still, I know that no one is interested. Leo sends out the paragraphs without changing a word. Later, we learn that the story has been picked up by seven regional papers, and one prints it under his name.

Even in my own language, I do not feel I can speak the words I want to speak.

My grandmother knew the rules of her village. You can see them as clearly as the fine white stones, drying in the sun next to the river, or the outlines of the shadows made by the old trees in the square. When she was a girl, she rose in winter and felt the cold, wrapped herself in wool, and stepped out into her mother's yard. In the sky above her, the mountain climbed stairs to the clouds. In the yard, the goats and the chickens were descended from the goats and chickens brought up by her grandmother's grandmother. In summer, they could let them out into the streets to roam from house to house. Everyone fed them.

In New York, the wind pushing its way through the canyons of tall buildings cut through her skin. Her sisters married men who took them to distant parts of the city; its tunnels and train tracks were stone and metal sharpness cutting their hands when they reached out for each other. What language could she speak, what language could she sing? The church offered the same prayers as the church of her village, but the building was not a small stone white-washed roundness, holding the bleached bones of her ancestors; it was made of red brick and wood, and the smell of incense mingled with the fumes of a foreign city.

This is how Steve and I make love.

It is now Thursday, the middle of the week. It has been days since we spoke to each other, but that does not matter. Eventually, he always calls. Tonight I have a feeling, so when Isabella asks me if I want to go out with her and her young lover, I tell her no, I am not feeling well, and this is true.

Close to midnight he does call, and he tells me he is in my neighborhood. Can he come by? I do not even have to say yes; he knows the answer already.

Once I saw him playing basketball. He plays in the amateur leagues, just glamorous enough to make the back pages of second-rate newspapers, enough to make him feel he is a kind of king. During the game, he ran up and down the court with the other players. The room shook with the pounding of their feet. Their bodies were too large; they looked like an alien species playing on another planet. When he raised his arms over his head to block a shot, I recognized every muscle that ran along the sides of his arms, every bit of the power that kept another man who was also twice my size from achieving what he wanted at that moment more than anything else. Those are the muscles I stare at when he holds himself over me, giving me pleasure.

He comes over and asks for wine. We sit across from each other in my little apartment, the curtains drawn, our faces illuminated by one small light. We are companionable, two players on opposing teams who have just met, as if we do not know each other, as if we like each other. He asks me a few questions about my work and tells me about the lyrics he is writing. As if they have nothing to do with what happens between us, he talks about other women he sleeps with, and the way he says it makes me believe it is so.

I never know when the game will begin. That is surely part of the excitement. We are talking one moment, relaxed, and the next, a tension creeps into his body that is instantly communicated to mine, though we continue to chat. Our voices slow, as though we have taken a drug. His eyes half close, and the next time he looks at me I have ceased to be myself.

Get up. He goes to the bed and I follow him. We have stopped talking, or at least he has stopped asking questions. He never asks when we have sex. He never gives me choices. Each time, he challenges me and I have to test myself, to see if I am strong enough to take it.

Kissing, if there is any, is only to make me anticipate what will happen. Usually, we do not kiss because it slows us down. Tonight, it happens right away. I take off my clothes while he watches, and then I feel that heavy hand on the back of my neck, pushing me down, down, until there is only the part of me that is necessary to the moment, ready, open, the whole focus of my being.

His body has become another language. His arms against me tell me where to move, how to position myself, when to shift rhythm. If he needs to speak to me, his voice is harsh. It is better this way, away from language, from Greek, from English. Why do I need it when I know everything about him, the color and scent of his skin, down to when he last had a shower, down to the invisible line of freckles that marks the place where his arm turns against the sun. The broad planes of his back are spaces of wilderness I can climb and conquer. I know where his skin softens on his stomach, and with my lips and tongue I have learned the darkest spaces of his body.

He tells me when to touch myself and when not to touch myself. He tells me when to ride and when I should hide my face against the pillow and be ridden. Tonight, he pulls me on top of him, quickly and violently, and tells me to come. I know I won't be able to, my mind filled with everything else, the room, the lamp, the neighborhood outside. Then he tells me he will slap me until I do, and I push down the fear of losing myself and throw myself out into the darkness.

Rites of passage are always associated with pain and endurance. The young man or woman who learns about the connection to the body, to how much the body has to say, can go back into a time before language and listen to what the secret voice of the self has to say.

Coming up through the tangled green of childhood, we learn to listen to everyone else, and maybe that is as it should be. But when do we return to listening to ourselves?

Their culture provides ways for men to find themselves in their bodies. They play sports; they test their strength. They learn to listen to instinct as well as reason, to balance trust in others with trust in themselves.

Women are not taught that their bodies can be a source of power to themselves, other than through the power to attract and manipulate desire. A woman's journey can take her as far or as long as she wants, but she must learn to travel in her own body.

At dawn, I stand at the window and watch the pink air burning slowly into blue. I smell the ozone of the rising heat and the thin layer of warm air off the bakeries coming to life. The sweat on my skin slowly cools, and I understand that the muscles in my arms and back are stronger than I thought they were. My body speaks to me and I listen.

Hours later, I move through the streets on my way to work, and the people are just like ghosts. Only my body is solid and real, powerful enough to pass through shadows.

Artemis

Once there was a goddess who had a temple by a river next to the sea, in what is now Turkey. She was so old and so powerful that the doors of her temple stretched to the sky and were lined in delicate filaments of gold. When they opened, wafts of incense and songs of priestesses fell out. Her pilgrims came from all over the world and brought offerings, small statues and hand-wrought jewelry. In their abundance and haste, some tipped into the river and were caught in the mud, where now, centuries later, they still turn up. She was a goddess of the moon, and her body was covered in shapes that could be the eggs of large birds, ready to burst, or breasts, or hillsides. Her hair was plaited and rich and her eyes looked ahead calmly, having seen so much already.

One day the goddess woke up and stretched her arms above her head to find her story had changed. In her new incarnation, she had become a goddess who likes to hunt, shunning the company of men. Roaming with her companions in the forest, she would pull back her bow and taste the metallic tingle of blood in her mouth. She swam at night in rushing rivers, naked with her women, their long hair streaming like grass in the water. During the day, they would toss a heavy bow to one another, catching it in one hand, arm muscles rippling. Chewing on wild garlic, they would halt when they saw prey, still as lions. This goddess lived by the moon and was worshiped for it; she was a goddess who knew what it meant to be both full and empty, a goddess of changes and phases, old but not as old as the first one.

Stepping over a few centuries as delicately as rocks on water, she has become the goddess familiar to us today. Wearing a crescent balanced precariously on her head like a tiara, her arm muscles shrunken, she has learned to skip. Trotting through the trees in a fetching little toga, she finds herself a virgin and afraid. No longer formidable or forbidding—a man can make her duck into a bush, tremble for cover. When she intervenes in the lives of mortals, it is on the arm of her far more glamorous brother, Apollo, whose icon, the sun, has long since outshone her silver moon. Sometimes she might murder a man who wanders upon her unexpectedly, but only in a fit of temper. When she demands a sacrifice, her voice is petulant, a whine. She is moody, hormonal, inexperienced—a teenager.

How did Artemis of Ephesus, the stately woman with the braided hair, mysterious, original, become Diana of the legends, pale and skinny? Maybe because she was a huntress, because she had not been tamed, she needed to be tamed in these legends, needed to find a twin to cancel her out with his more golden, masculine daytime rays. Her light becomes a reflected light, taken from his sun. We have been given many different goddesses, so it is interesting to notice which one remains. If I had to fashion my own Artemis out of all her faces and stories, who would she be?

My Artemis prefers the company of women, not out of fear but out of choice. While the other gods zoom up and down the countryside, pierced by the arrows of love, torn by the fires of anger, causing wars, interfering, ravishing, and arguing, my Artemis keeps her own company. She never pleads with Zeus or negotiates. Where did she come from? Not out of her father's head or out of a shell. My Artemis was there long before any of the other gods; she arrived on the scene as an adult, fully formed, standing before Zeus demanding nymphs, names, high holidays, and arrows. She hunts when and whom and what she wants. She never ever whines.

How far back are you willing to dig? Which stories will you choose? Which ones will choose you?

I call my mother and tell her I am not coming home for Christmas. Even in my own ears my voice sounds echoey, as if it comes from a long distance. Passing through the phone lines, it is seeking a way out. She can hear it wandering off, and she knows better. She tells me she is sending my father for New Year's.

Before I lived in Greece, I used to look at my mother's life as a seamless story with bumps along the way, all too familiar but with a basically happy outcome. I knew how she met my father and came to California. I knew about her glamorous life as a Greek-Californian Los Angeles mother. I just never knew that part of her story belonged to me.

She met my father when she was living in New York. She was working for Time Life as a researcher and living in Greenwich Village with her Italian friend, Anna. Like everyone else she worked with, she liked to smoke, she liked to drink, she liked to flirt with married men. One evening Anna had a date with a serious young Jewish doctor from Bellevue. My mother chose that particular Saturday to take the night off.

An August storm thundered overhead, cracking against the window, flashing lightning, pouring rain. My mother wore an old housecoat, and her hair was up in curlers. She was reading a horror novel and eating a tuna-fish sandwich. Just before the door opened, she got to the moment in her book where the heroine finds herself stalked by the killer. The woman in the book turned to face her killer; lightning flashed; my father stepped through the door. My mother says she jumped up and ran to Anna in absolute terror. This was his first impression.

She owned a beat-up old car. Spending her salary on essentials like clothes and a brownstone apartment and booze, she could not afford frills like insurance. When she found out that Anna's new boyfriend belonged to the AAA (the kind of thing a responsible young doctor from Baltimore would do), she asked for his phone number. She took to calling him at moments of car crisis or disaster, and he got into the habit of rescuing her.

A certain pattern was set early, of disaster and rescue, fear and comfort from fear. The first thing my mother says she liked about my father was that he was not Greek.

After a while, Anna went to Europe to visit her Italian relatives, and my father called my mother and asked her for a date. She reciprocated by asking him to a weekend in the Catskills with a group of her friends.

One of the group had a mother who owned a hotel that was empty just before the start of the season. They drove up together and shared a cabin. Her friends had known each other all their lives, and it was natural for them to bring a lot of food and liquor and to eat and get drunk. The first night, she said, she spent hours throwing up, my father holding her in his calm medical fashion, helping her through it without judgment or anger, just love.

My father arrives in Athens with one suitcase. We spend a few days in the city, touring the museums, and I find it is easy to step outside of my life again and become just another American tourist. The heavy muscles of the sculptures, the dead marble, all look charming and old. Oh! I think, rootless again! We eat at tavernas and order from the menus with style.

We decide to rent a car and go to Delphi to see what the oracle may bring for the New Year. A scientist, my father chooses Delphi for a much more practical reason; only a few hours from Athens, in the winter it will be cheap and empty. He remembers it from the last time. Although he asks me for other suggestions, I realize I am a terrible guide; I have forgotten how to be a tourist and regret the lost knowledge.

We stop at a village close to the top of the mountain, a few miles from the site. There is only one sign out for rooms, pointing down to the bottom of a stony path. The woman who answers the knock tells us the rooms are only half finished, but my father likes the idea that he can still rough it so we agree to rent one at a discount.

He takes a nap and I go outside onto the balcony. It is early evening. The rooms hang over a hill and I can see past the village down into the steep valley below, spread with tiny farms and houses. Clouds swallow the top of the mountain, swirling and evaporating as they dip down. The wind makes my eyes water as the sun sinks below the trees. The clouds turn purple and then red, the mottled color of peaches. Pushed by the wind, they form graceful shapes, like bodies merging into one another. It seems perfectly reasonable to see, in their limblike dances, figures of people, gods, and goddesses. I open my mouth and begin to hum. The vibration moves up through me into the wind, into the clouds. When the sky is almost dark, I go inside.

My father wakes up and asks if I am all right. I can feel the valley between us, stretching between his calm rational self and the turmoil I just felt. But I say that I am fine. We go out to explore the town.

The air has a hint of snow in it, and we hurry into the few open shops and galleries, looking at flokati rugs and paintings by local artists. Built like a fortress out of rough stone, one restaurant has remained opened. Wooden tables circle around a central pit fire, and we are served hot wine in old jugs. Colorful wool rugs hang on the walls, pushed faintly by wind whistling through the cracks. Our cheeks become red from the heat and wine.

My father tells me a story. When he was thirteen, he went to the last gathering of the veterans of the Civil War in Gettysburg. He had just had his bar mitzvah, very proud and fierce in his religion. His father was a patriarch, the owner of a moving company who boasted about his ability to break through union lines on the strength of a cane in his right hand. At the outdoor meeting, Roosevelt spoke and lit a torch for peace. I see my father, just becoming a man, standing next to his father, who is holding a cigar. The air is humid and the atmosphere thick with the green of July. He watches the men around him, part of the culture of war, and straightens his shoulders, a proud American boy. He tells me the veterans were so old, some of them passed out and died in the heat, right in front of him. I imagine them crumpling in their uniforms, lines of blue and gray tumbling down.

I know the rest of the story. How he walks out of his temple a few years later—when a recently arrived German rabbi blames American Jews for the death of their cousins in Europe—and goes from being the most religiously devoted in his family to a committed atheist; how he joins the navy and travels to Japan and China, where he sees the effects of bombs and starvation, and how the last wisp of the idea of that day at Gettysburg, like thin cigar smoke, disappears into the air; how he refuses to enter his father's business and becomes a doctor, a cancer specialist, choosing the most hopeless of cases on which to pour out his hope.

My father is telling me one story, but underneath is the shape of all the other stories I know he is not telling me. For a moment, I can see that visions do not all come in a moment watching the clouds, hoping they will tell you something. They develop with patience, growing slowly, like healthy plants. My father's story waits at the end of the field, but I am still hunting at night, scenting the quarry as it comes closer.

The next morning, we drive to the site. We take our time and look around. The tourist brochure describes the upcoming feast of

Saint George, the biggest festival on the mountain, and how many miracles are attributed to him. The figure of Saint George on a horse slaying a dragon and rescuing a maiden resembles another story. According to legend, Apollo also rescued the mountain's maidens when he killed a flesh-eating python and gave prophecy to the sibyl. Perhaps, before Apollo taught the sibyl, the python herself spoke to the mountain, predictions whispered to her by Artemis.

Out of the valley comes a powerful winter light, warming the marble. Does it matter who delivers miracles or how? We pick our way through the ruins, and this time, when we reach the amphitheater, I tell my father to climb the steps while I wait at the bottom. Then I whisper, *Can you hear me?* And his voice answers calmly, *Yes*.

For as long as he is in Greece, I feel safe and protected, as if I am in a circle of moonlight, and on my back I carry powerful arrows and a wide bow.

Isabella calls me the day after my father leaves to go back to America. We have not seen each other since before Christmas, and she asks me if I want to get together. She tells me she has spent the holidays with Alexandros, her new lover. Although less than a month old, the relationship has been intense; they see each other every day, and he has introduced her to his family. After an initial hesitation, they accepted her and now treat her like part of the family. I ask her if she is going to get married again. On the other end of the line, she just snorts.

We agree that I will come by Angelika's around eight, and we will go out to eat. Then we will prowl the town, like when we used to hunt around. We tell each other we will flirt a lot. I can tell Isabella thinks she may be nearing the end of her hunting days.

When I get there at eight she has not come home, and I get rushed at the door by Siobhan, an Irish model I remember from my own *pensione* days. She is full of worry and more than a little tipsy. Isabella had agreed to come home early to help her with her makeup for a photo shoot she is doing the next day. I say, *She's a big girl and knows what she's doing*, but I can feel my stomach drop and I know something is wrong.

I canvass the house for phone numbers. Someone has Alexandros's number, and someone else has the phone number of the friend who brought her to Athens, the young heir with a yacht, a party boy who likes to use his friendship with Isabella to meet a steady supply of depressed and beautiful young women.

Reached at the restaurant owned by his family, Alexandros says he has not heard from her since morning. No one answers at the yacht. There is not much else we can do but wait.

I find I am not happy being back in the *pensione*. Beyond my uneasiness for Isabella, I am uneasy in the rooms. The dinginess of the furniture oppresses me, the slight damp coming out from the walls, all the showers upstairs, the dramatic sweeping in and out of the girls. How had it ever seemed so glamorous?

Finally, we get a call. It is the head of Isabella's modeling agency, who also works with all the other girls. Isabella and the playboy were driving in his jeep, and they were going too fast. The jeep overturned. Isabella will be all right, but she has broken a few bones and needs a blood transfusion. The playboy is untouched. Out of remorse, he has agreed to pay for everything.

In Greece, there is no blood bank. Everyone has to call upon their relatives to donate. Even with all the money in the world, someone needs to give blood before you can get it, and those without friends or relatives to call on are considered destitute indeed.

Rushing over to the hospital in a taxi, holding the hand of the Irish girl who has become like a sister to me within the last hour, I realize Isabella has become my relative, closer to me than any of the cousins. She is most precious to me at that moment when we have already begun to drift apart.

The hospital is a frightening place. The outside presents a dull beige front, uniform and inhospitable. Inside, it is a mess. Siobhan and I step into a hallway and find a gurney smeared with blood. Chairs line up along the walls where patients and their relatives wait to be seen, some of them clutching open wounds, some of them moaning or just lying supine, being nursed by their sisters or mothers or wives. There is very little professional nursing staff in Greece. That, too, is considered the responsibility of the relatives.

We are ushered into a room where two young male doctors interview us about who we are. One of them reads a chart. The other one stares at our chests, makes a few jokes about how scared we must be and have we ever seen so much blood? but we don't laugh and just tell him we need to see our friend. Finally, the one with the chart who has not spoken indicates we are to follow him, and we do. We go down another hallway through a set of doors and find ourselves in the room where you give blood.

We want to see Isabella. They tell us she is sleeping now. First, we need to make a donation. The nurse seems very kind, settling us comfortably into a chair, painlessly injecting the needle. It does not take long. Fifteen minutes later, I feel exhausted. She tells us to rest before leaving. We insist on seeing Isabella. Another nurse comes in and bars the door, telling us to lie down.

I feel sleepy and my Greek blurs. I ask them if I can use a phone. They shrug, indicating a public phone outside. I beg them, *Please, I am so tired*. Finally, they relent. I call Leo at the office and explain what has happened. To my surprise, he agrees to come over immediately.

The office is close to the hospital, but it takes an hour before Leo finds us. He also gives blood, but he bounces off the chair with the energy of a large man. Telling us to wait, he strides down the corridor to find out what has happened to Isabella. He must have worked his reporter's charms on the doctors, because within a few minutes he has returned with the full story. Isabella has been transferred to a private American hospital, and we can go see her.

We take another taxi, both leaning on Leo, who barks out directions. Siobhan displays her warm gratitude by snuggling against his arm. Leo puffs his chest, enjoying his position as hero to the rescue. At the private hospital, the hallways sparkle and the walls shine. A receptionist in a uniform tells us the room number, and we find it immediately.

She looks much better than I had feared. Her leg has been hitched up on a pulley, and one arm wears a sling, but her fee-earning face, although pale, shows no sign of injury. She tells us she cried with relief when she realized her face had survived, although a broken leg could ruin her catwalk career. She jokes that she will have to engage in hand modeling, and holds up her elegant fingers for our inspection. Flowers pack every corner of the room, most of them from Alexandros and the playboy, with a few bouquets from work friends and other admirers. She tells us we just missed Alexandros, who returned home to fetch his mother, enlisted to act as Isabella's nurse.

We start to reconstruct our blood-donation saga, but she just says, *I don't want to hear another word about that horrible place*. She and Siobhan chat about the business. Most of the models must work illegally, and they have both heard about a raid that took place at a show Isabella had been invited to join and turned down; two of the models were deported, possibly as a warning to the whole community.

The Greeks won't do the jobs, but they don't want us to make too much money doing it either, Isabella concludes. *Oh, well, I'm out of it now*. We murmur not to worry about work or anything else but to recover as quickly as possible. We both kiss her on the cheek and she beams. She loves the attention.

When I arrive home I knock on Eleni's door. She invites me in for a cup of tea, and I recount the day's adventures. While I sit on the couch in her long front room, she stands at the counter slicing tomatoes. Holding a piece up, she insists I taste it, fresh from the farmer's market. Emily and her husband, Francisco, expect Ari for dinner and she suggests that I join them, *All the young people together*.

Instead of going out on the town with Isabella, I spend the night playing Monopoly and drinking beer with Emily, Francisco, and Ari. Francisco, a Venezuelan Indian with long silky hair and a soft voice, makes a surprisingly ruthless capitalist. After he has won all the hotels and houses, Ari throws the board at him in exasperation. When I laugh, I take in deep breaths of their house, the scent of babies, old honey, and bread and dusty cotton.

It has been weeks since I have heard from Steve.

Such a state of affairs can't last, or can it? Maybe it is renewed loneliness while Isabella is in the hospital. Maybe it is just fear of having slipped too close to happiness. Maybe it is going to work to file a story and having one of the senior editors, who is visiting from London, pat me on the head and call me a *good girl*. Maybe there is no rational reason and there should not be.

I am back at Steve's. We are on his bed and it is three o'clock in the morning. He tells me he is going to slap me and he does. I feel my head snap back, but I am on top of him and the pleasure rides over the feeling of pain. When he takes his hand back to hit me again, I raise my arm and strike him on the side of the head. *Don't ever hit me again*, I say, and I slide off him in a heap on the side of the bed.

We are quiet together for what seems like hours. A car passes under his window. I can smell the night air coming in off the ocean. The apartment creaks. I start to fall asleep.

It is his warm breath on the back of my neck, the tenderness of his kisses, that brings me back. I am aroused again, back in life. He has slid up inside me and his weight on my back is all I want in the world. Deep, deep inside myself, something turns over and pushes against the walls.

171

Isabella has called me to tell me she is going to marry Alexandros and stay in Greece. *It's a marriage of convenience*, she says, but underneath I hear something else. *Don't you think he looks good enough to eat?* She sounds happy and claims to want to try again. His family have already adopted her, even though she is twenty-four and he is only seventeen. Isabella will help Alexandros and his brother run the family restaurant, as a hostess. She invites me to come to dinner to see his place.

I remember when we first met Alexandros. After I came back from Larissa, Isabella and I paired up often, haunting the clubs favored by models. We always found a crowd and never paid for drinks. At the end of the night, very late, we would catch a ride to Ommonia Square, where the sandwich vendors ply their trade between three and five in the morning. The air fills with the smoke coming off the grills, onions and sausages sizzling. You can spot people getting out of expensive cars, their hair tousled and their shiny suits and dresses mussed. The women wait for the men to buy the thick, hot sandwiches. There have been times in the darkness of the middle of the city when the warm onion slipping down my throat seems like the most delicious thing I have ever eaten.

Isabella had fallen in love with a rich pretty boy with lips too thick and lashes too long. On the night she met Alexandros we had been at a bar, and this other boyfriend had communicated that they were breaking up by sticking his tongue down the throat of an heiress wearing a sequined dress. I followed Isabella out the door, and we sat down together on the hood of his car while she sobbed and plotted her revenge. She thought sugar in the gas tank would be just right again but settled for a key scratch down the front door, delivered as we ran off. We caught a taxi to a warehouse club called AuftoKinisi. There, she strode through the door as if she had never shed a single tear. Every man (and probably most of the women) wanted her. In the farthest corner was the most godlike man I had ever seen, all dressed in white. He appeared to be in his mid-twenties, and he moved without fear. He asked her to dance. Weeks afterward she found out he was seven years younger than she was.

At Alexandros's restaurant, Isabella wears a simple black dress, with her hair down and wild. She uses crutches but looks great. Her face is fresh and clean of makeup and she moves easily around the room, greeting people who come in. She is helping the brothers manage the place and has already rearranged the furniture, changed the marketing, and brought in friends of hers who have given the restaurant instant clout. She hugs me and seats me at the table closest to her, so she can sit with me whenever she gets a chance.

Isabella tells me she has decided to stop modeling. She has put money away for the first time in her life. Too many stories circulate, of deportation or of models who come to Greece for a short holiday and stay to earn easy money until they lose their looks and are stuck.

She tells me the story of a woman she knows who fell in love with an older Greek businessman who promised her everything in the beginning. He bought her a house and a car and paid for all her clothes. After a few months, he became jealous, at first of imaginary men, then of her friends, and finally of even her mother in Germany, whom she used to call. He locked her in the house, took out the phone, and never ever let her go out. One day she promised a workman she would have sex with him if he released her, and when he broke open the door she ran out screaming into the street and hid with friends until her mother arrived to take her home.

I tease Isabella about how she was the one who wanted to leave the most and now she plans to stay. She tells me she wants to take Alexandros home with her, to attend college in California. When he joins us at the table, he appears relaxed and tender and I think it is not my place to worry about her.

Isabella is a woman who always appears at home. She never equivocates, never changes her mind. If I dig, I can also see how she clings to Alexandros, how her brow melts when he smiles. If I dig even further, I can see a child who drew in breath one day and held it as her parents split from helm to stern, while the water closed over their heads and the ship went down.

I have followed her this far. Like a huntress, she has narrowed her sights on a target and is closing in. Waiting at the edge of the forest, I hold myself back. Closer than ever to what I thought I wanted in the first place, the sound of the night wind in the trees makes me want to run away. Isabella turns around and hands me a bow and arrow. Somewhere in the distance, we hear Greece drawing closer, like a deer crashing through the forest under a full moon.

FOR THREE GOLDEN APPLES

Imagine you have been born a daughter to a man who only wanted sons. He takes you to the forest, where he hopes you will be eaten, but instead you are rescued by a bear who teaches you to kill, hunt, and run. You embark on many adventures and are the only mortal woman remembered as a great fighter, someone with brawn. After you return home, your father concedes you are not a bad replacement for a son after all, but still suggests that marriage and a few grandchildren might be nice. Deciding that only a man who can outrun you deserves you, and to discourage suitors, you add that any who lose will die by your hand. Although the bodies piling up on the track have begun to rot, the contest allows you to stay single, to continue to rule your own fate, as warriors should. Then, one day, a man arrives with three golden apples in his pocket. As you run, he drops them and you pick them up, not because you are easily caught but because you think that even if their shine catches your eye, even if you pause to neaten the track, you can still catch up. But he wins the race and marries you. In the end, that is how you are remembered best.

Like Atalanta on her last run, the women in my family have sometimes paused on their path, looked at apples, dangerous and shiny, and been caught, turned aside from what we thought we wanted, our gaze distracted in mid-stride. It is not a sign that we have any less strength in our legs to run, but that it is easy to be diverted, easy to forget what you think you want.

One day, between February and March, I wake up in bed on my own. It has been a few weeks since I have seen Steve. Although I know I will see him again, for today I feel grateful. The light creeps under the curtains that cover the long windows at the front of the studio. It pushes a yellow line across the tiles, illuminating tiny dust balls. When the ray reaches me, I hoist myself out of bed and light the small gas burner that serves as my stove. My fingers create flames without flinching. Heating up the milk, I pour it over a spoonful of Nescafé and sugar, as the Soulas taught me, stirring up foam. At the corner bakery, Kyria Zaphridis hands over my usual small loaf with a smile. Taking the coffee and bread across the street, I push through the blue gateway into Emily and Francisco's courtyard. They have been up awhile, and the sun has warmed the paving stones. Emily sits at the round painted table they have pulled outside. She feeds the baby banana mush while Francisco and Ari work in the shed. They join us, dangling a new pair of earrings. Ari lifts them to my ears. Silver hoops with big green stones shine against my hair, and I gaze at myself in the piece of mirror they give me, looking like a different person.

Francisco has propped a radio up against the window so he can listen to it while he works. I hear the voice of the announcer in Greek, telling us about the latest government scandal and an upcoming concert of traditional songs. I understand almost everything, but there are gaps. Once-familiar words elude me, disappear. Moving into Greek and out of it again, I open myself up to the language like exposing skin on a warm day. The announcer on the radio says the word for electricity, reminding me. I kiss them all good-bye.

At this time in Greece, checkbooks and credit cards have yet to be invented. Every transaction has to be paid in cash. My electric bill is due, and I arrive at the office with a large wad of drachmas and a book. The line doubles back on itself, crossing the room. No one in Greece thinks the rules apply to them. We all become conspirators, trading rumors, looking for an inside angle. When a man tries to bribe the teller to let him go first, a woman in a floral housedress nudges me and shakes her head. Collective disapproval pushes him back. Two hours later, the housedress woman and I arrive at the front of the line together, like soldiers who have fought a battle. Feeling I have achieved a military victory, I turn toward work.

The UPI office clings to respectability, midway up Kolonaki Hill, home of Athens's rich. To get to the office, I negotiate the Plaka and cut across the university. A friend of Ari's has displayed his goods on a piece of black cloth in front of the main building. We chat about his new line, jeweler's gossip. As I climb the hill, intricate gold seashells and heavy chains glimmer in the windows of exclusive shops. Apartment shutters remain tightly closed; doormen guard marble entrance halls. In Kolonaki, no one hangs laundry out on the line because they all have maids or dryers. Even before finding out who lives at the top of the hill, Kolonaki's atmosphere seems hushed, expectant.

When I arrive, Leo is on the phone. On the other end, a friend adds detail to a story he published about a couple in the mountains who kept their disabled son in a kennel for forty years; Leo wants more color to resell it to a British tabloid. I clip some files and try to track down an expert on antiquities for an article on Melina Mercouri's latest volley of insults against the English, whom she accuses of stealing the Elgin marbles. When I reach the expert by phone, we speak two different Greeks, his the pure language of the well educated, mine a simplified version of that spoken by workers and villagers. Finally, I give up, embarrassed, and ask Leo to call. He tells me Isabella phoned and wants to have lunch with me in an hour, in the dead time between two and five.

We meet at our usual café, where the waiters wear black suits and the tables are covered in red cloths. Leaning on a cane, Isabella arrives from the agency, where she has picked up extra work answering phones. It is a little chilly, but she wants to sit outside so she can wear her dark glasses and look at all the other customers. She can spot habitués from her clubbing days: the fat industrialist who offered to pay her for sex; the rich daughter of a movie director who tried to become a model but was forbidden by her father; the clothes designer with his lover who he claims is only an assistant. We sip our coffees slowly, splitting a grilled sandwich, all of which cost as much as two full lunches in a *cafenion* in any other neighborhood. We agree to get together again soon and complain at the way the gaps between our meetings are growing longer and longer.

When I get back to the office, Leo tells me he has heard a story over the radio he thinks we should investigate at the airport. We had been there together a few weeks before, chasing a story about a TWA plane that had been bombed. Instead of exploding the plane in a big bang, the wrongly timed blast had only opened one hole in the side of the plane, just enough to suck out two passengers. They fell to earth between Italy and Greece, still strapped to their seats. Everyone else survived and we were interviewing passengers, many who had only just realized they were still alive, some who were shaking and crying, many Americans. I had wanted to pull them aside, take them home, and comfort them, but Leo kept reminding me we had to hurry to scoop the story. Now I ask if it is related to the bombing and he says no, something else.

A strange thing has happened. A family of Vietnamese refugees has landed in Athens more than ten years after leaving Vietnam. Promised safe passage to America during the war, they had ended up

in Yemen and had now restarted their journey to their original destination. Why, after so many years off the map, have they decided to
reenter history? They are in the airport without passports or money,
without a means of moving forward or going back, suspended and
officially nonexistent.

They have been living in the airport for a week. When I arrive
I find that the attention they have begun to receive in the Greek
newspapers has caused airport officials to announce a press blockade;
the family has been moved to a former storage room and is under
guard. Some staff tell me they have never heard of them; others say
they have donated sandwiches to keep them alive; others that passengers gave them clothing. The official story remains blank: yes,
they have landed; no, they can offer no further information. The airport corridors stretch out in front of me, turn abruptly, reveal closed
unmarked doors. Somewhere on the other side of a wall, children
hug each other while their father paces the room. Without a country or language, without passports or definition, they have only
stories—about their journey, their survival, their family. After an
hour of wandering, I realize they will keep their stories to themselves.
I have circled back on my mother's life, become a reporter, learned to
drink and speak fast. But where my mother would have found them
by now, learned their secrets, even bundled them out, I give up.

On the taxi ride back to Athens the driver picks up another
passenger, and the two of them start talking about foreigners, how
the American government has ruined the country, how the CIA
and the Jews and the Capitalists have all conspired together to keep
Greece from assuming its rightful place as the most glorious of
nations. Holding my tongue, I gaze at the identical apartment buildings until they become familiar. When we arrive, he starts to over-
charge me. As I hand him the correct fare, I confess I found his
conversation interesting, being Greek and Jewish and American,
before I slam the door. He idles while I walk off, as if his car were a
face I have slapped.

When I return home, the lights are still on at Emily's house. Eleni and Ari share the couch, while Francisco stretches on the straw mat floor. Emily roots in her closet for a sweater, throwing clothes across the bed. The baby is crawling on the floor, holding up a half-chewed cracker for all of us to admire.

Ari tells us a story about what happened to him the year after he finished his Israeli military service while training in South America, thousands of miles from home. In a remote corner of Argentina, far from any cities, he encountered a village celebrating a festival; the people carried flowers and baskets of fruit. Ari thought about the time of year and how much the ritual reminded him of home. When he asked one of the villagers about the meaning of the festival, they told him it was Succoth, a Jewish harvest celebration. He discovered they were part of a tribe who had escaped Spain during the Inquisition and had hidden in the mountains for hundreds of years. Ari said it was the strangest feeling, to come so far and find himself at home.

When Eleni and I walk back across the street together she hugs me and invites me to come visit any time. She has an aura of peace around her, one I have found rare among other Greeks, so easily split into civil wars and conspiracies. I watch her long white robe disappear into her courtyard, a bit of light in the darkness. When I get back to the studio, I spend an hour cleaning and making my home feel welcoming. Later, I climb into bed and look around the studio, glowing from the small light next to me.

At three in the morning, there is a knock. Steve leans over the threshold, waiting for me to invite him in. Although part of me feels like pushing him out of the door, the street, the neighborhood, the world, he has breached the circle and the night blankets the little houses in silence. I open the door and let him in.

I run my tongue up the ridge of Steve's back and close my eyes against the lamplight. Under my tongue, I feel the granite drying in the sun next to the riverbank where my grandmother spent her first years. I feel the rocks in her back that my mother described kneading out in her own childhood, pushing against the hard flesh.

Steve slams into me with so much force it brings tears to my eyes. In the watery half-light, I see the shimmer of the sea over the horizon near my grandmother's village. I feel the way each of us moved into water, how she used to dip her toes in and splash her face, and how my mother will go in for a quick dip only, and how I cannot get enough of water, how I stay in until my fingers are like pale raisins at the tips.

I push my face between his legs, breaking down my own boundaries. My grandmother's fearlessness brought her through dark waters and landed her on a hostile shore. My own mother moved from New York to the desert, where she hated the California glare of metal in the sunlight. I am burrowing to find a place, burrowing into my own earth.

Steve tells me to say something hard and obscene, and I find myself slip the bonds of language. The words that kept my grandmother caged for thirty years in a strange country and kept me out of half of my mother's life—and have teased me for months with my inability to enter the land to which they connect me—disappear. In their place comes an animal, sleek and swift, running across every border.

How long did my mother's engagement to the lawyer last? Weeks? Days? Months? I imagine it to be weeks, a short time. Perhaps the months leading to it and away from it match the months, summer to spring, of my year in Greece. There was enough time, after the engagement, for Daphne's fears to grow. She knew, on the day my mother told her that she and the lawyer had become engaged, that marriage was not what she dreamed it would be. Lacking the language of caution, Daphne could not express what she thought: *Don't do this, don't.* Like a root pushing at the surface of the ground, the words bumped at their happiness, threatened to rise between them. With a manicured palm, Daphne held them down.

Once the lawyer knew he had won her, once she had agreed to marry him, he changed. I imagine there were the first tiny clues, things that made her uneasy; he began to tell her how to dress, how to style her hair. Daphne kept silent because she wanted her to stay. My mother would have felt as if she were running through the air, pursuing freedom her own mother never had. She did not question whether her mother had laid down her life—like a rag to dry in the sun of her children's future—for my mother to become a Greek wife. When my mother went out in Athens after spending days in the strict confines of the village, when she swore in Greek or drank and danced, her body sang with its easy movements. It would have been some time before she noticed how she had circled back to the starting point. She crouched at the beginning of the race, heart pounding from running the track so many times before.

In the beginning, my mother would not have seen falling in love with him as a giving up of power. The decision to stay in Greece was a decision to break with the past, not a commitment to any particular future. At some point, though, she must have felt the trap closing in. If not in her words, then in her life, Daphne became the sibyl at whose spring my mother would have been more and more reluctant to drink. The truths that are hardest to take are the ones we know deep in our hearts but have taken care to hide from ourselves. Is it just my imagination, or was this the rift that began between them, the first opening of the gulf that would keep them apart?

This is what I discover through knowing, so many years later, how much they loved each other. Daphne knew what my mother did not: falling in love with certain men requires giving up half your soul. Some women are able to wrestle it back again, and have grown extra muscle where before there was only bone and skin. Some women never ever retrieve it.

To break the circle sometimes takes a sacrifice; sometimes you need to leave behind a limb when you climb out of the trap. In the end, my mother abandoned in Greece the woman she loved most in the world. Moving so swiftly to escape, she even broke out of her mother's house and her mother's circle, protective and strong. She could not have known the price she would pay for taking her own path, to lose a part of herself she would not recover for thirty years.

After being caught on the run, Atalanta was turned into a lioness by a friendly or unfriendly god. Transformed into what she never expected to be, perhaps she was more and more herself, four-legged but also swift, with a golden mane and sharp claws.

EASTERN CUSTOMS

Once upon a time there was a beautiful god with long glossy locks and eyes as deep as clear green pools. He was a god of the earth, a god of vines, of death and resurrection. Although a convenient story of his Greek birth was invented—the son of a mother who immediately dies, sending him wandering to Persia and Arabia—he was not in fact from Greece at all. He really came from the East, which is why he encountered so much resistance originally, as could be predicted from the way he looked. He had slim hips and liked to wear skirts. The interesting thing about this god was his amazing effect upon women. He made them wild with anger. When someone blocked their way, he caused them to run through the mountains, tearing men to bits and eating them. When he was around, women had arms the strength of outsize wrestlers, and they traveled together in large groups.

My favorite story of Dionysus involves his rescue of Ariadne. Abandoned on her island, she wonders how she ever fell for Theseus, with his square jaw. She makes patterns in the sand and rolls around at the edge of the sea, feeling the water lap at her skin and filled with a longing to get on a powerful horse and ride, to use her body to move and run. The island is so small, all she can do is pace and worry. One day, she notices a change in the weather, in the formation of the clouds. They shift and gather, looking down on her, causing breezes to appear that pull at her hair gently—all the signs of the arrival of a god. When he does appear, he offers himself to her. Lying down next to her on the sand, he lets her take her hand and run it through his long hair, and when he sees her lips tremble he starts to laugh. She wants to get angry, wants to complain. He tells her it is all right; he is the god of angry women, as well as all the other emotions that ride up in the body and come out through skin. Abandoned by Theseus, whose ship pulled away with all his promises, Ariadne is rescued by her temper's flare.

Dionysus lingers still; his deep laugh shakes each spring. To force life back through dead limbs of trees, his women sacrificed, sprinkled blood. In myths, they became maenads, tearing apart kings. Dionysus may have been parodied by the Romans, a fat little god of the vine, cheeks puffy with drunkenness, but his origins link death and sex, beginnings and endings, humans and nature. Some say his myth, re-created in festivals each spring and spawning theater, comedy and tragedy, translated easily into a new story from the East, another powerful king sacrificing his body to bring life. Maybe that is why, for Christian Greeks who still live in the land where spring evokes miracles, Easter remains the most powerful holiday, outranking Christmas or New Year's.

But before Easter comes Lent, because renewal has to be earned with sacrifice. And, as a reminder of the old god, Dionysus, before Lent comes *Apokreas*, Carnival, the last time for meat, when people stuff themselves as much as they possibly can and try not to be good in any way for an entire week.

Ari has come to invite me to what he calls the Greek Mardi Gras. In the last week in February, for five nights, Dionysus returns. Crowds swell the narrow Plaka alleys. People lug in big barrels and fill them with fuel, lighting up the streets with their flickering fires. The tavernas stay open all night, and the crowds move slowly, like thick liquid in a narrow jar.

Part of the excitement comes from danger. One of the traditions involves ridding yourself of anger and hostility toward those who may have hurt you. Realizing that passion cannot be coolly put aside but must be physically exorcised, the Greeks have a custom during *Apokreas* to wrangle with strangers on the street, who are supposed to fight back. No one should really get hurt; it is supposed to be done in the spirit of play. In Athens, the revelers buy oversized plastic hammers to bop one another on the head. Children buy water guns and throw water balloons. Teenagers use eggs.

Ari tells me he will come for me on the last night, the fifth and wildest. After he leaves, Eleni invites me up to her apartment.

She has been sitting with me on the steps outside her house, enjoying a few minutes of sun warming what is still winter air. She smiled at Ari when he invited me, but now she says she has something to tell me. *Don't go*, she says. *It's chaos down there right now. You could get hurt.*

It has been months since anyone told me to be careful about myself. Now I look at this woman, older than my own mother, with her handsome, lined face. When she talks she molds the air with her hands, and you can see other words come out from between them. Within her palms a red cyclamen blooms, the kind that grows out of the dry limestone of the islands. I find I want to tell her everything: about Steve, about why I am here. Although she is a stranger to me, when her eyes rest on my face, I feel I am real.

Eleni offers me another coffee. I tell her I will think about what she has said, though I know the danger, if anything, will lead me on.

I think of Eleni as a completely finished woman. Her husband has built her a house exactly to her specifications. Every view contains some part of her, a face she has painted, an arm sculpted, her books on the table, and her favorite western horizon out the window. I can see her going down to the sea with her sister, shorter and more ravaged than she is, more secretive and enclosed. The two of them swim together, Eleni moving gracefully through the water and the sister chopping at the waves with her blunt hands.

She has started to tell me a story about her sister, who has worked as a journalist but now sits in the house next door writing her autobiography. She tells me that the two of them grew up in that house; her father was a diplomat who was very involved in the early development of the Greek state. Eleni grew up in a completely different atmosphere from traditional Greek women. She and her sister were sent to Paris to go to school, and she studied law at the Sorbonne. Her sister published poems in French journals and was loved by many men and women.

When the time came, her sister fell in love with an elderly Greek poet and married him. They had one son before the husband died, and she settled into raising the child alone. A melancholy boy with a pretty face, he escaped the words that had belonged to his father and turned to music, taking up the flute. One day, a classical Indian musician came to Athens to perform, and Eleni's sister took her teenage son. The boy loved music so much he decided to study in India, leaving the year he turned eighteen. At first, he wrote every week. He had found a tutor in Delhi and everything seemed fine. Then there was a long period when she did not hear from him. Finally, he wrote to tell her he was in Tibet, in a monastery, and was very happy. A year later she received a letter from the authorities in Nepal, telling her that her son had died of an overdose of heroin in a hotel.

She went to Nepal the year he died, in 1968. For five years, she entered into what she imagined had been his life. She became a heroin user and a fixture in the international drug scene of Nepal. What finally saved her was meeting a Buddhist nun, who told her she was trying to bring her son back by conjuring his pain when she

187

needed to help him in the next life by remembering his strengths. She shaved her head and moved in with the nuns, curing herself of her addiction. Cleansed but ravaged, she returned to Greece and learned to play the flute. She never gives concerts but takes private students, which helps her to survive.

Eleni looks at me again, to see if I get the point of her story. *Why look for pain that isn't there?* she tells me. *You can't take someone else's pain as your own.* I start to tell her about Steve, and she tells me she has seen him leaving the house at dawn. She says one look told her everything she had to know about him. She is trying to remind me that there is more than one way off the island.

Ari and I dress in jeans and warm jackets and cover ourselves from head to toe. We walk down the Plaka around nine o'clock, and the night feels clear and cool. As soon as we get near, we can feel a kind of heat in the air coming out toward us. We enter one of the old streets and suddenly we are in a maze of bodies, carried along by the current.

Every few yards we pass someone selling the plastic hammers and water guns. Ari asks me if I want one and I say no, I just came to look, not participate. We hear some noise coming through the crowd and step off the street into a doorway. A shower of eggs sails through the air and hits the people who had been walking beside us in the backs of their heads, yellow gobs of yolk and white bits of shell sticking in their hair. All of a sudden, I do not feel afraid. I look at Ari and laugh. Sharp as desire, I want to be part of it; I do not want to hold back.

We leave the doorway, and I feel a bump on my head. I look up. A man who had been walking toward me, handsome and well dressed, has passed me with a sly boyish grin on his face. He has hit me and it does not hurt. Ari laughs at me, because I stand there, stupid and shocked. Then a woman passing by in a flowered dress hits him, and it is my turn to laugh.

We buy the hammers. First we bop each other, *pop-pop-pop* on our heads, the plastic bouncing off, leaving just a slight pressure that shocks for a second before it disappears. Then we begin to hit strangers.

There is no hard feeling in it. You hit someone, *pop*, and they smile at you. They hit you back and you pass each other along. The pace picks up. I hit an old man, a child, a mother, two teenage boys. I am sweating. I feel completely anonymous, free. There are so many people, no one can move quickly or get away. After a few blocks, I can hardly move, and I grab Ari by the hand when I see a side street where tables have been set up outside a café.

The crowd ignores those out of the flow. We find an empty table. Next to us a couple smiles at each other, eyes glistening. Next to them a group of friends shouts and laughs. A little boy sitting with his family dangles the candy hammer he has just acquired in front of his sister, who starts to cry. Her parents give her a toy gun and she quiets down. They share a bottle of wine.

Ari and I don't say anything to each other. We are panting, like participants in a mystery are supposed to pant, deeply and from our hearts. It is as if we have just taken off our masks and are returning to our daily selves. Already I can feel the pull to put on a dark robe again and go out into the crowds. All the wrestling of the months preceding this night mingles in my blood and rises to the surface of my skin. I can feel it evaporating off me into the night like sparks flying up from the fire, cooling and dispersing in the air. Ari and I are strangers to each other and strangers to everyone else in the city who has come here tonight. But we are intimate and open and safe.

Strolling back, I begin to realize that this is what coming to Greece has been. I have entered a role and participated in a drama; whenever I want to, I can drop my mask and go.

Everywhere in the world there are traps waiting for women. You might be hiking on a mountain, and a man with a knife enters your tent in the middle of the night. It happens. You might be following the signs in a faraway city, trying to find the temple, when you are hit on the head and pulled inside a doorway. The dangers waiting for you are entirely impersonal. They do not know who you are.

Women try to personalize their disasters. They marry men who take away their freedom, day by day. They fall in love with sons of mothers who love them too much and then find themselves being held to an impossible standard. They meet a man with long muscled arms who likes to hurt women, and they take him to bed again and again, asking him to see their face, please see it.

If you are lucky, something turns, and you realize you have brought yourself into these dangers. There are dangers you cannot help, which always exist. But there are also masks you have put on, and these masks can come off, leaving you free.

Once, when we were going through a box of old photographs, my mother pulled out a picture of her leaning over a balcony in a white sleeveless dress, big black sunglasses covering half her face, a martini in her hand. Next to her, leaning up against the bars, was a classically handsome man with thick dark hair and a blue T-shirt and a tan.

This is my mafioso boyfriend, she said. I met him when I was in New York, a few years before I met your father.

This boyfriend, it turned out, was an exciting date. The picture she showed me was from their trip down to Florida together. Beyond this she will not say—details about hotel rooms and hotel beds and at just what point before thirty this trip took place. But she does say that eventually he was too scary and violent for her, and she ended the relationship.

What did my mother know about what would happen to her in the future? She did not see her life as a story; she could not peer around the bend. When she found herself on a desert island, without food or water, did something explode inside her, warning her to run? Or did she sink into the sand, even for a moment?

There are certain points in your life when you think: okay, this is where it ends, where I am dropped off. But you never know what will happen, when the day will twist and deliver a god.

This is how my mother broke off her engagement to the handsome young lawyer who she imagined was going to take her down a path into a new life. She was so close to a fate that was not meant as hers that, she told me, she had booked her plane to return to New York, but only to announce her engagement, see her parents, and gather her trousseau. If things had not turned out the way they did, she might have ended up coming back to Athens, and we never would have known her as the woman she became. She might have been a matron living in Kolonaki; she might have worn gold jewelry and had five sons. For many years she would tell the story as a joke, laughing at herself, and for many years that is how I heard it. But now I know it could not have been easy; it was a change so strong it propelled her into a new life.

On the day before her flight my mother receives a visit, not from her fiancé but from his brother. The brother tells her he has come to arrange certain details before her departure. She invites him in, serves him a tray full of fruit dripping in honey, and cups of thick Turkish coffee. Or maybe she rushes him in, assuming that, as with his brother and their friends, she does not have to bother. She just puts the hot water on and boils up some powder and pours it into two cups she swishes out in the sink, leaving trails of old stains on the outside. Maybe she sits across from him with her legs bent at the knees, her elbows on the chair, looking confident and serene. Or perhaps she is nervous because here is a man she does not know very well, because now that she thinks about it she has hardly met the lawyer's family. She wonders what she looks like to him and why his hands rest on his knees so formally. These specifics are never included in what she tells us.

All we know is that, in the course of the conversation, he asks her about her dowry. And then he tells her what his family expects: fifty thousand American dollars. As she *is* an American, and as they *know* all Americans are rich, it should not be hard for her father to find the money that someone like his brother surely deserves. He lists his brother's accomplishments, then lists her lack of them, like tallying two columns on butcher paper at the deli: his and hers. Then he stands up, as if a conclusion has been reached.

My mother laughs at this point, because the joke is so obvious—the old-fashioned and obsolete Greek nature, and how easily she was fooled. She does not add the underlayers, either bitter or sweet: how her father had barely been able to pull himself up out of terrible poverty; how she had felt the lawyer's lips on her ear, promising her love as powerful as a wild horse. It must have been the final revelation after all the uneasiness of the last months. She also never adds how relief made her giddy as she saw him to the door, almost high with it. She could see so clearly the old and rusty trap. How close she had come to the snap, so close she knew it had happened for the last time.

She always finishes the story with a flourish. *The next day, I got on the plane and never saw him again.* There is never any suggestion of heartbreak or of sadness.

But now I know there was much more involved, and this is how I know. My mother left Greece and did not go back for twenty-five years. I know what it cost her to leave Daphne, because I was there when they met again thirty years later. The connection between them disappeared as if it had never existed. Severance like that does not arise out of an incident that meant nothing to you at the time.

But I also know my mother had discovered a secret in her year in Greece. If she had married the lawyer and stayed with Daphne, she would have been cementing herself into her mother's world—

married to an Athenian, not a villager; to a lawyer, not a waiter; but, still, married to a Greek man with Greek expectations. She and Daphne, mirrors of each other, would have been one version of the story—one way it could always turn out. So my mother was not just leaving Daphne, she was abandoning the tracks in the earth laid out for her.

To ride on the back of Dionysus, to climb off the island, my mother had to take on muscle. Like an extra layer around her heart, she padded the courage originally given to her with added weight, and it became a little hard. After starting down a path so familiar, she veered. Steering toward the open horizon changed her heart. One aorta closed forever, the other doubled in capacity. My mother left Greece, Daphne, the Kalidis girls, her own mother. She invented her own life.

As for me, I got rid of Steve. In the end, it was so easy.

The Real Magiritsa

Magiritsa means *little kitchen*. It is a soup that contains everything, and you eat it at the end of Lent's long fast. Every Greek family has its *magiritsa*; to heal such a long separation from meat, the soup must be particularly rich. Made correctly, it should have at least these ingredients: each part of a dead sheep left over from the main body—head, eyes, brains, feet, stomach, and entrails—a stack of green onions, and bunches and bunches of dill.

The word *magiritsa* evokes a love story in my family. The first Easter after my grandmother died, my father was invited to dinner with my mother's father and brothers. My mother had never brought her future husband home; my grandmother died before my mother was brave enough to introduce this man, neither Greek nor Christian, to her family. To bring him to them at Easter required courage. My father had an open mind; he attended church with the family, the way he was to continue to do throughout our lives, holding the candles. After the ceremony, at midnight, they went home. My grandfather and my uncles placed in front of my father a wonderful soup, a soup with the green richness of scallions, sautéed in butter to release a deep scent of earth, thick with meat, and more nourishing than anything my father had eaten in years. As someone whose own mother preferred processed American foods over the salty, juicy cooking of her shtetl ancestors, seeing adaptation as a better way to survive, my father would have recognized some truth in that soup, something of the flavor of his future life.

After he finished eating the *magiritsa*, so the story goes, my grandfather and my uncles gathered round and looked at one another with a gleam in their eyes. *Doctor,* my grandfather said, with the deferential irony of a Greek who in his heart defers to no one, *did you enjoy the soup?* My father, raised in an upwardly mobile household, with maids who taught him manners, said, *Yes, thank you.* And then, or so we were told, the family proceeded to name all the ingredients of the soup, one by one. My grandfather held up his spoon, at the center of which floated an eyeball, perfect and round. He asked my father if he would honor him by eating the most delicate part of the soup.

We always wanted to know what happened next. Once, when I was around fourteen and permanently touchy, I had one of my Beverly Hills girlfriends over. It was the week before Easter, and my mother had just done her Easter shopping. We must have provoked something in her, because my mother asked this friend if she could get something out of the refrigerator. When she opened up the gleaming white door, she saw two skinned lamb's heads staring up at her, twin characters out of a horror movie, red and white, every vein showing, eyeballs bulging. My friend screamed and shut the door. She never looked at my mother the same way again. So, knowing both the Greek delight in holding up blood and the American squeamish reluctance to see it, we begged to hear the rest of the story.

But my father was a doctor, someone who had seen his share of raw anatomy. We used to find the conclusion disappointing, because my mother would say, *Oh, he turned a little pale, but then he politely accepted and even asked for a second helping.* Now I think about how much that ending shows: two people measuring each other and agreeing without words to accept everything, the whole *magiritsa.*

In our family, we have restricted the key ingredients. My mother boils the heads for flavor but then removes them. She no longer leaves the eyeballs to float like delicacies. She washes the parts she chooses carefully and purees them in a Cuisinart, so that the meat blends with the greens into a sweet, milky broth, nurturing, warming, irresistible. When I was finally confronted with an old-world version of *magiritsa,* I found out how protected I had been all those years. To eat a Greek *magiritsa* is like poking through a corpse trussed up with onions. Arteries can be distinguished from pieces of intestine, aortas from eyeballs. Was it any wonder that when it came to eating the real *magiritsa* I gagged?

BREAKING THE FAST

In the story of Orpheus and Eurydice, a newly married couple encounters tragedy when the young wife flees a rapist and is fatally bitten by a snake. Her husband, Orpheus, plays the lyre like no other, mortal or immortal. He loves her so much he follows her to the underworld, where his music softens the rough beasts guarding the gates. His singing calms Charon, who ferries him across the river Styx, foot tapping. It even warms the cold heart of Hades, who crosses his legs in his dark suit and almost smiles. Orpheus convinces the gods to return his wife; they agree on condition that he climb toward the light without ever looking back at her. Because he worries that she might have changed, that her time in the darkness has altered her looks, he turns around once, just in time to see her dazzling face before she whirs away.

No one asked Eurydice if she wanted to leave.

In the dark, under the earth, she finds she can let go of the worries invading her since her marriage, whether Orpheus would always love her, how to hide her resentment at the hours of lyre practice he claimed to need, how to pretend not to miss her family. Without light or color, choices fade; the only thing that matters is the slap of the river Styx against the dark shore, the other ghosts who float without shadows. Perhaps, when Eurydice saw the first rays breaking over Orpheus's shoulder, she broke the rule, called his name, made him turn. Hurtling back to the darkness, she could have felt only relief.

I have spent the forty days of Lent avoiding the knowledge that the week of Easter is approaching. Like a promise I do not want to remember, I have slid away from the encroaching spring, clinging to winter. Not quite free of Steve, I feel I could trip at any moment. My sacrifice for Lent becomes my own happiness; neither swimming toward his shore or away from it, I tread water until I long to drown. Like a Greek woman who chews unsalted flat bread, swallows lentils without oil, my suffering fills me with grim satisfaction.

Greeks do not undertake Lent in an easy or lighthearted fashion. The dedicated fasters, the most devoted—almost always women—deny themselves everything, not only meat and all animal products but anything baked with yeast or cooked in olive oil. They survive on hard flat breads, plain beans, and a few winter vegetables. Greeks know how to savor their darkness, to hold it close to them and look it in the face like an old friend. Greek darkness lasts months after the land has rolled over to the light. It is a darkness of a people betrayed, a people who have betrayed themselves. It is the darkness of old paint on Byzantine icons, the darkness of eyes turned down at the corners, the darkness of young women dressed in black because they have been told they have no life left. If the sun insists on returning, as if it did not notice either history or tragedy, then Greeks must teach it by sacrificing more fully and more wholeheartedly than any other people.

When Easter does come, it lasts a week.

For me, the days leading up to Easter become a *magiritsa* week: every ingredient thrown in, frightening if examined too closely, full of peril but also nourishing, filling the blood with what it never even knew it needed. By the time Easter cracks over my head, I have been hoisted to the surface, eyes blinking from the light.

My mother's phone call from California wakes me up. *It's Palm Sunday*, she says, without much of a hello. I am lying in bed with a hangover, hardly realizing that it is Sunday at all. Her voice clears my head. At the end of the conversation she reminds me, *Don't forget to get a palm cross*. Every year she gets one, putting it in a glass on her desk where it grows dustier through the months. When I hang up, I look outside the window and see a procession of women, filing along the bottom of the street that leads to the church two blocks away—facing in the wrong direction. Then I look at the clock, which reads nine. The early ceremonies have already finished. These women have families, so the rites begin at dawn to give them time to work.

I put on some clothes and walk over. The walls around the houses of the neighborhood have been given a fresh coat of whitewash in honor of the holidays. Although it is a spring morning, the light reflecting off the paint looks like summer. The women who live on my block are coming back with their day's provisions, the last of the Lenten meals: beans, vegetables, flat breads. They greet me on my way over and I think, *Why am I doing this?* I am neither cooking nor being cooked for, neither providing nor with anyone to provide for me.

I reach the church to find the pews deserted, the basket holding the palm crosses for the faithful who got up on time empty. One old woman pushes a broom across the tiles. She smiles at me like a forgiving grandmother and holds up her hand to wait. She leans her broom carefully against the wall and goes inside the church. When she returns she has a branch of laurel, which contains its own powers of renewal and resurrection.

I take the laurel branch home with me and think that it works as a religion—a bit of what grows in the earth and whatever will not hurt you. I decide to get ready for work, even though it is Sunday. I know someone will be at the office.

After the initial excitement about having a real job, my UPI work has become routine. I wander into the office at odd hours, and Leo assigns me features for the wires. He repackages them for the British press and sends them out under his name. Occasionally, I find one I can rewrite and give to the *Star*. Sam and I meet each other when I go to his office, but, as expected, we do not see each other anymore outside of work.

Leo has asked me to look into a story broken by a friend on a left-leaning Greek paper. A group of women, or possibly men dressed as women, have assaulted a university student. They tied him up, stripped him naked, and covered his body with flowers. Then they painted RAPIST on the walls. Before they left, they called the papers and the police. No one saw the assailants except the young man. The police refused to believe women could do such a thing so they invented a theory: the perpetrators were transvestites. Others claimed the young man created the story and tied himself up in order to get attention. Leo thought it might make a human interest piece, and I would be the right one to tackle it. I have been trying to find out if any of the women at the university knew about the attack. Two days ago, I finally made contact with someone from the women's center, who told me she would reveal all if I met her in person. We set the meeting for noon on Monday.

At work, Leo tunes the radio to the main Athens news station. At one o'clock they break off, announce that for the rest of the week Easter liturgical services will replace the regular programming, and read the list of ceremonies and announcements from the Orthodox patriarchs. Leo mutters under his breath. *This country is really a theocracy.* We listen for a few moments to the high wailing coming out of the box; it transports me back to the church of my childhood, when I loved the sound of a language I could not understand. Now I am grateful when Leo turns off the radio.

The next day, I arrive at the apartment of the woman I spoke to over the phone. She introduces herself as a professor at Athens University, ushers me into her living room, and informs me that her weekly women's group will be gathering for lunch. One of them participated in the "action." Her apartment overlooks the city; I stare out at the view and run my fingers along her potted ferns, waiting for the meeting to begin. Gradually, the women arrive, various ages and sizes: a tall, blond Nordic woman, two American friends wearing silver bangles and scarves, a group of Athenian graduate students in loose clothing. Since the women come from different nationalities, we conduct the meeting in English. Everyone mills around the table, picking at the food.

Finally, the professor asks us to take a plate and sit down. She introduces the first speaker, and a small woman with short hair stands up. She looks about fifty and speaks with a heavy French accent. She relates how she was raped as a young girl and how afterward men followed her like wild dogs, nipping and harassing her. Describing herself as timid, she seems to shrink into herself. Then she says she met a boxer who tried to teach her about self-defense. When he fought, he knew he would get hurt, but he also knew the other person would get hurt as well. Sometimes that knowledge alone stopped a blow.

She places her legs apart, squares her shoulders, and half squats when she says this. She repeats it: *He knew the other guy would get hurt too.* When she speaks now, she looks powerful, almost frightening. Then she says, *If someone attacks me, he may hurt me, but he will also be hurt. This is shown in my body.* Ever since, she has traveled with confidence; no one even dares a catcall.

I think about all the men who have flashed me since I arrived in Athens. I think about the crowded bus gropers; the hard-on pressed up against your back when the crowd is too tight to move; the old men who pretend to bump into you accidentally in a busy street and, while apologizing, grab your breasts with a painful squeeze. What am I showing in my body?

When she sits down, a tall, heavyset woman with long braids stands up. One of the group of students, she proclaims she organized the action against the rapist. In her second year studying mathematics, a man in her class approached her about helping him with his studies. He appeared helpless, and she was a brilliant mathematician, fond of tutoring weaker classmates. Mostly, she felt sorry for him. He slathered her with gratitude when she agreed. Because he lived close to the campus, they decided to walk to his room, where he had left his problem sets.

Tagging behind her, struggling to follow her strides, he looked so small and pitiful it never occurred to her to be afraid. In his room, he made her a cup of coffee and told her he needed to find his books. She describes the chaos of papers, the bare walls, his fumbling. She sipped her coffee while he rummaged through his desk. Finally, he turned around. The room was lit by one bare bulb, so it took a moment to realize that he held a knife in his hands. Even in the low light, it gleamed like a sharp tooth. The knife transformed him into a different person, snarling and vicious, barking instructions as she trembled and cried.

He raped her and then he laughed at her, telling her as she struggled to get out the door, half terrified he would not let her leave, that no one would believe her. No one did.

In Greece, even in the 1980s, rape is not considered a violent assault but a crime of passion. Women create passion; men experience it. In police stations and in courts, women must explain first, before anything else, how they sowed the seeds in their assailant, what dress or word provoked the assault. When the woman told the police the story, they looked at her tall, ungainly body and said frankly that it seemed unlikely. When she cried and pleaded, they said that, even if it were true, it could never be proved, and hadn't her mother taught her never to go to a man's room alone? One police officer, short and round, sucked his teeth when she said she studied mathematics.

For a year, she held her story against her body, never letting it out. Like a fox, it ate at her entrails. One day, she saw the man's name written on the stall of a women's toilet, with the words *He's a rapist, be careful* written underneath. The fox leapt, struggled free. She took out a pen and wrote her own name and number, with *Contact me* underneath it. A pretty blond woman who was studying English called her and told her she had been through the same trauma, down to the refusal of the police to do anything. Two other women called. They agreed to meet. After crying and comforting each other, their anger grew, running back and forth among them, growling. By the end of the evening, they decided to both punish the man and brand him in public to save other women in future. They planned their assault and executed it perfectly. He had struggled and yelled, but they had held him down. The best moment had been when he lay trussed on the floor, naked, and they had covered him with flowers as he cried tears of humiliation. The English student had spray-painted RAPIST across his walls and the mathematician had called the police while he listened, making sure the authorities were on their way before leaving. Her voice catches in her throat as she describes their frustration at the way the story has been received.

She straightens like an orator and says that, whatever happens, at least the fox no longer bites her; she has released her fear. The women in the room applaud. Mingling afterward, I find the mathematician and promise to report her story in the international press; women around the world will feel inspired. Then I rush back to the office. Striding with aggression, feeling the Frenchwoman's rolling vowels stiffen my limbs, I am not bothered by anyone. In a rush I write the story, details extending it paragraph by paragraph. Then I show it to Leo.

He reads it too quickly. He claims a new directive he just received asks editors to reduce the number of features they send over the wire. Throwing it like a Frisbee, he tips back in his chair. *Maybe if it had turned out to be the transvestites, we could have done something with it, but this is just a story. It isn't news.* What is the difference between a story and news? Is it the difference between truth and a fact? Glaring at Leo, I will the chair to tumble over, but he rights himself and gets on the phone. I fold the story carefully, pocket it in my jeans, and scrape a chair over to the ticker, which is spewing out stories. Trying to make as much noise as possible, I rip the relevant stories off the roll and scratch labels on them for the file.

Sometime during the evening a release types itself out modestly, not even meriting a second glance. Perhaps it knows it will become the most important news story of the year, but to me it still looks like trash. Watching the stories march out and tearing off anything important, I clip an account of the American ambassador to Italy speaking at a conference on Mediterranean pollution, a piece about a financial audit of the British Museum that we might need for future Elgin marbles research, and three versions of Leo's story about an Armenian terrorist's attempt to kidnap a Turkish businessman on a Greek island. Without glancing twice, I throw out the four lines describing a report on unusually high levels of radiation in Sweden.

When I come to work on Tuesday, Leo announces he wants an early lunch. Since I strolled in at quarter to eleven, he suggests we leave now and return for an uninterrupted afternoon of work later.

We pick one of the local tavernas, on a tourist-free side street. A glass cabinet holds the day's specialties, and a counter separates us from the cook/waiter making the salads. Because it is officially still

Lent, the taverna has few customers. We pick out several plates of ready-made dishes: okra, green beans, even a bit of meat, which Leo relishes, cursing the church. The vegetables have the half-sweet taste of fresh food cooked for a long time in oil and tomatoes and lemon. Leo orders two beers.

First he tells me about how, six months ago, he met a woman on a train going to Yugoslavia. She was a Czech doctor, attractive. They started to write to each other and, after a couple of months, declared their love. Over Christmas, he went to visit her. He met her whole family, who treated him like a fiancé. At the end of the two-week visit, he realized he was engaged to be married. He asks me to congratulate him. Leo describes his plans for the future, how he wants to bring her to Greece, rescue her from her grim Eastern-bloc life. He orders another beer, and another. As he grows more drunk, he starts to tell me how lonely he has been and how he felt he could not honorably start a relationship with anyone else. To solve his dilemma, he confesses, he sometimes visits prostitutes. He tries to convince me the prostitutes are perfectly clean; doctors check them every week. Then he groans. He might be falling in love with one of them. Week after week, he returns to the same woman; he fantasizes about rescuing her also. Leo finally stops his monologue. He tells me he wants my advice.

I ask him if he is planning to run the story about the rapist. He says no. I tell him I have no advice to give him.

When we get back to the office, I write a story about Bhagwan Shree Rajneesh preaching to Greek fishermen in Crete. Adding my own embellishments to details garnered from Greek papers, I describe the way Bhagwan's followers wear diaphanous white dresses without bras. The humble fishermen flocking to the meetings admit they cannot understand a word of Bhagwan's teachings, but they like his entourage. The patriarchs have threatened to throw him out of the country. I show the story to Leo, who smiles as he shakes his head. *A theocracy, didn't I tell you? What's wrong with giving the poor lads a flash of tit for their suffering? Okay, yeah, this is good; we'll send this one.*

We work from two until after nine, while Leo's head clears. When his appetite returns, he sends me out to buy burgers. While I type, I continue to check stories appearing over the wires. Sometime during the afternoon, the story about the radiation in Sweden returns, but with more details.

The writer mentions towns where high radiation-level readings have been taken. At the official press conference, scientists claim no new theories. An hour later they reconvene; the Swedish government suggests a nuclear accident may have taken place in the Soviet Union. At seven, the correspondent in Moscow reports that the Soviet government has released no statements. Shortly afterward, he files another story: the Soviet Union has declared an official news blackout on the subject. Now stories race in from other parts of the world, other governments responding to the news blackout as an admission of guilt, urging a statement from the Soviet Union. When I leave the office close to ten, no statement has yet been made.

Home beckons, and I almost listen. Since the hour is late, Leo has given me money for a taxi. When I get in I decide it would be a shame to waste a good fare, and I tell the driver I want to go to Glyphada. We pass through dark streets, shutters and balconies closed. When we arrive in Glyphada, the center of the square is bright with neon. Suddenly I feel happy, energetic.

The three or four bars where Steve hangs out mark the boundaries of my territory. After months of chasing after him, I have become known to the general expatriate bar community, most of whom will buy me drinks when they spot me. They drink with the same people night after night; since I only go down there every few weeks, my novelty value makes me a welcome guest. Tonight, my bar mates are cagey. No one admits to having seen Steve. Then someone says he has been spending a lot of time at a place where a particular large blond English barmaid has been attracting his attention. This does not stop me; I hop right on over there. The woman behind the bar looks about forty, and she has fat red arms. She asks me if I'll have anything and I spend ten minutes drinking a beer by myself. When I walk out, I am ready to give up, but then I see Steve's car. I cannot wait for him any longer, but I take out a piece of paper and write a note and pin it under the windshield wiper.

Then I take a taxi and go home.

It is close to dawn when I hear the knock on my door.

Steve and I are on the bed, sweating. He has somehow gotten me on my back and he is towering over me, cock in hand. For a moment, this is just where I want to be. He is so large above me he blocks the view. His chest is taller than mountains, his hair, plastered to his forehead and floating out into air, looks like a dull sun. He is talking to me, telling me what to say. And then he tells me to call him master.

The words start to form on my lips. The *m* purses them together, and the *a* floats out. The *s* hisses along. But somewhere between the *t* and the *e*, the sounds explode into a laugh and the hard *r* is never completed. The word stays open like that, burst by air coming out of me in great heaves. Steve wilts in front of me, and I slide out from under him and sit up.

I never wanted to come in the first place, he says. *I was doing you a favor because you left that pathetic note.*

I cannot answer him. Part of me is terrified that he will leave, but a different force has taken over. When he says *pathetic*, my laughter bubbles over again. A voice in my head says in a heavy French accent, *You may get hurt, but he will get hurt too.* It is so funny because it is so pathetic; he's right. He pulls on his pants quickly, as if embarrassed to be naked. Buttoning his shirt, his fingers falter, and this makes me laugh harder. I am laughing so hard there are tears coming out of my eyes.

You're fucked up.

I am fucked up.

Steve puts on his shoes and walks out.

I am crying, not because he is gone but because I have wasted so much time with him. I pull on a T-shirt and start to make myself a cup of coffee. With tears still coming down my face, I draw back the curtains to watch the light rising behind me, etching the tops of the houses across the street, sparking on the rooftops like fire.

I turn on the radio in time for the morning service. Christ has just arrived in Jerusalem and cleared out the temple. It is only across the Mediterranean and two thousand years ago. The thought of it makes me smile.

The next morning, I call up Isabella and ask her for the name of her gynecologist. I want a complete checkup. The woman on the phone says she can arrange an afternoon appointment. I decide since I am awake I will go to work early.

When I arrive at the office, the boy from the *cafenion* is just delivering a tray of *turkiko*, heavy sweet coffee. Leo picks up a small cup and offers me one. He bounces around the room, rattling off the latest news. Gorbachev has admitted there was a nuclear accident in the Soviet Union, in a place called Chernobyl, not far from Kiev. Leo and I spend the morning watching the wires and drinking coffee. Neither of us does any other work.

Every quarter of an hour, the same report, with variations, appears out of Kiev. Some casualties may have occurred. Residents in Kiev are assured they are not in any danger. There have been no reports of mass evacuations. From around Europe, correspondents measure the level of radiation and outline government statements about possible danger to the population. Some hint at rising panic, telling of runs on canned goods in parts of Europe closest to the disaster.

When the president of Greece makes a statement, Leo types up a summary and processes it through the machine. Papandreou's voice sounds confident, calm. Though there has been an accident, the citizens of Greece are safe, Leo types. He snorts. *Socialist government, Soviet disaster; of course he's not going to say there's any danger.* He calls the American military bases to see if they have better local information. They tell us they have been monitoring the radiation levels continuously and see no increase from normal levels. When he slams down the phone, he barks, *They've got their own agenda; they want the world to believe radiation's good for you,* but he types the story anyway.

Leo gives off an elated energy, a reporter's high. News, however bad, pumps through his arteries, sharpens his eyesight, quickens his fingers. Relegated to a sidekick, I still feel strong and fearless. In the newsroom, we are safe.

In the afternoon, we hear the first reports of a cloud of radiation spotted in the atmosphere by international meteorologists, heading in the direction of France and England. Parents are advised to keep their children indoors at all times unless absolutely necessary. Governments predict possible famine in Eastern Europe and plan to ship in massive amounts of food to contaminated areas. The correspondent from Kiev has been transferred to a safer part of the country.

The gynecologist's office is just around the corner from UPI. At three, I remember my appointment and wrench myself off the wire. As I arrive, the receptionist pushes past me, clutching her bag. She tells me all in one breath that she is going home to her family to make sure everyone is safe and what a thing to happen just before Easter and she has a million things to do but her mother wants to leave the country.

I am alone in the office with the doctor.

Up on the wall, framed pictures of palm trees and the Rockies create a familiar airport-lounge panorama. The doctor stands and apologizes for the desertion of his support staff. He has a handsome, fortyish face, clean-shaven and square. He shakes my hand, noting my admiration of the photographs. He shot them himself, on a golfing trip to America. I compliment him on his American-accented English, and he tells me he studied at Cornell. We chat about the East Coast versus the West, golf versus tennis. Then he tells me to take off my clothes and lie down on the table. He puts on his gloves and tells me to hitch my legs up. He puts cream on his fingers and reaches inside me.

Ah, he says, *you have a beautiful tight vagina.*

I am not sure I have understood him, but then I realize I know just what those words mean. I find I am incredibly tired. It is hard to take an aggressive stance lying on your back with your legs up, notwithstanding my performance with Steve the night before. Instead, I simply remain silent and wait for it to be over.

When I am dressed and sitting in front of him, he asks me some questions, who I've been sleeping with and how often. I lie and tell him I am engaged to be married. He smiles. Then I tell him I have fallen in love with another woman and that I need to make sure my fiancé hasn't given me anything, because when I told him, he confessed he has been sleeping with five other women. The doctor frowns. He does not ask me any other questions. He just says he will run some tests, but everything looks fine. On the way out, he hands me a paper bag.

This is a douche, he says. *Every woman should use one.*

Thinking about all the advice I have been given during the past year and by whom—all the men who have told me what to do, assuming I have the mind of a child, a little doll, inside my woman's body—I feel tempted to punch him. Instead, I take the package, feeling it burn my fingers.

I run down the stairs to the street and find an open trash canister. I dunk the paper bag over the lid, hearing the satisfying crunch as the package hits the pile. Rubbing my hands over my jeans, I turn toward UPI. Leo and I stay until eight, until the news everywhere repeats itself ten times. On the radio, Papandreou's voice intones the same message over and over, in between long stretches of liturgical singing, the Orthodox high-pitched nasal wail. Impatient for another day's news, we agree to return early.

As soon as I reach home, I take a shower. Naked, I climb between clean sheets and fall asleep.

On Thursday, I wake as soon as the light touches the curtains, dress quickly, and skip breakfast. We file variations on last night's stories and watch the panic mounting around Europe type itself out in a march of paragraphs. At eleven, Leo receives a phone call and announces we will break early for the holiday. He wants to take the whole building to lunch—me and John, the old society reporter, and anyone else we can round up. An Australian stewardess he used to know has a six-hour layover and wants to get together. All thoughts of marriage are temporarily forgotten. It feels like the eve of a war. We close the office at noon. Who knows when we will ever open it? The liminal time of the holidays obscures a deeper suspension of reality. We have all entered into unknown territory, without having been asked if we wanted to go for a ride.

Leo takes me in a taxi down to the bay. I realize I have become like other Athenians, living among the white hills and valleys of the city, close to the sky, dipping down to the sea only when necessary. We have John with us, who entertains us with gossip about Athenian high society, politicians' mistresses, and businessmen who like to wear drag. Rarely in the office, he does his research by going to lunch with a series of wealthy matrons. Although he only files a few stories a year, Leo keeps him on the payroll for precisely these moments.

John has invited an American military officer, who brings his half-Greek son. At the table, Leo and the Australian woman sit on

211

one side, the budding young soldier and I on the other, with John and the officer at either end. We order a round of beer and then another. Before long, we are all drunk.

Leo seems to want to impress the Australian, a magazine ad of a stewardess, lithe and blond and sweet. He speaks a rapid Greek to the waiters, who rush back and forth to take care of us, amazed that anyone has appeared today at all. We are sitting outside, and perhaps the waiters just want to spend as little time in the open air as possible.

The cook invites us inside to inspect the fish. When we emerge, the light has changed. Down in front of us, the water lies flat as glass. It has a strange gray-green tinge to it, the milky color of the sea under clouds. The sky above remains a stubborn blue. The officer tells us that the Americans have predicted the cloud will never come to Greece. I turn around and see it just behind me. At the edge of the northern horizon, clouds tower in dark storm columns. An ashy mix of black and white reaches high into the atmosphere, pushing at the lid. Even though I think this could not be *the cloud*, I suddenly shiver. Invisible systems of life swim in my blood; tiny cells sleep innocently inside me, cocooned deep in my ovaries. Life has its own agenda; it waits for me to pass it on. More than being a daughter, someday I would like to have one. Particles drop from the sky to find her, like Zeus romancing Danaë as a shower of gold. The radiation is an unseen hand I want to block.

After lunch, we go for a defiant stroll on the beach. Half a mile from the taverna, we come across a large dead fish. Almost five feet across and round, it looks like a small whale that has lost its body, a giant face with no tail. We wonder whether something has cut it or mutilated it, like a boat's rudder, if technology slapped it and sliced it. (Years later, I discover it was a sunfish, a giant creature with tiny fins, a strange and lovely monster of the sea.) Why has it washed up on the shore? What is it doing here? Without discussing it, we turn around at the sunfish, ten minutes after starting out.

Still thinking about the sunfish, I find a dog pacing outside my door when I return to the studio. It seems to want shelter. I am used to all the strays and yet I feel responsible for this one. The dog's rib bones protrude through its coat; it looks at me with begging eyes, hopeful and submissive. My first instinct is to rush it indoors, away from danger and bad air. I pretend that all it wants is something to eat and give it a loaf of bread. The dog declines the food. It wants in. I whisper that it should be glad to belong to a species without invention, part of the innocent hordes who try to survive in our atmosphere. I give it a few pats and slip through the door, trying to block out its whimpers.

Instead of letting the dog in, I pack.

Instead of getting on a plane, to fly away with the Australian to cleaner, more distant shores, I climb on an old bus bound for Larissa.

Instead of going south, I go north.

In another day, Easter begins in earnest, and I have waited to celebrate it in the land of my ancestors since long before I knew such a land existed.

When my mother left Greece, she promised to write. For years, she inscribed a line of accents at the top of all her letters, asking her cousins to distribute them where they belonged, since she could write Greek words but not the correct accentuation. She returned to Queens, left quickly for Manhattan. After she married, she traveled even farther, to California. Twice a year she cooked Greek dishes, at Christmas and Easter, and drew crowds of every nationality but Greek to sigh and coo over her food; they had been languishing in the months between without it. Her cooking was like a sequined gown, brought out only for special occasions. We saw its sparkle and never knew how it hung in the closet, next to the ghosts of all the other meals that might have been, other labors not performed.

Greek had been her first language; she spoke it for four years before ever learning English. When we grew up, we always asked my mother for definitions, synonyms, new vocabulary. She retains a professorial facility in English; every morning, she completes *The New York Times* crossword puzzle before finishing her coffee. None of us knew how much strength it had taken for her to choose one life over another, her house filled with books, each word a passport, an opening, a way out. We watched her like the weather, basked in her sun and hid from her storms. We never realized how much her moods mirrored another place, another country, how darkness threads through light.

Like Eurydice, my mother always felt the pull of the underworld. Close to the light, she often turned back to visit with the shades. Treading over her earth carelessly, we could not see her communing with ghosts. Their names never crossed the threshold, those characters we never knew: Daphne, the Kalidis girls, our Greek cousins, even her own mother, our grandmother. While we bounced red balls across the cement, jumped into the pool, filled the house with our noise, we never heard their silence beckoning.

EASTER

No one knows what really happened in the Eleusinian mysteries; no amount of archaeology or speculation has been able to pin down what was so fiercely guarded, long before the birth of Christ. Those who participated were made to swear never to share the secret; the only way to discover the sacred knowledge was to go to Eleusis yourself and take part in the ritual, to know in your body what you could never speak with your tongue.

We do know the mysteries were dedicated to Demeter, goddess of life and death. Participants were told about the immortality of the soul; those who died reappeared in a better place. Not long ago, only two thousand years, not far from Greece, another story was brewing—one of sacrifice and renewal, blood and harvest, the death of a king giving life to everyone. Greece had been prepared for the story already, a good place to start a new religion. Unfortunately, the message arrived through Paul, who displayed his impatience with the past when he arrived at Ephesus and tore down Artemis's golden temple. Paul added his own embellishments: women should hide their power, cover their heads in church, stand behind their husbands, keep their mouths shut. As Paul laced women tightly into one plain dress, the goddesses slunk away, disappeared. Nymphs turned into saints, itching under the collar. The Virgin became the only mother. Priests put on skirts, and women shut the door on their longings.

Greece became so religious that when the West moved in one direction it moved in another, causing a schism to open up in the earth, a great hole that to this day makes travel between West and East difficult. During Easter, a gap opens—a link between cultures, between goddesses and a new God, spring and eternal life.

In my family, we have always had two Easters: one American and one entirely our own. The first Easter, TV Easter, we shared with all our friends. TV Easter wore pink and white, produced yellow bunnies and lavender eggs. It smelled sweet and tasted like sugar, quick on the tongue and gone in a moment. The real Easter never happened at the right time. It was the color of blood and gave off an odor of frankincense and strange meat. During real Easter, a small window would open and my mother would step into it and come out the other side a different woman, someone with powerful hands and secret knowledge.

Those who participated in the Eleusinian mysteries may have been afraid before they walked into the grounds, holding their torches aloft. They may have wondered what would happen to them, may have known their lives would change without knowing how. Part of me has waited for Easter this year through months of worry and doubt. During Easter I felt I would encounter the core, uncover the mysteries, travel to the origin. I did not realize the strongest feeling I would have by the end of the week would be a desire to get as far away from Greece as quickly as possible. Easter did change my life and bring me back full circle, but not in the way I expected.

In Larissa, my cousins welcome me with open arms. They plan to celebrate Easter as they would any other year, and my bus reaches town by midafternoon, in time to help prepare. People in a disaster are not just brave; they have no choice but to continue as if life goes on. Someone plants a bomb in a bank; people switch branches.

We spend the day indoors, cooking and watching the news. The Soulas tell me that their friends feel cynical about the government line. Costas's wife, the one who looks like a movie star, passes through the living room periodically and tells us to turn down the volume because she has work to do and can't concentrate with the noise. Her voice, usually so soft, sharpens to an anxious twang. Later, religious programming and soaps replace the news broadcasts.

Midway through the afternoon, the rain starts. Heavy, thick as fists, it pounds on the roof. The movie star emerges from the kitchen again, nervous. She has never seen rain like this, she says, unnatural at this time of year. She keeps repeating how it never rains on Easter. She orders us to get out of the house and go to church. While we dress, the movie star asks me whether I have ever been to church. I start to explain about my mother's faith, which survived her excommunication. But then my aunt adds, in a kind voice as always, *Isn't your mother a pagan, isn't your father?* She actually says *unbeliever*, but the meaning remains the same. I am not quite sure how to continue; stories crowd my mouth, jostling to get out.

When they were young, both my parents were passionate about religion. My father, according to his family, was so orthodox he would not allow his sisters to leave the house on a Saturday night until the first star shone. When he went to school he could only read and write in Hebrew, and he was so proud of spelling his name in English on the first day of class, it took him a moment to notice the others mocking him for being so far behind. According to my mother, it was a sign of her love for her religion that, growing up, her first crush was on the priest.

My mother once said to me, *God is about saying yes. Religion is about saying no.* By the time they married at the Ethical Culture Society in New York, my parents had long left the faiths of their childhood. My mother was excommunicated for marrying a Jewish doctor. At their wedding, some of his relatives danced, some of them asked why there was no real food, and some of them never showed up. A few of hers were there, but mostly the pictures reveal good-looking men and women, looking drunkenly relaxed despite their jackets and ties, the kind of New York friends of my mother's who always talked fast and who embodied the word *smart*. The reception was at the Overseas Press Club in Manhattan, and my mother wore a short white dress. I once tried it on. The bust hung off me and I could barely get it over my waist. The fashion in bodies changes.

Despite Manhattan and Ethical Culture, we were all baptized; when my brother was born, my mother took him back to the big Greek cathedral in Manhattan, and her aunts and cousins all came. Long before we had any choice in the matter, we were held over a basin and our relationship with water was established—both in and of it, part of a people with a longing for the sea. Because we had been baptized we were allowed to take communion, and although my mother had exiled herself, she was faithful to our possibilities and took us to church once a year, on Palm Sunday.

Once my mother stopped to pick up a decrepit alcoholic woman as we drove through Beverly Hills. Her sweater on backward, the woman teetered at a busy corner. My mother halted abruptly, despite my thirteen-year-old glare. We drove miles to take her home, my mother chatting with her amiably, helping her to her door before going away. Back in the car, rolling down the windows after maintaining a sulky silence, all I could say as I fanned the air with wide sweeps was, *Mom, why did you pick that stinky woman up?* She just looked at me. *You never know who might be Jesus.*

My Greek vocabulary will not stretch to form the story; neither the language nor my relationship to it can bridge the distance that prevents my aunt from understanding either the woman behind the wheel or the one too dizzy to find her home. Instead, I tell her that we have all been baptized and attend Saint Sophia's in Los Angeles. I do not mention my mother, who has done something that seems inconceivable as I stand in the Soulas' apartment with its marble floors and carefully tended furniture. My mother has made a choice, has kept what she has wanted from her mother's past and discarded what tasted too sour or cost too much. How can I explain that to these relatives who never got a chance to decide for themselves which pieces give good flavor and which are too gristly to swallow?

I notice, when we step outside, clothing covers every inch of our body; the Soulas have even lent me a hat and gloves. Whatever the government says, we do not plan to take chances. The Soulas decide to take a bus to their mother's village, on former farmland at the edge of town. The small church knows them well; they say I should see it. Shrinking from the rain, we wait at the bus stop, because neither father has yet allowed them to have driver's licenses; they will have to wait until they are engaged. When we arrive, we enter the church. Wooden seats line the wall, carved and worn. Only men rest on the seats, mostly older farmers with craggy faces. The women stand in the middle, like cattle in a barn. The priest emerges from behind the saints. His long braided beard hangs across his belly, his hair braid reaches down his back.

He commences by asking us if we know why this disaster has been visited upon us. He gives details of the horrors we have already experienced and the horrors to come. Then he points his finger at the back of the church. *It is because of women*, he says, *who show no respect anymore.* He points to us. We are wearing pants and shoes, not skirts. The Soulas grab my arm and pull me out. Later, they try to laugh it off. They tell me it was a country church; *Pay no attention.* But when we attend a Good Friday procession later in the evening, I look at the gold and silver of the big town church, look at the male saints in their warrior garb, look at the priests who do not look at the women and the women who are all looking at them.

Late that night, after church, my cousins and I leave my aunt and find a group of friends drinking a round of forbidden ouzo. The rain has stopped and we step outdoors, defiant, but defying what we do not know.

My mother told me that when she was a girl and had her crush on the priest, Good Friday was her favorite part of Easter. Dedicated women and girls could volunteer to weave flowers for the tomb of Christ, to be lifted in a procession around the church. The earth would display its offerings, fragrant and delicate, and each perishable bloom would be placed, with nimble fingers, around an empty offering.

When we were growing up, Greek Easter started on Palm Sunday, not Good Friday, with our once-a-year communion. We were always sleepy, doped up, too early in the morning to know what we were doing, forced out of T-shirts into stiff, unfamiliar clothes. My mother never joined us when the line departed the pews to swallow the wine; she hung back, sending us to wait with strangers. At the right moment, we knelt in front of the priest, who intoned the names we gave him; mine was always the same, not the one given me at birth but my grandmother's name, the first Greek word I ever learned. We swallowed the sweet wine and chewed the bread quickly, eager to return to the sunshine, heathens again.

After church, we crossed the street to the Greek store. Part of a small collection of Greek shops in a neighborhood far from our own, the store was filled with scents that evoked another country. They were waxy and rich like oregano and sesame, oily like garlic and olives, sharp like feta. We hopped around while my mother ordered what she wanted in a language we never understood. We were kids who knew only odorless supermarkets, places where everything was prewrapped and prepackaged. On the way back in the station wagon, the brown bags wafted out the scents of the shop, swirling over us, a cloud we could follow back through time all the way to the mountains.

When we reached a suitable age, she took us with her to the Mexican neighborhoods to search out the illegal meat markets. She knew butchers who sold her lamb year after year, who got her the bootlegged heads, bellies, and intestines. Over the years in California, my mother had developed her contacts, her college Spanish finally coming in handy. At home, the lamb's heads went into the refrigerator, next to the orange juice. Then she would pull out an iron vat that had been passed to her by her own mother. It was nicked but intact, stained around the rim with red dye, like watermarks on paper.

During the week she would cook and prepare, chop and arrange. We stood by her side, handing her what she wanted. She would not explain how it all fit together; we had to learn by observing. In the supermarket, she bought eggs in bulk, four dozen for the guests arriving later that week. The packets of dye were always plain Rit, but in the water they were transformed into the color of blood. She boiled the eggs and dropped them in the dye, staining them a shiny deep crimson, the red of the earth. Later, she would weave a bread into the shape of a cross and bake it with an egg decorating each corner.

To confuse us even further, Easter always occurred on Saturday instead of Sunday. All day, the house was invaded by the last of the cooking, the *magiritsa* and the bread. At dinnertime, instead of eating, we were sent to bed. At bedtime, instead of sleeping, we were woken up to go to church. Driving to church was like entering a tunnel, the streets unfamiliar, empty, and dark. We always arrived late, to miss the sermons, in a gang of Greeks and non-Greeks, the friends who came for the unusual ritual and the food. By the time we pulled into the parking lot, other once-a-year Greeks were spilling out onto the pavement, gossiping above the words being broadcast from inside the church.

Squeezed up against one another, each person held a candle, pressing to see the final procession, the swinging censer, the altar boys holding saints aloft. All the lights died. We stood in pitch blackness, as full of suspense as if we had never done it before, while we waited for the first candle to be lit from inside. One by one the candles carried the light out, and the air mingled the scent of incense and singed hair. *Christos anesti*, we sang, *Christ is risen*; even my father sang the words we had memorized. We carried the candles with us in the car, their glow dispersing throughout the city. Then we arrived home and feasted until four in the morning. We were the first kids we knew to stay up past midnight.

My mother's Easter beckoned me like a mirage toward Greece. Now I find I am in Larissa, in the shadow of her parents' mountain, and I want to bury my head under my pillow and stay in the dark a little bit longer. The noise coming out of the kitchen shoves my shoulder; the women have been up for an hour, banging pots and boiling water for eggs. The mothers have assembled their daughters, and the six women move in a precise ritual, their hands working the meat they have not touched for forty days, their nostrils filling with its scent. I groan and turn over but I can see through the blinds the men outside in front of the garage, wrapping entrails. They toss the rope between them, stuffing it with bits of meat ferried down to them by one of the Soulas—*koukouretsi*, the most delicate sausage. When the yeasty scent of bread tickles my nose, I rouse myself and ask if I can help. Everyone smiles as they bustle; it feels better to be touching food, bread, meat. They seem solid and unchanging.

On the radio, we hear that milk products may no longer be safe. A right-leaning newspaper has printed photographs of mutated vegetables, twisted and frightening. The headline reads, *Will this happen to our children?* One of the Soulas switches off the radio; we

222

cannot listen to any music so close to the end of Lent. Instead, we keep breaking into the silence, beginning a conversation and letting it die away. The movie star hums; she taps the bottom of the cage in the kitchen holding two yellow canaries and makes them sing. On this holy weekend, she instructs us, there must be no talk of disaster. We should celebrate. She hands us a bag of onions and five knives. With water pouring out of our eyes, we chop in some kind of relief.

It rains on and off all day. Although dim, the dusky light extended the day and we are relieved when it finally fades to night. At last, the mothers call us to prepare. Dressing tangles us together; someone picks up the wrong lipstick or asks to borrow a scarf reserved especially for this occasion. The women snap at one another, on the verge of tears. Finally, we smooth the last silk, zip the last skirt. As if in defiance, the women wear heels; their legs peep from under airy floral dresses that leave bare skin open to the night. When we step outside, the rain has cleared and the night feels fresh, a few clouds scattering over a thin moon. We take it as a good sign and walk to the church, picking our way carefully around puddles.

When we enter the courtyard, so many have gathered that we have to join the crowd outside. Men pile firewood on the ground. Priests process, swinging incense. We have arrived earlier than my family ever did, and we stick together, warm where our bodies touch, cold where air creeps in. Finally, in the last few minutes before midnight, the lights cut out. Each of us clutches a candle, our own piece of fire. The glow rises inside the church and reaches us in a hail of candles, neighbors catching each other's light. The warmth moves down our fingers. With great gulps of breath we sing *Christos anesti* and the words vibrate inside me, as recognizable as childhood. The men light the bonfire. Everyone throws firecrackers. Loud noise pierces the night. Faces flash like eerie masks, grinning to drive back darkness.

Because human beings have grown careless, forgetting the way we once carefully balanced what we wanted with what we owed, we have let a plague out of a jar. Digging into the warm womb of the world, men tried to fashion their own star, believing, because God looks like men, men look like God. They brought fire that lights without healing; burns without teasing out spring. In the green glow of the sparklers, the Easter revelers shout at the night, as if to say, *We meant this by fire, this by light. We never meant the other.*

We carry our candles through the streets; they flicker into the distance as people move off. When we reach the apartment, we find the table already laid out carefully: white plates with gold trim, a heavy cream tablecloth. The settings are spaced neatly, one for each member of the family including me, silverware and linen napkins aligned. The room looks festive, ready as every year for those who have sacrificed and survived to share another triumphant return of life. At the center of the table, a bowl filled with red eggs gleams.

When we had our Easters in America, we always played a game with the eggs. Each person picked one, weighing it in the palm, seeing how it felt. Then, commencing with the eldest male, one diner challenged another, bumping first one side of the egg and then the other against the egg held in the other's palm. If yours cracked, your opponent could hit you back. The survivor would play against the next winner, all the way down through the women and children. The person who held the winning egg received luck throughout the year. Beginning with the prominent, the round finished at the bottom of the pile. Obviously designed by women, the pecking order ensured that blessings landed on young girls while seeming to defer to male elders. Why did none of the men ever notice the pattern? To go first, they abandoned good fortune.

We click glasses full of ouzo and break the eggs. The youngest Soula cracks one side of my egg and I crack hers. With one good half each, she holds hers steady and I tap my smooth side against hers. Her egg shatters into a web of red and white, and the Soula wraps mine in paper, telling me to keep my luck safe. Looking at my half-broken egg reminds me how much we hold each other's future in our hands.

After we break the eggs, my aunt brings out her *magiritsa*. I suddenly feel tired; half an egg, some bread, and two glasses of ouzo slosh around in my stomach. Everyone else lifts their spoons, full of appetite. I look down into the bowl. Segments of arteries, dark chunks of liver, round noodles of innards, bump against the green onions. Pushing the meat into a pile, I sip on the broth. My cousins express concern, ask if I am unwell. I tell them my stomach hurts and pick at a piece of bread while they consume the rest of the meal. I cannot eat the real *magiritsa*.

The next day, the family plans to picnic on the plot of land they own on the bay at the foot of the mountain. The first time I went there, after abandoning my language program two summers ago, the land looked rich and abundant. The summer blew the last leaves of winter out of my body and I stayed with them for a month, camping and cooking, swimming in the morning, sleeping in the afternoon. We ate watermelon lifted off the back of trucks that trundled through the back roads every day, speakers broadcasting a melodious invitation, *kalo krio karpouzi, good cold melon*. Sometimes we mixed it with slices of feta cheese, the sweet and the salty. Bloated and sticky, we ran into the sea and floated in water clear all the way down to the multicolored pebbles ten feet below us. The air seemed to sparkle, rolling off the mountain like a fresh breath. Now, as we pull out of Larissa in two carloads, the air carries a sluggish haze from the smoke of last night's bonfires. It has a gray tinge to it, like lung tissue.

An hour later, we reach the spot. New grass sprouts under the trees; the aunts open the small cement hut that houses the only sink. When we lived out there, the uncles and aunts put their cots in the hut; the girls shared a giant tent, which we have left home.

All around us, neighbors have erected spits and tables. While the women fix the equipment, the men pull a skinned lamb out of a trunk, skewering it with an iron stake. A metal handle rotates the spit, allowing the heat to baste the outsides into an even, leathery crispness. Everyone takes a turn at the handle except me. I linger in the shack next to the girls preparing the salad, watching them slice tomatoes in their hands, cutting them neatly without ever putting them down. They dispatch a cucumber and an onion quickly and slice the feta into even chunks. When Costas calls to bring some garlic, I hurry across the ground. The air feels humid; it sticks to me like an unwanted friend.

The Soulas set the table under the tree. Smoke from all the roasting lambs drifts overhead; the leaves lift and fall in a slow breeze. Yiorgos eats a piece of raw garlic, crushing it in his gold back molars; Costas opens a bottle of wine. He fills each glass and we all toast; fresh lamb steams on a platter surrounded by bowls of salad, bread, and fruit. When I swallow the lamb I wonder if it glows in my stomach. The haze obscures the mountains above us; if I could leave the table and start hiking, I might reach Retsiani by sundown. To keep myself sitting down, I have to grip the bottom of the chair. This moment has waited for me all year, sitting under the shadow of my grandparents' villages, surrounded by a table of my kin, eating an Easter feast. Now I find I have lost my appetite completely.

After lunch, they drive me to the bus station. I kiss them all good-bye, hugging them as if I will never see them again. They hand me plastic bags filled with fruit, ask if I have enough money, jostle the bags, joke about my trip. Used to seeing daughters come and go, they have practiced the short good-byes and elaborate greetings those left behind need to survive. When I climb on the bus, I close my eyes and keep them closed until slamming brakes wake me.

Midway to Athens, a traffic jam appears in the middle of no-where. We find ourselves behind a long line of parked cars and buses, stretching into the distance. When I look out the window, fruit groves and empty fields offer only the zap of cicadas. One of the men stands up and says someone should investigate. The driver heaves himself out the door and does not return. Some of the other men leave to find him.

Finally, one of them pokes his head in the window and says, *Afti einai ei xthesini anthropi*. The words in English sound flat, missing the way the *phi* caresses, how the *xth* gathers against the teeth, like a good piece of fruit: *Those are yesterday people*. The cars on the road have been there since the night before, when the road was washed out in the flood; because of the holiday, no one could come to remove the mud. Now, they tell us, tractors are on the way. Some of the drivers have contacted distant relations among the local farmers, who have agreed to clear the road.

Within an hour, the mud has been lifted. When the engine rattles on the bus, I know I am leaving behind a language that can create poetry in the simple story of a stuck line of cars, my part in a land that has survived so many disasters.

This is how we lose magic, generation by generation. My grandmother made Easter eggs burnished a deep red, dedicated the first one to the Virgin Mary. Now sacred, this egg could not be thrown away. After Easter each year, she would have to find ground to bury it. She was a woman who had come from a land pocked with the buried eggs of her foremothers. She moved across the waters and had to entrust her offerings to the shifting soil of New York. When her husband lost his business and they lost their home, she had to tuck them up behind the fire escapes of smaller and smaller apartments. The thread connecting her to the earth and across time loosened and snapped.

Now my mother uses supermarket dye to make her deep burgundy eggs. She has kept the iron pan her own mother used, its edges permanently stained, like a red watermark. She puts her eggs into bread, which she shapes like a cross and passes out to her friends and family—Greeks and non-Greeks, believers and nonbelievers. The egg for the Virgin Mary has gotten lost with all the others. As for me, I have never yet dyed an egg red, but every year, in whatever country or city I am in, I find a Greek church, and I know the words of the song at midnight.

Priests Will Faint

If the beginnings of myths fracture in too many different directions, the endings are even worse. Everyone agrees that Theseus leaves Ariadne on the island without food or water. His trajectory is clear and straight after that: battle, kingship, love, right until his death. As for Ariadne, does she throw a rock or wave good-bye like an idiot? Does she die of thirst or is she rescued by Dionysus? I know which version I prefer.

Europa, another daughter of a king, attracts the fancy of Zeus. He disguises himself as a bull, with a white hide and flowers in his horns. Nibbling on the grass, pawing delicately as a ballerina, he lures Europa to his side. A big girl with strong thighs, she decides to climb on his back when he bends down for her. No one disputes what happens next. The bull's gentleness vanishes; he snorts and tosses his head and gallops across the sea, carrying her with him. Does she shriek and cling to his mane? Or does she toss back her hair and enjoy the splash of salt water on her bare legs? After they make love, she gives birth to a continent. Whether or not you picture her collapsed in a heap of shame or lying on the grass, head against the flank of her lover, chewing on a long piece of grass, determines everything else. Endings count.

Do I have to write this part? It is only fair to tell you: after all this, I did go back to Glyphada. But it is not as bad as you think, different from what you expect.

After Easter, I return to the American bar one more time. Maybe it is to do a story; a rise in terrorist threats has not kept the American soldiers from their off-duty rituals: *Babes and Beer, not Bombs, at Bobby's*. Maybe I don't have an excuse. With the usual bad luck, I have found Steve, who has invited me to join some friends at a local taverna.

We arrive after midnight: three dancers from an international troupe, two basketball players, me. At the adjacent table, a man eats alone. He has dark curly hair and wears jeans and a T-shirt. A leather jacket drapes the back of his chair. By the time we finish the first bottle of wine, Steve has his right hand on my knee while whispering to the dancer on his left, a tall blonde with large cheekbones. He asks how she feels about sleeping with others. His left hand drops; now he grips both of us. The man from the table looks up from his bill. *Love*, he says, *is something sacred, not a game*. I rise to go to the bathroom and slip out the front door. I am standing looking at the empty highway when the man from the table next to us walks by me. He asks if I need a lift.

We are on his motorcycle driving back to Athens. He instructs me to hold on to his body, and at first my arms cross his torso formally, as at a dance. The leather warms under my fingers and I relax into his back. When I look up at last, a late full moon has risen ahead of us. We drive into Ommonia and buy sandwiches. Then he asks if I would like a tour of the city.

Under the moonlight, the dirty apartment buildings have all returned to their original startling white. The wide boulevards sleep soundly. As if we were a boat on a dark river, we wind our way along them, ignoring the flashing yellow traffic lights. The bike carries us into the hills and then down into the canyons again. He takes me to secret parks, where he tells me about the statues dedicated to hero thieves of the War of Independence or shows me bunkers where resistance fighters held out in the Second World War. He points to places where bodies fell from starvation, shows how the trees were stripped of leaves. We pass the Jewish museum, run by a solitary American, someone he knows, and then ride by the oldest church in the city, circling the market stalls covered in cloth. All night, his body shifts under my hands, muscles like rocks heating in the sun. His hair brushes my cheek, silky, chamomile-scented. He offers his broad back and I can hear his heart beating through the leather. When he hands me off the bike, his palm feels steady and gentle, the grip of a man holding a child. Somewhere under the moon, I have fallen in love with him, but my veins run gently as a summer stream.

At dawn, he stops in front of a *cafenion*. The old woman proprietor has just opened, and she lifts the chairs off the tables with a grunt. He helps her finish and she welcomes us in. She fetches the day's first bread from the bakery next door and gives us sweet coffee with hot milk. While we eat he tells me his name, Alkibiades. He teaches philosophy at the university, a full professor. He has just completed three months of research on Mount Athos, investigating ancient prophecy.

Why do you think they keep women away from there? he asks me. I know that the rules against women are so strict that the monks will not allow even female animals to breach their peninsula, eating only roosters and rams. They maintain it like an island fortress, as if protecting themselves from a great danger. While no woman has trodden that rock in six hundred years, any man from any country is welcome without invitation.

Alkibiades tells me that the monks have preserved copies of very ancient manuscripts, chronicling the rituals of the old cults of the goddess, and that they have suppressed this information ruthlessly.

While researching Byzantine religious visionaries, he picked the wrong tome, a dusty manuscript. After this accidental discovery, he secretly dug further. The manuscripts predict the future, and they underline the same message: as long as Greece strangles its women, the land will remain blighted, bereft of blessings. He plans to write a book about his findings.

Then he asks me about myself. His face opens in the early light, turns to me fully. A shadow beard stains his jaw; when he laughs, hazel eyes ray with lines. Unlike almost everyone else I have met this year, he does not seem to have his own agenda. While he listens, his eyes stick to my face, never wandering. I tell him everything, including what happened with Steve. Unlike Sam, he offers no judgment, just the comment that he's seen that guy before and developed a strong dislike of him, which is why he interrupted our conversation and why he thought he should offer me a lift. Long after our coffee has grown cold, my voice scratches my throat and he says he will take me home.

Because Alkibiades knows endings rewrite beginnings, when we reach my apartment, he does not invite himself in. Smiling, he regards me through thick lashes, pulling my hair back from my face as if I were beautiful, not the wreck I seem to be. My smile back marks my gratitude and my love, my launch off into new waters. I hug him deeply, for a long time. He kisses me on both cheeks, delicate satin butterflies brushing my skin. We shake hands good-bye, an in-joke.

The old monks are not as clever as they thought. One day, enough men will go to their fortress, not as allies but as spies, and they will take out their knowledge, their power, word by word, line by line. They will change the ending and transform the story.

Without ever knowing about Alkibiades, my mother confessed something strange, years after I left Greece. In Athens, she had one more boyfriend, a man she never mentioned, a police officer who had been a resistance fighter in the war. *I never knew anyone like him; he was such a wonderful man, so good to me and impossible for me.* When he was in the Nazi camp, he survived by secretly keeping strong, doing furtive calisthenics at night in his cell, and by planting vegetables in the prison yard. He was wise and funny and told her she was beautiful, that he loved her hair and eyes, loved her gap-tooth. *No one ever said that to me before. He taught me that love in the first moments of the morning was the sweetest love of all.* She said she saw him once in New York where he had come for a conference, but that she had just started work and things had changed. Another kind of love lingered in my mother's past, and she had never told me about it. What did I have to uncover in myself before that story was ready for me?

By coming to Greece, I had fished into my mother's story, trying to find the beginning. Down in the water, I felt a current pull me, believing its black water. After Easter, I began to swim in the other direction and released a tide of stories, new versions of what really happened.

When my grandmother first arrived in America, she did not settle immediately in New York. At first, she followed her older brother to New Hampshire. Her first job in America, my mother says, was threading a spindle in a factory for *seven American dollars and a buffalo nickel.* Her teenage fingers, nimble with years of sorting herbs and seeds, flew across the table. The factory would have been a square room, filled with other girls, none of them speaking English. Walking to work in the morning, my grandmother must have felt the dawn urge her forward, her first money in her pocket, her first American steps, free from the eyes of the villagers watching her shuffle. My mother says she still has her mother's union card; she promises to send it to me. She has kept the card her whole life, a promise unfulfilled.

When she finally reached New York, my grandmother enrolled in a public college to take courses in English. Although the story about how she refused to go to the post office herself, sending her children to drop off official papers, reveals a woman hunted by her own fear, she started down her path bravely. She traveled alone through the crowds, jostling against strangers, holding her books. English tasted like a new peach, the first of the season, wet and sweet. One day a man followed her home, and after that, her older brother and cousins, the men who decided for all of them, said they would not allow it. The first hour she passed at home with her sisters instead of in the classroom, she could picture her teacher leading the lesson, the words that might have been hers scurrying away. When the hour closed, she heard a metallic slam, reverberating down the years of her life. My grandmother hid that story behind the official one we had always heard: how she met my grandfather through village connections, married him, and launched her troubles.

One version of my grandmother's loss shadowed my year in Greece. Because of the silence that ended her life, her pain and her early death, she left behind a strangled voice, a lost village, a broken connection. Perhaps she mourned her mother's house, the herbs in the fields, the sky in all its abundance. Another possibility presents itself; maybe when she got to the new world, she felt desire nudging her, making her want to run, hard and fast. Perhaps, instead of wanting her village, she wanted the world. She felt as far from it in New York, behind the metal gates and cement torrents, as she had felt in Retsiani, hemmed in by *ta matia tou kosmou*, the rules of her ancestors, without language to lead her like a thread through the maze, an escape plan. All the while, I thought the longing pointed to a return, a reunion with history; perhaps her legacy in my blood, passed through my mother, was a swift forward momentum.

Although I knew about her childhood in Queens and her years in Manhattan, I had never pictured the day my mother packed her things and crossed from one island to the other. Now I see her putting the books in boxes that her mother used to scold her about. She straightens her back and finds her mother standing in the doorway, watching her. The tears in my grandmother's eyes rise for so many things: her daughter's leaving, the impending loneliness, living in a house without another woman's company. Maybe my grandmother also regretted the lid my mother taped over the books, the words that never would be hers. Kissing the cross around her daughter's neck, and then her cheek, she blessed her and released her.

When the borrowed truck blinked out of the tunnel and my mother saw the small city towers refracting the early summer light, she knew she had finally crossed the right water.

Heroines' adventures end abruptly—they marry, bear a soldier, offend a god. It is up to us to discover the lines that run on after the man, after the island, after the escape from the houses of their fathers.

Virgins and Goddesses

Under the Acropolis in Athens, at the back of a cave, lies a shrine to the Virgin Mary, candles reflecting off an icon hung against the rock. An ancient Athenian lady, so round that her body has lost all shape and so dark that her skin blends into the black wool of her widow's scarf, tends the site. She sleeps on a cot against the wall, waking in the night to keep the candles lit. She rolls out of bed in the morning in her long johns and wool socks, puts on her slippers, and slides a candle into an iron holder, just as the last candle she placed in the middle of the night sputters. If you went there in 1955, you might see the same woman, or a woman who looked so much like her it could be the same woman. If you go there twenty years from now, you will see her again.

The shrine under the Acropolis originated long before Christianity, before the golden age of Athens, before the Acropolis itself. When the northern tribes invaded, they encountered goddess worshipers who ruled the large flat rock overlooking the sea. Drunk and violent, with better weapons, the invaders reduced the inhabitants to a small remnant. Zeus thundered over the horizon and Hera receded into a carping middle-aged housewife. The last of her tribe hid in the heart of the rock, commencing a long tradition of secret worship, so ancient its origins have vanished. Even the women who light the candles with such fidelity do not realize they preserve a small fragment of a large cloth, once a thriving worldwide religion.

The Acropolis rose with its elegant columns, and the statue of Pallas Athena, that tomboy rebel, stood above the cave in her golden armor and her biceps. The shrine under the rock lived its quiet steady life. The Caryatids with their demure faces, locked in marble servitude for what must have seemed like forever, blushed in marble; still the shrine burned incense. Christianity marched in and threw heathens out of temples but overlooked the harmless site, hardly noticing when the women just started calling their goddess by another name. The site changed hands again and became a mosque. The women burrowed farther underground. In 1687, a Venetian soldier lit a cannon and sent a ball hurtling through space. The Turks housed all their munitions in the marble fortress; the soldier consoled himself that war is war when he saw the shards of wood showering down the hill. Although the Acropolis lost its roof, the women returned to the cave a few years later and began again. While they were there, a city built itself.

Feminine power is hidden under the Greek culture, as in so many others: a shrine under a rock, the distant rush of an underground stream. It survives munitions explosions and urban catastrophes, while it lights a candle day after patient day, waiting for daughters to follow the light.

Athens has succumbed to fallout chaos. People want to buy as much uncontaminated food as they can grab. In the supermarkets, riots break out over the last can. I hear stories about rich matrons buying extra freezers to store the frozen food they hoard. Eleni tells me I must take a shower every time I go outside, and in the beginning I wash my clothes religiously. I do not think about the water.

At the office, a woman freelance writer who drops in occasionally grabs me for lunch. Years ago, she was living in Toronto and fell in love with a handsome Greek cabdriver, who told her he wanted to be a photographer. They married and tried working together for a while; he made pictures and she wrote. After they had a baby, differences over child-rearing split them and they divorced. He moved back to Greece. When their daughter reached seven, he invited her to visit him. The child flew over in June. By September she had not returned. When the woman phoned her ex-husband, he told her that by Greek law a child needed the consent of both parents to leave the country and he would never give his. She boarded a plane and moved to Athens.

Now, she tells me, she would like to take her twelve-year-old child out of Greece. *We don't even speak the same language.* She worries the radiation will enter the food chain; cans and freezers cannot stop it. The poison will last for generations and it will work its way up into everyone's body, no matter what they do. She urges me to leave. I tell her I think I will, although probably not for the reason she believes.

Leo suggests I write about the riots. He speculates that if we exaggerate the violence, we can compete with other items from around Europe. I tell him I am quitting. He tries to talk me out of it, offers me an above-the-counter position. *I'll pull some strings for you at the head office.* Thanking him politely, I shake his hand. When I step out the door, I do not look back.

After that, I realize I am really leaving. While the land returns to summer like a flower opening to light, I slowly say good-bye. Meanwhile, Athens reassembles itself—tables appear on the sidewalk, clothes become lighter, the first tourists appear carrying backpacks, harbingers in shorts and T-shirts. Having suffered so many disasters, the Greeks quickly forget Easter's blooms. Men open their shirts four buttons and women hike up their skirts, bouncing on the way to work.

Isabella and I celebrate with a farewell trip to the sea, passing Steve's stop without a quiver. We lie out on rocks, both of us soaking up the rays that burn gold sparks on the water. Ari takes over my apartment, and I move in with Emily and Francisco, my one bag still just one bag. I call up the philosopher and wish him well. Eleni and I share a bottle of wine, and I thank her for all she has done for me. I have dinner with Sam. With summer, Greece seems familiar and strange, a mirage again.

The day before I buy my ticket to Los Angeles, my mother calls me. She is coming to Greece.

When my mother arrives off the plane, she looks like a ghost come to life. The air buzzes around her. Her lipstick leaves a red poppy on my cheek; when she embraces me, clouds of perfume rise off her silk dress. She tells me she has come to find Daphne. When she discovered I planned to leave, she thought it might be her last chance. She has never mentioned Daphne's living in Greece; I only ever heard of her as *my friend Daphne I grew up with in New York.* Handing her bags to the taxi driver, who hefts them with a groan into his trunk, she tells me Daphne was her best and greatest woman friend. She has been waiting all this time to contact her. Then she adds, *We haven't spoken to each other in thirty years.* Her voice trembles.

Stavros and Meropi, the cousins who put me up when I arrived, have invited us both back to their apartment. I could not ask my mother to stay on Francisco's floor. During the year, I visited them periodically; Meropi fed me *pasticcio* when I looked a little pale, heaping my plate with noodles, tomato, and ground beef. Stavros would swing into the kitchen and ask about my work, but we felt awkward together. I had declared myself to be one of theirs but did not follow the rules. Now that I am returning to America, we can rearrange our relationships, back into visitor and native, outsider and insider. Together with my mother I am once again both relative and stranger, doubly deserving of *philoxenia.* While they greet my mother with loud kisses, their daughters pull on my leg, showing off their new toys.

A tenant has vacated the upstairs apartment, and they donate it to us for the week. Although I have never seen her far from a washing machine, now I watch my mother wash her silk dress in the sink and hang it on the balcony to dry. She arranges her expensive soaps and shampoos on the tiny counter in the bathroom and buys a converter for her iron and blow-dryer. When Stavros and Meropi invite us down for dinner, she does not listen to protests and moves through the kitchen, marshaling the children, helping to cook. I watch her move with ease in this environment, taking her sense of herself with her everywhere. I wonder how it becomes so easy.

On the second day, my mother announces the time has come to call Daphne. I cannot believe Daphne exists in this city, only a few miles away, like a character in a myth who has come to life. Her childhood with my mother always appeared too distant to be real. I had never really heard more than the outline of my mother's year in Greece: her arrival, cashing in her ticket, her engagement, her return. Now the details start to leak from their tight container. Daphne, I discover, wrote her for years. She sent her letters to New York and California and then stopped writing, never having received a letter in return.

Daphne was so beautiful, my mother says. *You have to understand. I married your father and moved to California. I got fat.* Here she reaches up to push her hair back over her eyes. Gray peppers her curls, and her deep green eyes reflect the light. I think she looks beautiful, as always. I have just begun to understand how a secret life can undermine what appears strong on the surface, the way water can eat the foundations of a rock until it becomes an empty cave.

My mother has an address for Daphne from one of the last letters. Not trusting it, she tries the operator and double-checks the name. The operator gives her a number. When my mother calls, she asks me to hold her hand. I hear her scream with recognition and talk rapidly in Greek and English over the phone. They arrange a lunch date. Of course, she wants me to accompany her.

The next morning, my mother rises early to prepare. She pulls out all her best props—her Beverly Hills clothing, her perfume. She looks glamorous, pale gray silk and matching eye shadow. My cousin offers to drive us over, but of course my mother wants to arrive in style. She hires a taxi and directs it to Kolonaki. As we drive higher and higher, I imagine all the times I have prowled these streets in the last year, how often I met Isabella for coffee in the snobby café even when it was more than we could afford. We pass the offices of the magazines where the models worked, the bars where we would be offered expensive drinks. Under the rubble of my year in Greece, older layers hide. When the taxi driver delivers us to the marble-fronted apartment building, my mother pulls back. Her mind holds a picture of Daphne at nineteen, her hourglass figure and porcelain skin. Shaking her head slightly, she sucks in her cheeks, powders her face, and gives the driver a big tip.

When we get to the door, my mother asks me to ring the bell for her. Her hand holding mine feels moist. We take the elevator and find the one door at the top of the building, the penthouse suite, and ring. The door opens. For a moment all I can see is creamy white carpeting and gold-tinted mirrors. A tall woman in a white silk dress stands in front of it all, her head topped with enormous honey-colored beehive hair, her ears tagged with heavy gold shell earrings. Her liquid blue eyes well with tears. She embraces my mother, and then she engulfs me in a pair of strong arms, crushing me against a giant Chanel-scented chest. When she pulls back, I can see that she must have once been very beautiful. Now, her face has tiny red lines webbing her cheeks, unhappiness etched on either side of her mouth. I think of my mother's wrinkles, soft pillows where she has smiled.

Darling, Daphne says, her voice husky in the way of women who have smoked their whole lives. *This must be—?* She looks at me fully. My mother has already warned me not to explain how long I have been in Greece, that I was here a whole year without getting in touch, without calling.

She leads us into the living room, lined with plush carpets and gilt cabinetry. Gesturing with her long fingernails, she explains how new government regulations have impacted the textile business; her husband has an ulcer from juggling producers and distributors. Although she apologizes for her humble offerings, her husband's wealth speaks for itself. Daphne seats us on a white leather couch and sends an aproned maid into the kitchen to fetch us coffee, which arrives on a bronze tray painted with scenes of classical Greece. Daphne squints at my mother, who gazes back at her. She lights a thin brown cigarillo and takes a deep puff.

Do you know how many letters I sent you, hoping one of them would get through? Not someone for small talk, she launches into a dramatic recounting of how she waited and waited, how she felt her heart break. *I am still not willing to forgive you.* My mother says, *Oh, Daphne!* and takes her hand. Daphne lets her fingers wilt in my mother's palm. *However, I am willing to forget and put it behind us now.* Twisting her cigarillo stub into an embossed ashtray, she brushes ash off her knee. *Here, let me show you something.* Each word sounds bitten off and chewed slowly, continental English with a slight hint of New York, nothing Greek. She slides back one of the mirrored glass doors and pulls out a small shoebox. The simple cardboard looks out of place in such elegant surroundings. Almost as if she can read my mind, she says, *Of course we have to keep this place like this, for my husband's reputation, but I have never cared about any of it, one way or the other.* Before opening the box, Daphne lights another cigarillo. Then she takes off the lid to reveal a pile of letters, faded blue aerogram envelopes, neatly wrapped. She lifts them up. Underneath, I can already see the dark outline of photographs.

These are the letters that were returned unopened from the States. Here—she hands them to my mother, who hands them to me—*you*

242

might as well have them now. My mother looks at me and raises her eyebrows. *And these, darling, are all the photographs of my life with your mother. Have you ever seen them before?*

Of course I have not. A bouffant siren, Daphne flashes a whole new vista in front of me. All this time, at the top of the hill I walked up every day to work, the stories were waiting for me. Daphne, the one my mother left behind, has guarded the source, tended its bubbles. Here is the one of my mother standing in the road of her father's village, dressed in a black woolly skirt and black sweater. She wears boots, and her legs are scratched. On her back she carries a bundle of sticks. Her tanned face beams into the camera. In another photo, she sits next to a younger, more Marilyn Monroe version of Daphne in a booth, two men escorting them. They lean casually against the rich dark leather, and the table in front of them is laid in smooth, silky white. Elegantly cut glasses, half filled with liquid, cluster around an ashtray. The smoke from still-burning cigarettes curls around their eyes. A sophisticated crowd, they offer bored half-smiles to the camera. Finally, Daphne hands me the picture of my mother leaning down to hug a tiny bird of a woman, dressed all in black. My mother kisses her, and her lips are puckered, full, suspended in air. The woman scowls out at the camera, as if she does not know how to smile. *This is my grandmother*, my mother tells me.

Daphne spends the rest of the lunch filling my mother in on her stories. While we crunch lettuce, a rare romaine, she describes moving her mother into her house while trying to raise five sons. In the back room, her mother built a shrine, spending all her time at the religious markets to buy new icons to decorate the walls, red holders for the candles she lit daily. *My mother said a prayer for me every day. Why? What did she think was wrong with my life? I gave her everything she wanted, but by the end of her life she only ate bread and water.* Daphne says when her mother died she felt relief. My mother asks about children. *Five sons, Daphne, how wonderful*. Daphne laughs.

Don't give me that Greek bullshit. Do you know how much I wanted daughters? She looks at me. *Those sons hover like vultures, waiting for their father to die. They've already spent their inheritance on women and booze.* My mother asks if they married. *Married, divorced, remarried. The youngest are still angels, but how can I trust them after their brothers?*

My mother trades a few stories, not too many. The conversation takes on the natural rhythm of two friends resuming where they left off only the day before. The past slips between the eddies of their words, forgotten. Daphne offers us a plate of sticky honey-and-nut pastries. We tour the apartment, the interior rooms much more simple, in shades of green and blue. *We have an apartment in London, and I buy everything at the Harrods sales.* At the threshold of the guest room, Daphne insists we stay the night. *In fact, you should leave your apartment and stay here.* My mother refuses, her voice as steely as Daphne's. She even lies, telling her our plane leaves sooner than it does. At the door, our departure is delayed by noisy, demonstrative hugs, lipstick kisses, dramatic sighs. My mother promises to write, and Daphne checks twice to make sure she has my mother's number. Daphne's driver takes us home, so we hold our tongues until we reach my cousins'. In the apartment, my mother flings off her heels and throws herself back on the bed. *Oh, God, she hasn't changed, bossy as ever.* She sounds like a loving but exasperated sister, the first time I have ever heard her use that tone. My mother is taking off her slip, and she looks at me as if I were an image, the picture of her whole life from end to end. *I haven't done so badly*, she says.

(After this, Daphne and my mother talk on the phone every month from wherever they are in the world: Los Angeles to Athens, London to New York. Many years later Daphne comes to my wedding. Magnificent in a two-piece tailored mauve suit, she sits at a table with some VIP friends of my husband, still smoking a cigarillo in a long ivory holder. She entertains everyone with her husky voice and afterward writes us a large check. Too broke to hire a room, we hold the postwedding party in our apartment, weeding out the polite guests from the committed revelers. To our surprise, Daphne joins the party, one of a huge crowd squeezed into two small rooms, everyone wildly drunk; for months afterward my husband and I will try to get the cigarette ash out of the carpet. She and my mother stand in a corner together, talking and laughing over the noise. Sloughing off their society-matron propriety, they become the girls they were, eyeing the men who fling off their shirts, trading comments about the other women's clothes.)

The next morning, my mother makes a few more phone calls: relatives, people she has not seen since we came as a family when I was sixteen. She has not come this far not to visit the village, and she tells me we will make a loop: rent a car and go north, and then, telling everyone we have to leave five days before we really do, take a trip south to the seashore, all by ourselves.

We are planning to leave the next day, so Stavros tells us he wants to take us out into the city. Somehow, I do not want to travel to familiar places, and when he says the Plaka, I cringe. We find an expensive restaurant, a place I have never been on my scrimped budget, where the waiters in neat polyester swivel their hips for the tourists. At any moment I expect someone to break plates. The food has a plastic tinge of precooked meals, no glistening oil, and the bread tastes stale, but a wall of windows reveals a panoramic view of the Acropolis. After lunch, my mother tells him we want to explore. The kids kick each other and start to scream. Stavros and Meropi agree to leave us if we promise to take a cab back (in the family circle again, they worry about our safety; protected women need protection). Seeing them off, my mother sighs with relief. *How lovely to be alone together.*

We amble down the Plaka and find the flea market, the weekly spread of stalls selling clothes and kitchen goods. Far from the tourist lanes, the cheap practical items attract Athenians, who bargain hard. At the fringes, less fortunate sellers spread sheets on the ground and display eclectic offerings, knickknacks found, hoarded, or stolen—used clothes, an old stereo, plastic vases. My mother halts in front of a toothless old man selling battered icons. She picks up a frame with a printed picture glued to the surface, frayed paper and chipped wood. *These are my mother's saints.* She buys it from the man and gives the icon to me.

Two men gaze out from the picture, their almond eyes the sad brown of all Byzantine saints. Dressed in matching robes, with identical beards, they are alike but not the same, brothers. Fourth-century doctors who were martyred for their faith, they watch over the sick, patron saints of those who pray for healing. *My mother prayed and prayed to them.* The saints stare at me as if to say, *Sorry we couldn't help her.*

I carried them with me for years from place to place. Perhaps I misinterpreted their message; they wanted to tell me not to trust my first impression. My grandmother did not pray to the saints only for herself, she prayed for other people. More than knowing how to cure the evil eye, my grandmother knew how to cure evil, how to take others' pain away, how to soften suffering. She learned this from her mother, and her mother learned from hers before her. In the mountains, she would have known the name of every herb, what to use to take away fever, to end heartache, to cure madness. Locked into the streets of Queens, where only a few brave trees grow, she still practiced her ancient knowledge. Women flocked from all over the community to see her, even non-Greeks who heard about her from their friends.

The next morning, we leave for our trip. Stavros has given us elaborate instructions for exiting the city, watching as we write it all down. As soon as we pull away from the apartment, my mother tells me to chuck his guidelines and get out the map; we will chart our own course. *Here's the thing about Greeks*, she says. *If they insist, you agree. Then you do what you want anyway.*

We open the windows and feel the wind loosening our hair, freeing our skin. The trip has strict boundaries: only six days in the north—two for the city, and two for each of the villages. The wisdom of this plan becomes clear as soon as we arrive. The Soulas dance around us, admiring my mother's clothes, weaving my arms with theirs. The uncles stutter like shy boys, young again as they blush at my mother's kiss. Everyone complains dramatically when we tell them we only have two nights. They want us to stay for weeks, but my mother has come to Greece for her own reasons and I have already said good-bye. After one day in each house, three meals each, distributing and receiving gifts, we kiss everyone loudly and get back into our car.

On the road up to the mountain, my mother and I sing over the radio, wailing together. We have started in the late morning; the beet fields steam gently in the rising sun. Few other cars pass us. When a tailgater pulls up behind us in a tanklike battered sixties car, complete with fins, my mother ignores him. She tries her LA tricks, hitting and releasing the brake to scare him off. He speeds when we speed, slows when we slow. Finally, she pulls over to let him pass. I catch a glimpse of him as he roars by, a middle-aged man with slicked-back hair. On the single-lane highway, he assumes his place in front of us and immediately slows down. My mother curses. *Malaka!* She waits for him to resume speed, but he slows further. Finally, she passes him, giving him a wide berth. Again, he rides up behind us, sitting on our backs. Her temper rises to the surface, boils over. My mother speeds in front of him and throws her palm up and curses again. *Na xatheis. Go to hell.* In Greece, an open palm carries more weight than a curse; he drops behind us. Soon he returns, and this time my mother swerves to the curb, slamming on the brakes. We slump back in our seats while the car clicks and cools. He disappears into the distance. *Sometimes I hate this country. He just couldn't stand the fact that we were two women, driving alone.*

(Five or six years later, I have returned to Los Angeles to take a job I despise in a large media corporation. I live in an apartment not far from the sea, and I drive everywhere. One day, a business meeting near my house finishes early, and I decide to grab a bite before heading to my next destination. An hour's distance separates the two offices, Torrance in the south, Thousand Oaks in the north, and I feel pressured, in a hurry. My panic drains out of me as I step into my deserted apartment. Eating my sandwich, I drift into my bedroom and pick up an inviting blue cover, a book of poems by a famous modern Greek poet, Odysseus Elytis, *What I Love*. Opening it, I begin to read: *Somewhere there is an island which always dreamed me:* When my watch reminds me of the time, my pulse starts racing again. I throw the book into the car with me and begin to drive. The words echo in my head, swirling dangerously. On the freeway, I glance at the cover again, gulping poems between traffic jams. By the time I cross over the Santa Monicas to the valley, I am hiccuping sobs and giggles while the traffic zooms by me. Finally, I toss the book into the back, and it takes me until Ventura to pull myself together. My working day ends with the meeting. On the way back, I roll off my nylons and slip off my heels. I hitch my skirt over my thighs and rub my bare feet on the carpet. I open the windows and pick up speed, plotting how to quit my job. Then a strange thing happens. I am on the freeway, breaking the speed limit. In the distance the golden hills shine in the late-afternoon sun. The air off the tarmac tastes warm and salty. I think about how far all the cells in my body have come to be in this moment, making these choices. And then I think if I turn around now I will see them, and I am afraid to look in my rearview mirror, to find the back seat crowded

248

with ghosts, the tiny birdlike women dressed in black, the voices who want me to turn up the radio, the ones who love the feeling of the car under their hands, the hard grip of the steering wheel, the ones who want me to step on the gas.)

When we climb the road to Retsiani, we find the house my mother's uncle still owns. His wife is like a little bird, bent and delicate. She serves us sweet coffee and grapefruit rind preserved in honey. My grandmother's brother looks healthy, well-fed, with a full head of thick white hair. He tells us about the farm, the land he has acquired. My mother describes her children, telling him about universities and American education. He hears my mother explain about how well I have done in school, and without looking at me he says, *Tell her not to think too hard, it will spoil her beauty.* I am helping to clear the table and I look at my mother, who winks at me and smiles. Why argue? We know we can leave any time; that freedom has been bought for us at the cost of someone else's life.

After lunch, they take us outside for a tour of the property. We see the small hut where my grandmother was born, a low-lying whitewashed building with a red tiled roof, now turned into a stable. He tells us how the family once lived there, all together; the girls must have felt like gold no one could trade, a useless treasure unless exchanged for something like a cow or a field, practical and edible. My mother and I stare at the stable, where everything began. Chickens run across the straw, chased by a rooster. She asks about the Kalidis girls. One of them married a judge, he tells us, another married a poet, and the third married a diplomat and went to live in another country. It is the first time I hear my mother talk about the relatives on her mother's side, and I wonder if they meant so much to her, as much as Daphne, that she had to let them go. When my uncle shakes my hand good-bye, his calloused palms feel like hard wood.

When we reach Nivolyani, my grandfather's village, only a few families emerge onto their porches. Many of the houses remain shut, now holiday homes. One of my grandfather's brothers had a son who remained in the village, the last one to work the land. Because this cousin has two sons, I have only seen him occasionally, but my mother was very close to him when she lived in the village, and his outdoor face, leathery and worn, cracks into a hundred lines when he smiles to welcome her. His older son is getting married, and they have invited the fiancée's relatives over for dinner. The family expects most of the guests to arrive at dusk, but some of the men came earlier in a pickup truck to join the younger son, George, on a hunting trip. The one getting married, Mikeli, has a clerical job. Tall and frail-looking, he has grown the nail of his pinkie long as a girl's to show he no longer works with his hands.

The women are busy roasting a lamb, making *pitas*. The fiancée has joined them early, to prove her skills in preparing a large feast. She folds dough into triangles, stuffing it with cheese for *tyropitas*. My mother and I pitch in, chopping the wild dandelion greens for the *xortopitas*, which they will cook outdoors in a stone oven. We even turn the spit, basking our faces in the low flames. I look at the women who are my mother's age, and the deep lines in their faces reveal years of hard labor.

In the afternoon, the men return from the forest, their jeep trussed like an altar. On the roof, a spread-eagled deer drips blood down the side windows; on the front, a wild boar lies motionless, wrapped in rope. My mother and I decide this would be a good time to take a walk.

She remembers how, when she lived here, one of the women we saw chopping lamb entrails had a pet rabbit. The child fussed over the rabbit and loved it very much. One day she came home to find the rabbit gone. Silence greeted her queries about her pet; at dinner that night, her mother presented it to her on a plate.

We head toward the top of the village; near the last house, a voice calls out to us. An old man, almost blind, hobbles toward us, demanding to know who we are. My mother gives him her name and then says my grandfather's name, her father. He claps his hands together; of course he remembers her. After he invites us to share a cup of coffee, we duck under a low threshold and blink at the sudden dark. A much younger woman, his wife, stands in front of the only table in a bare room. While he introduces us, she lights the burner to heat a brass beaker, spooning out the black grains. Huge, plain, with a crumpled, punched-in face, she nods when we address her. When she goes to a neighbor's for milk, he tells us how they met. Long past the age he thought would attract a bride, he lived for years in the field in the company of goats. Her father invited him to inspect a new herd; her beauty encouraged him to swallow his shame and ask for her hand. *The day I married her was the happiest day of my life, and every day after that I've lived in paradise.* His wife returns, stooping under the door; he wraps his arm around her hips. An aviator's cap covers half his face, his nose drops to a toothless mouth, but his eyes squint with delight when he regards his wife. *I thank God on my knees for her, every day I thank God I can be so happy I know so little about the human heart.*

Walking back to my cousins', my mother looks at me. It is as if she knows the story of my year, the story I hope I never have to tell her. *See that man? No woman should ever settle for anything less.*

As we approach my cousins' house, I see a line of broken bricks in the middle of the lot next door, the remains of a wall. My mother asks me whether I notice the outline of a house. *That's your house,* she says, and I ask her what she means. *I mean yours and your cousins'. It was left to my father and his youngest brother, Crazy Panos, but Panos burned it down a long time ago. If you ever want to come rebuild it . . .* Then she tells me the story.

Crazy Panos lived in that house after his parents died, and he was not yet thirty when it all went wrong. One day, no one knows why, Panos poured gasoline all over the house, set it on fire, and walked out. Perhaps he woke up to smell the cheese fermenting under the stairs, the animal hides under the wood. He thought about taking the flock into the fields, marching them up the mountain. Instead, he put on his best suit, assessing himself in the mirror. The clear liquid splashed over the wood, the straw beds, the onions drying in the corner. Behind him, the flames made a *swoosh*, but he had already begun to walk. In his shining leather shoes, he strode out of the village, down the mountain, across the beet fields, to Larissa. By the time he reached the main square, his shoes were scuffed and his suit dusty. Surrounded by the new hotels, the bars and lights, he could almost taste the sweet and salty promise of the city. He spent the night leaning on the fountain, breathing the clatter of heels on pavement, the waiters' swift movements.

With the dawn, the glittering windows turned to eyes, measuring him, weighing him up. In Larissa, giant flocks of tiny black birds settle in the trees and rise in clouds with the dusk. With the first light, they started to land in the branches, one by one. Before the flock could assemble, a noise startled them back into the air. Panos had reached into his pocket for the revolver he carried from the village, held it against his head, and pulled the trigger. What was left of his head crashed against the pavement.

Why? My mother looks at the skeleton of the house, now framing a vegetable patch and some chickens scratching in the dust. *Maybe Panos was gay*, she said. *Maybe he was just different.* We do not say but both think it—the ruined house is better left in ruins, an open yard next to living people a better legacy. The cousins beckon us from their backyard, where the table has been set for dinner. That night we sleep on straw beds and I dream about Panos. The next day, we turn toward the south.

By the end of the first day, we have breached the border of the Peloponnisos. To save time we decide to cut through the middle of the peninsula, down a road marked on the map by a dotted line. We measure it—twenty-five unpaved miles—and think, *How hard can it be?* Five miles in we realize our mistake, but we forge ahead. The empty hills confront us, hiding modern-day bandits, men in cars who will try to run us down, take our money, worse. As we drive, I remember all the trips we took across the country, from Los Angeles to New York. Often, my father flew later and my mother took the wheel alone, five days with three kids in the car. Instead of filling the gas tank safely, when it was half empty, my mother liked to increase the drama by leaving the fuel gauge on red past the sign where it said LAST GAS. Once, in Wyoming, the car sputtered to a stop on the off ramp with a lightning storm gathering overhead. Ahead, like a miracle, a one-pump gas station guarded the middle of nowhere. No wonder we watched her every move.

Greeks are a people addicted to risk, to extremes of emotion. Living so long under arbitrary yokes—the gods, the priests, the Turks—they have learned to duck their heads low, to expect the worst. Yet they are constantly brave, throwing themselves in the face of danger. Growing up, whenever we said anything positive or American, like *This is going to be a great day*, we spit out the words *ptu-ptu.* The sound felt awkward on our lips; we had to shape them a funny way. We still carry the habit; lovers and spouses who stick with us long enough pick it up eventually, noticing how it works. The old gods hang around, along with all the new ones; if you stop watching out for them, they pounce.

After thousands of years of true danger, what can you do when you have found a safe road? You search out your risks where you can. My mother and I could have turned back. Why didn't we? We stuck to that road, eyes on every curve and every cloud of dust. When we bumped onto the paved road at last, the smoothness felt almost disappointing. For more than an hour, we had used everything in us, all our senses, alive and aware. She looked at me afterward, recognizing some part of herself that she had passed on, a capacity for danger she had always suspected in me and fought against, as if she could protect me from wearing her own skin.

We drive to the very bottom of the peninsula, to a town called Monemvassia. Built on an island linked by a thin bridge to the mainland, Monemvassia became a tiny fortress, fought over by all the nationalities plying the open waters just beyond it. A rocky mount houses the ruins of an ancient village; the newer seventeenth-century settlement grew around it. Strong walls kept out waves and pirates. We abandon the car in a lot outside the gates and cross the wooden bridge to the island.

Inside, we discover a *cafenion* built of stone and wood, walls draped in brightly colored red and pink wool blankets. A woman behind the counter offers us breakfast and then puts on a tape. A sweet, mournful voice fills the room. We rest our elbows on the table, drinking in peace—the voice singing in Greek, the melancholy guitar, the sun against the wood, and the woman who owns her own business, her arms pushing a rag across the counter. When we pay her we ask about the voice and discover her name: Arleta, a famous protest singer who sang in cafés in the time of the colonels and whose lyrics about love and children conceal subversive messages. We buy the tape.

After breakfast, we stroll through the town, peering through archways and round windows to sudden glimpses of a bright blue sea. The villagers have placed flowers in every corner, red geraniums in blue pots, clematis and basil. They have created a world of brown wood and stone opening onto sudden flashes of color, a landscape of bones and bursting life.

I remember now why this is a beautiful country.

Later, we take a ferry to Crete. We want the deep south, the very edge, the end of the country. We start on the northern side, packed with tourists and NO VACANCY signs. Like every Greek, my mother knows the rules are not for her and finds us a room with a giant tiled bathtub and our own terry-cloth robes. *Don't think about how much it costs, shelter's shelter.* Too many bodies on the beach and too many neon signs push us farther south. We cross the center of the island: miles of farms, villages dabbed into the corners of the hills. My mother gets out of the car when we stop for lunch and gas. Her mountain dialect comes back to her, and the proprietor pulls a jar of special olives from behind the counter and offers us a small bag free. When we find our way to the coast, the horizon opens and the sparkling water beckons.

We find rooms in a *pensione* in a tiny village on the sea. The owner is a meticulous widow who keeps the rooms sparkling clean and who drinks her coffee with us the next morning. After four days, we know all about her family, especially her son. We exaggerate our disappointment, crushed we won't have a chance to meet him. She measures me up, and then she smiles. My mother and I grin back at her. While I hold my hand over my mouth, my mother haggles over particulars, his salary, weight, and height. I have to grab her arm when she asks for a picture, and then she says, *Maybe later.* Back in our room we collapse together, laughing until tears come to our eyes.

We stay for five days, and each day follows the same routine. In the mornings, we have breakfast in the harbor, yogurt and honey and fresh bread. In the afternoons, we stroll down to the beach. My mother rents a snorkel and mask and plays in the shallow water, and I swim for half a mile up and down the coast.

The water lies in the warmest heart of the Mediterranean and feels salty and buoyant against my skin. I find I am no longer afraid to go out into the deep and can swim without being able to see the bottom. I am no longer afraid of drowning.

Looking at my mother in her black bathing suit, snorkel floating just above the water, her body held up as she moves slowly in her exploration, I think how easy it is, now that she is no longer the part of me I have to fight against. She rolls in the water, moving with the same grace that carried her through the mountains to this place. We have different bodies and different desires. I want to move quickly

255

down the coast, feel the water part with the force of my body, cover distance. She feels happy to look deeply at one or two spots for a few hours and then sit on the sand, reading her book. We have come to a truce, the truce of two women who have been on a hard road and have come to respect each other's fight.

At night, eating our dinner in the one open café, flirting with the waiter, we have time to sit together or explore the village. This is the first time she tells me about her year in Athens. It is the beginning of the story.

BREAD

When I was growing up, I knew only one story about my mother, and that was the mother story. It began when I began, and its twists and turnings followed my own. The farthest edges of my horizon were the mountains and valleys of her warm body. In her big sunglasses, carpooling us to school or wearing a sweatshirt while she patted ground beef between her palms to make a burger, she did not look that different from the other Los Angeles mothers we knew.

Sometimes, we would see another side to her. Sometimes, my mother would dance with a glass on her head, full of water, and the glass did not fall or break. The music was strange, its rhythms more ragged and mournful than the music we heard on the radio, and my mother would dip down in time to the bouzouki strums, snap her fingers about her head, glide past gravity with confidence and grace. Sometimes, we would hear her speak a language that was not our language; sometimes, she would cook food with an aromatic taste of tomatoes and garlic, food from a time that was long gone.

My mother's silence about her mother offered us few stories at all. We knew the story of the icon because we would kiss it before

257

any long journeys. We knew she carried the Madonna with her for months on end. But we also knew she made it to New York, and since we were new-world children, making it to the new world was the happy ending. She got to New York, she became a mother who became our grandmother, and so the story ended.

Behind those layers, there were other stories that would never be told but would have to be searched out. In my year in Greece, I had not tried to find my mother or my grandmother. I had stumbled into my own mistakes and my own pain. But there at the bottom, feeling lost and worthless, I found something I had never known. The women in my family, like many lost women, had a kind of courage that will never be sung, that perhaps, until now, until these daughters, has never been told.

There are some recipes you cannot pass on. They are secrets that can only travel from mother to daughter and cannot be written down. We have one in our family for bread. The dough we make has a light blond color, and the bread bakes like heavy gold. We weave it into the shape of a cross, which disappears when it rises. The final bread is round, full of the hills and valleys of its braids. The sesame sprinkled on top browns. Inside, the meat of the bread stays moist and sweet. It is the kind of bread to make grown men sigh with happiness, the kind to bring families and communities together. And it is not a recipe we have ever shared with anyone. Yes, we have given out certain ingredients, a version of the recipe, but no one has ever been able to reproduce our bread exactly. All over Los Angeles, there are disappointed women, women who have tried to get it just right and who have failed. They will never know the secret ingredient, the one we reserve for family, a treasure.

My mother once told me why she did not like to write her recipes for us.

She said that she used to beg her mother to copy the recipes down on paper. Her mother knew many things, but she was never comfortable with words—she did not read and did not like to write. Finally, painfully and in great detail, she dictated her recipes, things like a palmful having to be explained and quantified, what felt right in the hand translated into new-world measurements, cups and ounces. Did my mother have a premonition? Was it true, as somehow she has always implied, that by writing down her recipes, my mother stole something before her time, took the easy way and tried to pin down what is learned only by being alongside another woman, only by feeling the same weight in your own hand, the same texture of bread against your own skin? My mother had left her mother's house. Maybe my mother is afraid that the heartbreak, the distance that written recipes imply, added to all the others, contributed to her mother's end. Either way, a week after the recipes were written down, my grandmother was dead. As for my own mother, she refuses. If we want to know the recipes, we have to learn them on our own, following her step by step, learning them by heart, writing them with our bodies.

And this is just what I have done.

Acknowledgments

I would like to thank the following people for their help, stories, and encouragement: Alba Ambert, Helen Cohen, John Cookson, Diane Darby and Keith Jafrate of the Word Hoard, Elke Wolf Davidson, Jennifer Hengen, Rachel Klauber-Speiden, Ike Pappas, Jim Pappas, Holly Prado, James Ragan, Blossom Rosen, Anna Stearman, Alice Tomic, Susan Tomlinson, Martin Winter, my US & UK tribes, and my family, especially Nestor and William Davidson. For vital interventions, Anna Eirini, Diane McDaniel, and Sophie Volpp. Grateful thanks to Tim Ward for his love and support.

Established in 1978, The Women's Press publishes high-quality fiction and non-fiction from outstanding women writers worldwide. Our list spans literary fiction, crime thrillers, biography and autobiography, health, women's studies, literary criticism, mind body spirit, the arts and the Livewire Books series for young women. Our bestselling annual *Women Artists Diary* features the best in contemporary women's art.

The Women's Press also runs a book club through which members can buy, every quarter, the best fiction and non-fiction from a wide range of British publishing houses, mostly in paperback, always at discount.

To receive our latest catalogue, or for information on The Women's Press Book Club, send a large SAE to:

The Sales Department
The Women's Press Ltd
34 Great Sutton Street London EC1V 0LQ
Tel: 020 7251 3007 Fax: 020 7608 1938
www.the-womens-press.com

Sue Woolfe
Leaning Towards Infinity

A passionate and daring exploration of motherhood, genius,
love and betrayal, *Leaning Towards Infinity* tells the story of
three generations of women, bound together not only by the
inescapable ties of family but also by the mysterious and
intriguing world of mathematics. Witty and exciting, this novel
was the winner of both the Commonwealth Writer's Prize and
the Christina Stead Prize for Fiction.

'Extraordinarily rich . . . Woolfe's name can
sit beside Gabriel García Márquez's with barely
a blush' *Daily Telegraph*

'What a glorious and tumultuous novel'
Fay Weldon, *Mail on Sunday*

'Written with the clarity and elegance of a
numerical theorem' *Literary Review*

Fiction £6.99
ISBN 0 7043 4658 3